STAR WARS®

—[CORUSCANT NIGHTS II]—

STREET OF SHADOWS

Michael Reaves

LUCAS BOOKS

DEL REY

BALLANTINE BOOKS • NEW YORK

Star Wars: Coruscant Nights II: Street of Shadows is a work of fiction. Names, places, and incidents either are products of the author's imagination or are used fictitiously.

A Del Rey Books Mass Market Original

Copyright © 2008 by Lucasfilm Ltd. & ® or ™ where indicated. All Rights Reserved. Used Under Authorization.

Excerpt from *Star Wars: Coruscant Nights III: Patterns of Force* copyright © 2008 by Lucasfilm Ltd. & ® or ™ where indicated. All Rights Reserved. Used Under Authorization.

Published in the United States by Del Rey Books, an imprint of The Random House Publishing Group, a division of Random House, Inc., New York.

DEL REY is a registered trademark and the Del Rey colophon is a trademark of Random House, Inc.

This book contains an excerpt from the forthcoming book *Star Wars: Coruscant Nights III: Patterns of Force* by Michael Reaves. This excerpt has been set for this edition only and may not reflect the final content of the forthcoming edition.

ISBN 978-0-345-47754-5

Printed in the United States of America

www.starwars.com
www.delreybooks.com

OPM 9 8 7 6 5 4 3 2 1

For
Jim Bertges

acknowledgments

Once again, thanks go first and foremost to my editors: Shelly Shapiro at Del Rey and Sue Rostoni at LucasBooks, who invited me to walk on the wild side of Coruscant again; to Leland Chee and the other galactic wonks who never got tired of continuity questions; and, as always, to George Lucas for the whole shebang.

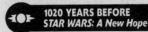

THE STAR WARS NOVELS TIMELINE

1020 YEARS BEFORE
STAR WARS: A New Hope

Darth Bane: Path of Destruction
Darth Bane: Rule of Two

33 YEARS BEFORE
STAR WARS: A New Hope

Darth Maul: Saboteur*

32.5 YEARS BEFORE STAR WARS: A New Hope

Cloak of Deception
Darth Maul: Shadow Hunter

32 YEARS BEFORE STAR WARS: A New Hope

STAR WARS: EPISODE I
THE PHANTOM MENACE

29 YEARS BEFORE STAR WARS: A New Hope

Rogue Planet

27 YEARS BEFORE STAR WARS: A New Hope

Outbound Flight

22.5 YEARS BEFORE STAR WARS: A New Hope

The Approaching Storm

22 YEARS BEFORE STAR WARS: A New Hope

STAR WARS: EPISODE II
ATTACK OF THE CLONES

Republic Commando: Hard
Contact

21.5 YEARS BEFORE STAR WARS: A New Hope

Shatterpoint

21 YEARS BEFORE STAR WARS: A New Hope

The Cestus Deception
The Hive*
Republic Commando: Triple Zero
Republic Commando: True Colors

20 YEARS BEFORE STAR WARS: A New Hope

MedStar I: Battle Surgeons
MedStar II: Jedi Healer

19.5 YEARS BEFORE STAR WARS: A New Hope

Jedi Trial
Yoda: Dark Rendezvous

19 YEARS BEFORE STAR WARS: A New Hope

Labyrinth of Evil

STAR WARS: EPISODE III
REVENGE OF THE SITH

Dark Lord: The Rise of Darth
Vader

Coruscant Nights I: Jedi Twilight

10-0 YEARS BEFORE STAR WARS: A New Hope

The Han Solo Trilogy:

The Paradise Snare
The Hutt Gambit
Rebel Dawn

5-2 YEARS BEFORE STAR WARS: A New Hope

*The Adventures of Lando
Calrissian*

The Han Solo Adventures

 ## STAR WARS: A New Hope
YEAR 0

Death Star

STAR WARS: EPISODE IV
A NEW HOPE

0-3 YEARS AFTER STAR WARS: A New Hope

Tales from the Mos Eisley
Cantina
Allegiance
Galaxies: The Ruins
of Dantooine
Splinter of the Mind's Eye

3 YEARS AFTER STAR WARS: A New Hope

STAR WARS: EPISODE V
THE EMPIRE STRIKES BACK

Tales of the Bounty Hunters

3.5 YEARS AFTER STAR WARS: A New Hope

Shadows of the Empire

4 YEARS AFTER STAR WARS: A New Hope

STAR WARS: EPISODE VI
RETURN OF THE JEDI

Tales from Jabba's Palace
Tales from the Empire
Tales from the New Republic

The Bounty Hunter Wars:

The Mandalorian Armor
Slave Ship
Hard Merchandise

The Truce at Bakura

6.5-7.5 YEARS AFTER
STAR WARS: A New Hope

X-Wing:
Rogue Squadron
Wedge's Gamble
The Krytos Trap
The Bacta War
Wraith Squadron
Iron Fist
Solo Command

8 YEARS AFTER STAR WARS: A New Hope

The Courtship of Princess Leia
A Forest Apart*
Tatooine Ghost

9 YEARS AFTER STAR WARS: A New Hope

The Thrawn Trilogy:
Heir to the Empire
Dark Force Rising
The Last Command

X-Wing: Isard's Revenge

11 YEARS AFTER STAR WARS: A New Hope

The Jedi Academy Trilogy:
Jedi Search
Dark Apprentice
Champions of the Force

I, Jedi

12-13 YEARS AFTER STAR WARS: A New Hope

Children of the Jedi
Darksaber
Planet of Twilight
X-Wing: Starfighters of Adumar

14 YEARS AFTER STAR WARS: A New Hope

The Crystal Star

16-17 YEARS AFTER STAR WARS: A New Hope

The Black Fleet Crisis Trilogy:
Before the Storm
Shield of Lies
Tyrant's Test

17 YEARS AFTER STAR WARS: A New Hope

The New Rebellion

18 YEARS AFTER STAR WARS: A New Hope

The Corellian Trilogy:
Ambush at Corellia
Assault at Selonia
Showdown at Centerpoint

19 YEARS AFTER STAR WARS: A New Hope

The Hand of Thrawn Duology:
Specter of the Past
Vision of the Future

22 YEARS AFTER STAR WARS: A New Hope

Fool's Bargain*
Survivor's Quest

25 YEARS AFTER
STAR WARS: A New Hope

Boba Fett: A Practical Man*

The New Jedi Order:
Vector Prime
Dark Tide I: Onslaught
Dark Tide II: Ruin
Agents of Chaos I: Hero's Trial
Agents of Chaos II: Jedi Eclipse
Balance Point
Recovery*
Edge of Victory I: Conquest
Edge of Victory II: Rebirth
Star by Star
Dark Journey
Enemy Lines I: Rebel Dream
Enemy Lines II: Rebel Stand
Traitor
Destiny's Way
Ylesia*
Force Heretic I: Remnant
Force Heretic II: Refugee
Force Heretic III: Reunion
The Final Prophecy
The Unifying Force

35 YEARS AFTER STAR WARS: A New Hope

The Dark Nest Trilogy:
The Joiner King
The Unseen Queen
The Swarm War

40 YEARS AFTER
STAR WARS: A New Hope

Legacy of the Force:
Betrayal
Bloodlines
Tempest
Exile
Sacrifice
Inferno
Fury
Revelation
Invincible

*An ebook novella

dramatis personae

Aurra Sing; bounty hunter (female humanoid)

Baron Vlaçan Umber; art patron (male Vindalian)

Baroness Kirma Umber; noblewoman (female Vindalian)

Darth Vader; Sith Lord (male human)

Dejah Duare; artist's assistant (female Zeltron)

Den Dhur; Whiplash partisan, former reporter (male Sullustan)

I-Five; protocol droid

Jax Pavan; Whiplash partisan, former Jedi Knight (male human)

Laranth Tarak; Whiplash partisan, former Jedi Knight (female Twi'lek)

Pol Haus; sector police prefect (male Zabrak)

Typho; Naboo captain, security specialist (male human)

Ves Volette; light sculptor (male Caamasi)

prologue

Padmé had never known how much he loved her.

She had died, as far as he knew, in a lonely, far-off place, on a planet that, if not the hell envisioned by the superstitious beliefs of sundry worlds, certainly came close. That was as far as he'd traced her final journey: to Mustafar, a globe still in the throes of creation, where rivers of fire and molten rock stitched across a landscape of basalt and obsidian, and where specially designed heat-resistant droids mined the lava flows for rare and precious minerals. A terrible place, a world of eternal darkness, of soot-filled skies and mephitic gases. No one deserved to die in such a place, especially not Padmé. If she had to die, she should have spent her last hours on a world of sunlight and song, like their mutual homeworld of Naboo, a world of green and blue, not black and red.

But she had gone to Mustafar, gone after the Jedi Anakin Skywalker, on a mission so secret, she'd said, that not even her bodyguard could accompany her. And he, believing that she would be protected under the aegis of the Jedi, had let her go.

And had never seen her again—alive.

Captain Typho, once head of security for the Consular Branch of the Naboo Senate, castigated himself for his decision as he stood with the rest of the mourners, watching the flower-covered casket moving slowly down the esplanade. It had been his job as a soldier to protect Senator Amidala, to shield her from attacks by clandestine Separatist agents. He had known there would be more attempts on her life. He had known it because there had been previous ones: the bombing of her starship on the very day of her arrival on Coruscant; the deadly kouhuns released into her sleeping chamber by a changeling assassin; her near execution in the arena at Geonosis.

Even had he not loved her, he would have sacrificed his life to protect her without a second thought. That would have been his duty. His love for her only compounded his culpability. She had gone on her mysterious mission with Skywalker, and he had not gone with her. And now he had to live with the guilt of his survival, a curse infinitely harder than the relatively easy task of dying for her.

It was true that, had she lived, there still would have been no chance of his love for her being requited. Padmé had, after all, been a Senator, and before that the planetary Queen. He was but a soldier; the difference in caste had been far too great. But it hadn't stopped him from loving her. No power in the galaxy, not even the Force itself, could have done that.

After the funeral, Typho milled aimlessly about in the crowd, still stunned, still trying to wrap his mind around the fact of her death. Still reviewing, over and over, what he might have done differently, if he could possibly have persuaded her to reconsider that last journey . . .

Pointless. Fruitless. These self-flagellations served no purpose. Execrating his actions would not bring her back, nor would it honor her memory. Had she known how he had felt, had she known of his love for her, he knew Padmé would have wanted him to move on, to release her, to live instead of wallowing in despondency. And he was willing to do that.

But first, he told himself, *there is one last task that must be performed . . .*

Padmé Amidala must be avenged.

He had heard conflicting rumors, snatches of conversation during the chaos immediately after her death. Most of the government factotums and officials were caught up in dealing with larger issues; although to Typho there could be no greater concern than his personal feelings regarding Padmé's death. He knew that the diplomatic reverberations, especially in light of Naboo's already tenuous status of autonomy in the eyes of Palpatine's new regime, were gigantic. For the circumstances of the Senator's demise were, to put it bluntly, suspicious. There was evidence—compelling evidence—that she had died a violent death.

Of course, this was not meant to be known by the population at large. But rank did have certain privileges, and Captain Typho had learned some things about Padmé's last hours. There were conflicting reports, of course, but all the autopsy reports were in agreement on two things: that she had been strangled, and that the child had died with her.

But exactly how the former had been accomplished, no one was quite sure. The evidence of strangulation had been there, and obvious: the fractured hyoid bone, damage to the larynx, and compression of the trachea were all clear indications of fatal throttling.

But . . .

There were no signs of bruises on her neck, no scratches or signs of congestion . . . no indication of exterior trauma at all. Her throat had been pristine. It was as if she had somehow been choked to death *without* physical contact. And there was only one power in the galaxy that Typho knew of that could accomplish such a thing.

The Force.

Padmé had gone to Mustafar to meet with the Jedi Knight Skywalker. And all evidence indicated that she had been killed through the Force.

It could not possibly be a coincidence. Even if Skywalker was not the murderer, he had to have been connected somehow. In any event, he was the best and only lead to follow.

Typho knew what he had to do.

He would go to Coruscant. He would find Anakin Skywalker. And depending on what he learned, the Jedi would live or die.

And then, perhaps, Padmé would rest easier.

—[PART I]—

PLANET NOIR

one

"I think it's safe to assume," the droid said, "that we've been set up."

A fusillade of laser and particle beams erupted from across the room, aimed at the five of them, as if to punctuate the statement. Den looked at Jax. "Aren't you glad your father gave him that neural upgrade?"

Another series of beams struck the huge hyper-condensor unit behind which they were hiding. They were protected for the moment, Jax knew, but eventually, if the stormtroopers' lasers and charged-particle bursts kept hitting the unit, the duralumin housing would overheat, quite possibly upsetting the stability of the ultracold Tibanna condensate within. Should that happen, I-Five estimated the explosive factor as at least a 7.5, which would certainly vaporize the building they were in, as well as a sizable chunk of the surrounding urban landscape.

"That's only a rough estimate," the droid explained. "There are too many variables to factor for me to refine my—"

"Seven-point-five is more than enough for me," Jax assured him. "Den?"

"I'm good," Den agreed. The little Sullustan was crouched beside I-Five. "You definitely know how to motivate people," he added to the droid.

"Less talk. More shooting," Laranth said. The Twi'lek Paladin had a blaster in either hand and was crouched near the far end of the unit. "I say we go—*now*."

Jax couldn't argue with her logic. The longer they remained pinned down, the less chance of survival they and their client had, not to mention however many hundreds of thousands of beings would die if I-Five's 7.5 scenario really was in the immediate future. Not that Jax had any doubt of it. The droid had an annoying habit of being right just about all the time.

"Okay," he said. "Laranth, take the right; I-Five, the left. On my signal—"

"Hey, what about me?" Den asked.

"Stay here with the undersecretary." Jax spared a glance at the corpulent, trembling form crouched beside Den. Before the Empire had superseded the Republic, Varesk Bura'lya had been a midlevel government official assigned to the Bothan embassy on Coruscant. Immediately after the Republic's fall, he had become a fugitive, along with thousands of other representatives of various species on the city-planet. True, no particular effort was being made to hunt them down, and in a global metropolis that was home to literally trillions of sentient beings, one stood a very good chance of living a lifetime (thousands of lifetimes, in fact) without ever coming into contact with an enemy. But one overall characteristic of the Bothan species was paranoia, and Bura'lya had no shortage of that. So he had contacted the Coruscant resistance movement known as the Whiplash, and arranged for safe passage offworld through the Underground Mag-Lev, a dangerous and circuitous secret route that delivered enemies of the state to spaceports and sympathetic starships via safe houses, private conapts, and other clandestine means.

Jax Pavan, one of the last surviving Jedi and a partisan of the Whiplash resistance, had been assigned to help ferry the Bothan dignitary to freedom. All had gone well until they'd reached the final checkpoint, in the dimly lit interior of a carbonite-processing plant. Here they'd been greeted, not by the resistance members they'd expected, but instead by a brace of Imperial stormtroopers.

They were smart, he had to give them that. Knowing that a droid was part of the party, they'd staged the attack in the depths of the carbonite-cracking plant, taking advantage of the low-level background radiation that would confuse I-Five's bio- and energy sensors for the moment needed. They hadn't known that there would also be two Jedi to contend with, however. The Force had warned Jax and Laranth of the trap, which is why four troopers now lay dead on the floor. If the Bothan hadn't, in his panic, gotten in the way, Jax was certain that the rest of the troopers would also be dead by now, and Varesk Bura'lya would be about to board the spice freighter *Big Score* and become a fading unpleasant memory instead of hiding behind the hypercondensor unit, caterwauling about his imminent demise.

Now he looked up at Jax, the fleshy tendrils that protruded from his upper cheeks quivering in fear.

"You were hired to protect me!" he squealed, his voice scraping unpleasantly along the Jedi's nerves. "Your job was to help me escape from this overbuilt rock! Is this what you call *escape*?"

"Well," Den observed, "that depends on how metaphysical a definition of *escape* you want to go with . . ."

Another volley of beams struck their shelter, scorching the air and leaving the unpleasant tang of ozone in Jax's nostrils. There was no more time, he knew; they had to make their move. He opened himself to the Force, letting it expand his awareness, feeling its strands groping outward, beyond the bulk of the condensor unit, giving him an accurate "picture" of the chamber they were in and highlighting the locations of the eight concealed stormtroopers who had them pinned down.

"On my mark," he said again. ". . . *Go!*"

Laranth hurled herself from behind the right side of the condensor's bulk, blasters in both hands firing, her eyes as cold and hard as chips of comet ice. I-Five burst from concealment on the left side, the lasers in his index fingers zapping beams of coherent light at their adversaries. Jax let the Force lift him, let it carry him up and over the huge, shielding slab, his vibro-sword parrying the blasts as he landed, batting them back toward the astonished troopers. This was much harder than it looked. The durasteel blade had been woven with cortosis, a mineral strong enough to resist energy blasts, but its similarity to a lightsaber ended there. A scarlet ray struck low on the blade, more by luck than by aim, and the vibrogenerator in the hilt shorted out. Even through the insulation the jolt was painful. Jax knew immediately what had happened, as did the troopers; they could see the blade's edge lose its high-speed blur. Jax dropped the weapon and extended both hands, palms-out, in a Force strike that hurled three of the troopers back against a wall. Even as he did so, however, he could sense another trooper lining up on him—

Laranth stepped into the edge of his peripheral vision, firing her blaster. The beam struck the blast meant for Jax. The air sizzled with multicolored ionized energies, flickering corposant danced along his arms and momentarily wreathed his brow, and the sound was like a thousand fire wasp nests being broken open at once.

Jax's vision was momentarily dazzled by the pyrotechnics. I-Five's photoreceptors, fortunately, were not. The droid fired rapidly, his laser blasts unerringly accurate. In a matter of moments it was finished. The eight stormtroopers lay sprawled in various ungainly positions, on the floor or across slurry pipes, control consoles, and other large pieces of industrial apparatus. The three hesitated a moment, wary of another possible attack. Then Jax said, "It's over. Stand down."

Laranth nodded and holstered her blasters. The hard-bitten Gray Paladin's connection to the Force had no doubt told her, just as his had told Jax, that the immediate danger was past. Simultaneously the droid lowered his arms. Jax knew that I-Five had swept the room for life signs and booby traps with his sensors, and that the readings were null.

"That was exhilarating," I-Five said. "Have I mentioned lately how much I enjoy the organic predilection for violence and carnage? No? That might be because—I don't."

Jax grinned. "Okay," he said. "Let's get our reluctant client to the spaceport and on that spice freighter before anyone else shows up wanting to play." He raised his voice. "Den! Secretary Bura'lya! Let's go!"

There was a moment of silence, and then Den's voice came from around the corner of the hypercondenser: "I'm afraid that might be a problem."

Jax felt himself go cold. Had they come this far, only to have the being to whom they'd promised safe passage die at the last minute? Had a stray energy bolt ricocheted from a reflective surface somewhere in the room at just the right angle to kill the undersecretary? Jax reached out with the Force, just as Den continued, "Bura'lya's fainted. And—" The Sullustan peered around from behind the unit, his nose wrinkled. "I think he's had an . . . accident."

I-Five said, "My olfactory sensor confirms that Den is correct—assuming that *had an accident* in this case is a euphemism for—"

"It is," Jax said. He sheathed his useless vibrosword and sighed. "Come on. Let's get him cleaned up before we put him on board."

two

There were no further impediments in getting Undersecretary Bura'lya on board the freighter *Big Score,* unless finding a new set of pantaloons in the spaceport duty-free that fit a Bothan counted as such. Once the ship had lifted, and I-Five's illegal patch into the orbital grid feed had confirmed its slot for hyperspace insertion, the four headed back to their current quarters, in the downlevels sector known as the Southern Underground. This was several thousand kilometers from Jax's previous neighborhood, the Blackpit Slums, near the equator and not far from the ruins of the Jedi Temple.

Their living quarters were, for a change, relatively upscale, which meant, as far as Den was concerned, that the roof didn't leak and slugthrower fire hadn't riddled the walls. Lately. As a result of the unexpected generosity of Kaird of Nedij, the former Black Sun assassin who, thanks to Jax, had been able to exit the criminal organization and return to his homeworld, they had enough credits to live comfortably for a while. Unfortunately, the same plan that had aided Kaird and saved the lives of himself and his friends had cost Jax his lightsaber. He had used it to trigger a small-scale nuclear explosion in the deserted Factory District in order to escape the clutches of both Darth Vader and the Falleen Prince Xizor. It seemed to have worked; several months had gone by, and Jax had felt no untoward "plucking" of the psionic threads that constituted the way he experienced the Force—at least, nothing that carried with it the sense of Vader's renewed attention. The Sith Lord evidently had assumed that Jax and his companions had not escaped the blast.

"It's not like you really *need* another lightsaber," Den pointed out. "After all, there's no surer way of saying *Look, I'm a Jedi!* than to go waving one around.

"Besides," he added, "don't you still have that other gizmo that Nick Rostu gave you?"

The "other gizmo" was an energy whip: a length of flexible, conductive metal that could be charged with a plasmatic field, which Jax had used in his battle with Prince Xizor. Ironically, the Black Sun operative had been wielding Jax's own lightsaber against him— and not too shabbily, either, Den remembered, considering that Xizor didn't have the help of the Force with it.

"The lightwhip? Yes," Jax replied. "But it's not very good for close work, or multiple opponents."

"Even so," Laranth said, "I agree with Den. A new lightsaber will just tempt you into more overt demonstrations of the Force. If you want Vader to know you're alive, then by all means find another one."

The green-skinned Twi'lek was standing by the partly opaqued window, looking down at the street below, as she spoke. She was dressed mostly in gray:

leggings, tunic, and vest. This wasn't surprising, since Laranth Tarak was one of the few surviving members of the Gray Paladins, a splinter group of Jedi who had believed, even before the overthrow of the Republic, that the Order relied entirely too much on the Force as a metaphysical panacea. Since the lightsaber's use was nearly always augmented with the Force, they advocated proficiency in other weaponry as well. To an amazing degree, Laranth had honed her skill with the pair of DL-44 blasters she wore; Den had never seen her miss. If she shot at something, that something either vaporized, blew up, or fell over; it was a surer bet than a perfect twenty in sabacc.

Of course, Den mused, she obviously used the Force to warn her of lasers or particle beam blasts that were about to be fired at her. No one was fast enough to block something traveling at or near light-speed. But Den was pretty sure that, if one could somehow turn off Laranth's access to the Force, it wouldn't affect her speed and accuracy all that much.

The Twi'lek turned her head slightly, and Den could see light reflect off the shiny scar tissue on her right cheek. That and the burned stub of her left lekku were souvenirs of the atrocity known as Flame Night. As a reporter, he hadn't been able to stop himself from asking once about her part in it. "And don't tell me I should see the other guy," he'd cautioned.

"You can't," she'd replied, "unless you dig up his grave."

She didn't smile as she said it, but then, neither Den nor anyone else in the small group could recall seeing Laranth ever smile. There was no question in Den's mind but that the Twi'lek's nerves were wound tighter than the carbonite nanofibers that tethered skyhooks to the surface of Coruscant. He was glad she was on their side. He hoped she'd stay there. He'd hate to be facing the business end of her blaster.

There was only one other member of the group who could probably match the Paladin's deadly accuracy: I-Five. As others remarked more than once, the erstwhile protocol droid, who had been Den's friend and companion since the Battle of Drongar—and who had dragged him halfway across the galaxy to Coruscant and this current thrill-a-minute existence, he reminded himself wryly—was a rather singular droid. The word *unique* had even been applied. The reason for this was as simple as it was complicated: I-Five was more self-aware than any other droid that Den had ever encountered, not to mention a sizable chunk of sentients it had been the reporter's misfortune to come across over the years. This could be partly explained by some of the modifications that Jax's father, Lorn, had made in the droid's synaptic grid and creativity dampeners. But Den and the others couldn't help but feel that the droid was somehow journeying beyond even that, toward a consciousness that couldn't be entirely the result of programming. If he wasn't already there.

Den shook his head. He'd been slipping more and more into such esoteric reveries these days. It wasn't a good frame of mind to stay in, especially since a large part of his current existence consisted of trying to smuggle various contraband and fugitives from the streets to the spaceports and eventually offworld. One had to be alert; one had to live in the moment and take care of business in such an environment. Philosophical musings could rarely be indulged.

Not that he was given overly much to such things anyway. In his former life—which was how he often found himself thinking of it these days; it seemed as misty and faraway as a half-remembered dream— he'd been a reporter. A newsbeing who had worked on some hot stories in his time, covered some danger- ous fronts, been more than once in "humpty deep poodoo," as some of the Ugnaughts who'd been his source for juicy newsbits back on Drongar had so col- orfully put it. Drongar had by no means been the best of them, but it hadn't been the worst, either. He'd covered the Clone Wars from Eredenn Prime to Jabiim. He'd won awards, citations, and scrolls of merit for his stories from the front. It had been hard work, dangerous work, exciting work.

These days, the memories of those times seemed like a pleasant walk in Oa Park.

Den was jarred out of his reverie by Jax's voice. The former Jedi was saying, "—may be right. Still, given that there are more beings on Coruscant than on any other fifty inhabited worlds, I think the chances of being noticed with a lightsaber are thin, especially downlevel. And I'd rather have it and not need it than the other way around." Jax turned and addressed another being standing in the shadows of the conapt's foyer. "How about it, Rhinann? Can you find me a lightsaber?"

Den watched as the Elomin stepped into the lighted room. Haninum Tyk Rhinann was typical of his species: tall, angular, and bipedal. He wasn't quite as hirsute as a Wookiee, but he came close. His nose tusks, stubby horns, and wide-set eyes all protruded from a fleshy lump that could only be recognized as a head because it sat on top of his short neck. He was depressed. This came as no particular surprise to Den or any of the others; Rhinann was *always* depressed. Formerly Darth Vader's personal aide, he had fled the Dark Lord's service, finding sanctuary at the last moment aboard the freighter *Far Ranger* with Jax and the others, just before the droid factory had been destroyed by the exploding reactor.

Rhinann, like the majority of his species, was a scrupulous, fastidious, meticulous, and punctilious being. For the Elomin, the reason and joy of life truly was in the details, and it had been that passion for order and precision that had convinced Vader to designate Rhinann his aide-de-camp. Unfortunately, along with that painstaking attention to minutiae came an outlook of extreme suspicion upon his life in general and his employer in particular. Den remembered reading somewhere that expatriated Elomin were prone to psychoses of various sorts—including, it seemed, paranoia. Rhinann had become convinced that Vader would sooner or later have him killed for some minor infraction or dereliction of duty, and it had been that fear as much as the very sensible desire to avoid imminent de-atomization that had driven him to jump ship.

Since then, Rhinann had been an unwilling fugitive. He yearned to return to his homeworld of Elom, but his share of the credits bequeathed by Kaird wasn't nearly enough to persuade a merchant ship's captain to carry one passenger all the way to a world on the Outer Rim, far from the trade lanes. And so he'd stayed with those who had rescued him. His exacting nature and near-fanatical attention to detail had easily dictated his job within the group; Rhinann was the go-to being, the procurer. Whatever was needed—from delicacies such as Geniserian sand monkey flambéed in foyvè oil to please a client's epicurean palate to an outmoded widget essential for repairing an aging holoproj unit—Rhinann could put his hands on it.

Except, it seemed, a lightsaber.

"It's not possible," he said dolefully, in response to Jax's query. "The weapons of the Jedi were destroyed along with the Jedi. There are rumors that some lightsabers remain in private collections of the extremely wealthy. But the only one that I am certain truly exists belongs to Darth Vader, and I doubt he'd part with it willingly."

"Good call," Den said.

"A crystal, then. I'll build my own. It'll be more in tune with my—"

"Adegan crystals, as well as Corusca, Ilum, and others, are all under strict trade and commerce interdiction, per the orders of Emperor Palpatine."

"I'll grow one, then." But Jax didn't sound quite as determined as he had a moment before, and Den was pretty sure he knew why. Although as recently as a couple of standard years ago, what he'd known about lightsaber technology and Jedi tradition would have rattled around in a green flea's ear, he'd learned a lot since then from listening to Jax and Laranth, as well as from Barriss Offee, back in their days on Drongar. He knew that the use of naturally occurring crystals, as opposed to synthetic ones, was one of the ways

Jedi had distinguished themselves from the Sith. The ostensible reason was that the synthetics weren't quite as pure as the crystals mined from the caves of various worlds, and there was always the chance that one could fail at a critical moment. And, since practically every moment a lightsaber was activated was perforce a critical one, Den could see the merit of the argument. He wondered, however, how much of that was based on experience and how much on doctrine. It was well known that the Jedi had, by the time of the Republic's downfall, effectively hobbled themselves with their dependence on rote and cant. As nasty as the Sith had been in ages past, Den had to admit that they'd been more practical by far in many areas.

"That may be possible," Rhinann said, in answer to Jax's last statement. "It will take some time, however, to assemble all the necessary equipment and materials. In the meantime, I suggest this." He withdrew from beneath his robes what appeared to Den at first to be an antique sword. The blade was slightly longer than a meter in length and pale silver, almost white, in color. The metal was not chased, although, Den realized, there did appear to be delicate whorls and patterns woven through it. They almost seemed to move, like oil on water.

The hilt was ornate but functional. It looked like it was made of electrum, a rare fusion of silver and gold. Mounted in the guard were two small faceted crystals that scintillated even in the relatively dim interior light.

All in all, very pretty, Den had to concede. Even impressive. But insofar as being able to block a blaster bolt, it seemed about as effective as a pointed stick.

Jax seemed somewhat nonplussed as well. Both I-Five and Laranth stepped forward for a closer look. There was wonder in the Paladin's normally grim face.

"A Velmorian energy sword." She looked at Rhinann incredulously. "You couldn't find a lightsaber, but you could find this?"

The Elomin shrugged. "Things are tough all over. I was able to obtain this in an online auction from a member of the Velmorian royal family who had fallen upon hard times."

Laranth shook her head and took the sword from Rhinann. Den watched as she extended it. He didn't see her do anything to activate it, but the length of the blade suddenly blazed with a cold and crackling silver flame.

"There's something you don't see every day," Den murmured.

The Paladin carefully handed the energy sword to Jax. He held the weapon up, admiring the coruscating shifting waves of power. It was quite different from a lightsaber, and it lacked the latter's purity of design. Still, it was obviously a weapon to be reckoned with. It seemed much more akin, as far as the mechanics of it went, to the lightwhip.

"It's activated by a pressure pad in the hilt," Laranth explained. "The generator feeds plasmatic energy through the crystals and along the blade. A magnetic feedback loop contains it."

Jax relaxed his grip experimentally, watching the

superheated gas retreat, leaving the blade as it was before. He held his other hand close to the metal. "No heat," he murmured.

"The containment loop keeps the plasma from direct contact with the blade. Otherwise it would melt."

Jax squeezed the hilt, triggering the plasmatic coating once more. He swung the weapon a few times, testing its weight and balance. "Easy there, big fella," Den said, backing up quickly.

Jax moved through a few steps of one of the seven forms. There was more weight to the energy sword than there was to the lance of pure energy that was a lightsaber, of course, but nothing that he couldn't compensate for easily enough. Since it was a sheath of energy surrounding a solid blade, it obviously did not have the same frictionless edge that a saber had. He wondered how it measured up against a vibrosword.

Well, he thought grimly, *if life continues to be as interesting as it has been, I've no doubt I'll find out. Sooner, probably, than later.*

three

"It's only a rumor," Dejah said nervously. "Put it out of your mind. Your only obsession must be your work—now, especially."

Ves Volette shook his head, the short, golden fur covering his shoulders and neck rippling in reaction to the tense muscles beneath the skin. "Normally, I would agree with you," he said. "But I can't ignore this. I *must* ascertain the truth."

His partner looked at him with an expression difficult to read, even for Ves, who had been with her for the last seven years. "Tonight," Dejah said, "will be the crowning achievement of your life and your art—thus far, at least. You can't allow anything to distract you."

"Not even genocide, Deej? Not even the extermination of a species? *My* species?"

"You don't know if it's true. It's just a rumor. You—"

"I can find out," Ves said, "easily enough." He turned to the uplink terminal next to the workbench; it was only a few steps away, like everything in the small studio behind the gallery. The gallery itself was large enough to hold six of his latest pieces; any more would seem cramped. Each piece needed its own area within which to radiate.

Ves called up a holoproj of the 'Net and entered his query. It didn't take long to find the news item he sought.

MYSTERIOUS DISASTER STRIKES CAAMAS

SCANS HAVE CONFIRMED THAT THE POPULATION OF THE CORE WORLD CAAMAS HAS BEEN DECIMATED IN A PLANETARY APOCALYPSE OF UNKNOWN ORIGIN. ORBITAL INVESTIGATION TEAMS SAY THE MOST PROBABLE CAUSE IS A CLUSTER OF HIGH-YIELD ACTINIUM BOMBS, NO DOUBT OF SEPARATIST ORIGIN, THAT HAD BEEN DRIFTING THROUGH THE CORE SYSTEMS SINCE THE END OF THE CLONE WARS. IT IS ESTIMATED THAT 70 TO 85 PERCENT OF THE POPULATION HAS DIED FROM THE EXPLOSIONS AND SUBSEQUENT FIRESTORMS . . .

Accompanying the news story were holos of the devastation. Ves could see the charred remnants of cities. Entire forests, encompassing thousands of square kilometers, were still ablaze, the obscuring smoke visible from high orbit.

My world is gone, he thought. Not literally; the globe was still there, orbiting around its sun, but the Caamasi civilization would likely never recover. The Empire could try to spin the disaster as a result of leftover munitions from the war, as if any sentient with even a Level Three education couldn't realize how slim the odds of a bomb cluster just happening to hit a planet, even in the Outer Core, were. The truth was there, for anyone who could read between the data lines.

Amazing, how calmly he was accepting it. That, of course, was due to shock. He hadn't accepted it, not at all. Not yet. He wondered clinically if, when his brain finally let it in, he would go mad.

Caamas. His world. His people. Reduced from shining civilization to near barbarism—the few that were still alive—in less than a day.

And the Emperor had given the order.

Of that Ves Volette was certain. He was apolitical, but he wasn't stupid. Only a ruler as paranoid and ruthless as Palpatine would be threatened by a planet of pacifists. His people had done nothing wrong; they had merely exercised their right, under the Galactic Constitution, to protest the extreme restrictions and tax hikes the Empire was levying on art, science, philosophy, and other modes of consilience.

His people. Quiet, reserved, knowledgeable, compassionate . . . it had been said that the Jedi, when attempting to formulate the consistent ethos that eventually became the Jedi Code, had gone to the Caamasi for guidance. No more. No one would visit his once-beautiful homeworld now, save possibly to stare in outraged shock at the devastation of a planet that once had been a beacon of rationality.

Ves gasped and staggered, suddenly beset by a *memnis,* a sense-memory so intense that, for a moment, the small and cozy surroundings of his workshop vanished, to be replaced by his home in Jualya Village, the picturesque hamlet in which he'd grown up, nestled in the rolling hills of Kanupian. He was standing in his den, looking out at the tartapple orchard, admiring the opalescent tints the rising sun was striking off the glossy leaves and silver skins of the ripe fruits. He could hear songfish piping in the nearby stream.

He remembered the actuality, when it had taken place: three standard months before he had left Caamas and came to Coruscant to light sculpt, to capture in controlled photons universal emotions, feelings common to nearly every sentient being of the galaxy, to display and, he'd hoped, to sell his work. Although Caamasi were overall nonmaterialistic, they weren't foolish. As the philosopher Hyoca Lans once put it, "The problem in galactic society at large is not that there are too many poor sentients—it's that there are too few rich ones." There was nothing wrong with capitalism—as long as it was accompanied by some form of egalitarian ethos.

The *memnis* ability was a primordial, ingrained aptitude coded in the Caamasi genome, unique to the species. They typically occurred at times of great stress, and were nearly always linked somehow to the stressor. He'd only had one before, as a child, when a beloved nest uncle had died. Ves frowned in puzzlement. This *memnis,* this recollection of a pastoral moment not long before he'd left Caamas—how could it possibly be linked to the mundicidal horror of which he'd just learned?

He soon found out.

Ves felt a sudden . . . *disturbance.* A soundless roar, a lightless flash, a vibrationless tremor, not moving, yet somehow propagating nevertheless at terrifying speed toward him. The *memnis* shattered, fragmenting into sharp shards like the psionic equivalent of brittle duralumin, hurtling toward him, accompanied by the silent screams and cries of an entire world dying.

He understood at last what was happening. Caamasi typically shared these grief memories with others of their kind, in an attempt to spread, and so dissipate, the sorrow. What he was feeling right now were the *memnii* of millions of others of his kind, a wave front of agony, confusion, despair, and disbelief that transcended time and space. His individual sense-memory had been symbolic, an expression of the population's peace and tranquillity that had been so suddenly and horrifyingly decimated.

Myriad experiences ripped through his mind like emotional shrapnel. There was no resisting it, no hiding from it. He felt every Caamasi on the planet die.

Dimly, a thousand light-years away, he heard Dejah shouting his name, felt his worried partner help him over to the davenport to lie down. But lying down or standing up made no difference; there was no escape or respite. It was all he could do to hang on to his self, to keep his consciousness from being torn to tatters and sucked into the maelstrom.

Finally, after untold eons of horror, it began to subside. Ves came back to himself, to his own focal point in the cosmos, shuddering and sweating, but alive and, by some miracle, still sane.

Deej was sitting beside him, worry creasing her brow. "Are you all right?" When Ves managed to nod weakly, she exhaled in relief. "What happened?"

"A *memnis*."

Deej looked at him. Being a Zeltron, she had some experience with empathic resonance, and she had been with Ves long enough to be familiar with the concept of shared memories. "I didn't know they could be that intense."

Ves briefly explained what had happened. His partner and friend looked horrified. "After such a shock, you can't put on the exhibit tonight. We must postpone."

Ves shook his head. "No. It is more important than ever now that we open as planned. As long as one Caamasi lives and can create, the Emperor has failed."

Ves lurched to his feet, his head feeling as if a comet had just impacted it. Dejah stood as well, offering her hand in concern, but Ves waved it off. "Offer my apologies to the clientele; tell them that illness prevents me from attending." He moved over to his workbench and activated the plasmatic flux inducer. An oscillating hum quickly rose to the edge of hearing; a parabolic cone of blue light, a meter tall, materialized. Ves fed torsion into it, adjusted the ellipsis. The flame of plasma twisted and gave a low, electronic moan.

Ves glanced at the wall chrono. "It's almost time," he said. "You'd better get ready to let them in."

Deej hesitated, then nodded in defeat. "All right. I suppose you know what you're doing." She exited, closing the door.

Ves concentrated on the torqued spearhead of light. He added neon, krypton, xenon; the plasma flushed red, green, blue. He adjusted tinctures, spun the result through various arcs.

Simplicity—that was the key, of course. The emotional power lay in that. Dejah was right; Ves knew exactly what he was doing.

He was building a cairn.

four

Jax breathed slowly, deeply, as Master Piell had taught him. With each exhalation he pushed his awareness out farther, letting the threads of energy that were his connection with the Force expand.

Many of the Jedi, his tutor had told him, had experienced their unification with the Force in various symbolic ways that they likened to aspects of the real world. For example, Master Piell had always found the metaphor of water best suited his link to it. Jax, on the other hand, felt and "saw" the Force as threads, or strings, stretching and reverberating through space and time, connecting everything. For him, to be aware of another's aura was to see the person swathed in a cocoon of variegated light or darkness. To sense something at a distance, tendrils of Force established themselves instantaneously between him and the object he sought. To augment his own physical powers, such as running or leaping, he let himself be lifted and carried by them, or used an invisible "lasso" to bring objects within reach. Now he sent those threads questing outward, probing and searching, until they encountered that which he sought.

As though it in turn sensed his contact, the floating remote droid let loose a volley of laser beams aimed at him, simultaneously zipping from one midair position to the next as it fired. Jax, blindfolded, whipped up the energy sword, countering each burst by knowing, before it was fired, which direction it would come from. *One . . . two . . . three . . . four . . . five . . .*

The sixth, and last, beam stung him painfully on the right side.

"Blast!" Jax pulled off the blindfold and spoke the deactivation code for the remote, which drifted to the floor. He sat down on the extruded lip of a wall couch and looked ruefully at the weapon in his hand.

"I see it's remote one, human zero," a voice said. Jax looked up to see I-Five in the doorway of the small, enclosed courtyard in which the Jedi had been practicing.

"I'm beginning to think that Laranth is right," Jax said. "The Jedi should have practiced more with other weapons." He grimaced. "Don't tell her I said that."

"On the other hand, no one but a Jedi could have blocked five out of six beams."

Jax shrugged. "It makes no difference if it's the sixth one or the first one that kills you. Dead is dead."

"I wouldn't know. I do know, however," I-Five said, "that you're much better with that sword than you think you are."

Jax glanced down at the weapon, saw his distorted reflection looking back at him from the blade's surface. "Yeah? How do you know th—?"

I-Five suddenly whipped up his left hand, index finger extended, and fired a laser beam at Jax. The beam splashed off the ionized fire that suddenly coated the length of the blade, which Jax had automatically raised to block the beam.

"That's how," I-Five said. "The speed of light is just under three hundred thousand kilometers per second. You are currently seven-point-three meters from me. Your Force-augmented anticipatory reflex action is obviously working fine. You just have to let it."

Jax grinned. "You sure you're not carrying a Jedi Master template somewhere in that droid brain of yours?"

"Maker forbid. I'd like to think that even preprogrammed mechanical intelligences are less rigid than the Jedi were."

Jax's smile faded. The droid projected concern. "My apologies, Jax. Even protocol droids can be indecorous at times. I was out of line."

"I'm not upset at your opinion. What gets to me is—you're right. Every living species in the galaxy knows that one either adapts or dies. It's not a difficult concept. Why didn't the Council understand it? Why couldn't they recognize the danger until it was too late?"

"Assuming for the moment that the question isn't rhetorical," I-Five said, "all I can offer is an observation your father made once, more than twenty-five years ago. He was a Temple employee, as you know, and had an opportunity to observe his employers closely. Even before he became so biased against them for what he felt was your kidnapping, Lorn was under no illusions about Jedi stagnation and complacency.

"He told me of references he'd found in datafiles to someone they called the Chosen One . . . a being whose coming was foretold and said to be imminent, who would restore balance to the Force. Perhaps they were waiting for this being to come and accomplish for them what they were unable or unwilling to do for themselves. It was your father's opinion—and I've watched the behavior of enough organic sentients in my travels to heartily agree—that whenever they give up their own judgment to some sort of fanciful higher power, instead of looking for answers within themselves and their actions, they are the worse for it."

Jax nodded thoughtfully. Of course he had heard the rumors that Anakin Skywalker, protégé of the noted Jedi Obi-Wan Kenobi, was this Chosen One. But Jax had no way of knowing. He had not been privy to such exclusive information. Only a rank-and-file Jedi, he had barely achieved Jedi Knighthood immediately before the Order's destruction. But it made as much sense as anything else in a galactic society gone mad. Though he had been one of the very few Padawans who had been able to call Anakin Skywalker friend, Jax had not been then, and was not now, under any illusions about the powerful young Jedi's mood swings. He remembered once sensing Anakin's aura, perceiving it as strands of blackest night stretching multidimensionally in every direction.

Why hadn't the Council seen it, as well? Or had they just chosen to ignore it?

"You may be right," he finally told I-Five. "Or at least, partly right. I doubt we'll ever know for sure."

A sudden mental onslaught struck him, unexpected

and powerful enough to literally knock him to his knees. *Something* had just happened, somewhere in the galaxy. Something involving such monstrous pain and death that it had set the threads connecting him to the Force to vibrating like the Balawai Creation gong. He sensed millions upon millions of lives extinguished in some kind of global holocaust. Dropping the energy sword, he cupped his face in both hands and moaned.

"Jax?" I-Five's hands were made of hard alloy, yet their touch was gentle as the droid took him by the shoulders and turned him, leaning down to peer intently into his face. "Are you all right? What's happened?"

"Death." Jax was barely able to croak the word. "Death's happened. The cry in the night. Mass destruction, somewhere. They're all . . . all . . ."

He couldn't finish the sentence. The crushing weight of the tragedy that had been thrust upon him barely left room enough for respiration. Somewhere, on some world in the known galaxy, millions upon millions of people had cried out as with one voice— and then had fallen silent, forever. Although the room still seemed to be spinning on its axis, he struggled to his feet. I-Five began to remonstrate, but Jax pushed past him and headed for the front room.

He hoped he was wrong. Hoped with all his heart that this massive disturbance in the Force had been due to something else, *anything* else. But he knew it wasn't so, and his certainty was given added corroboration when he saw Laranth's face. As expressionless and closed off as she could sometimes be, still he recognized the haunted look in her eyes. He knew it mirrored his own.

"Caamas," she announced tightly.

The location of the catastrophe was almost as great a shock as the initial psychic tsunami that had convulsed the Force only a few minutes previously. *Caamas?* A world populated by beings who had repeatedly raised the bar for other species through their remarkable achievements in the arts and philosophy? Jax stared in utter disbelief. It made no sense. The Caamasi were gentle, educated beings, for the most part. Their world was one of the very few to maintain a planetary militia instead of a regular professional army. Only someone as paranoid as Palpatine could possibly think that . . .

Jax realized then what it was, what it had to have been, and the realization left a sour taste of bile in the back of his mouth. Of course. Caamas was the perfect example, guaranteed to pound home the message that the Emperor was too firmly ensconced to be overthrown. His action would demonstrate that if he was crazy enough, or just plain cruel enough, to obliterate a world of scholars and artisans, what was there to stop him from doing the same thing to Corellia, or Alderaan, or Dantooine, or any of a thousand and one other planets?

Nothing whatsoever, as far as Jax could see. And that, of course, was the point.

He felt, to his surprise, a sudden surge of anger against the Jedi—against his own people. Why had they closed themselves off, shirked the duties and responsibilities that had been theirs for thousands of generations? If they hadn't, perhaps none of this would have happened. If they had been more receptive, they might have sensed the threat in their midst before it struck. A burst of awareness that manifested itself through the Force with absolute surety. Suddenly Jax *knew*. He didn't know why, he didn't know if it had anything to do with the echoes of the dead and dying Caamasi still reverberating in his mind, he didn't know if it was totally unconnected and just a random flash of insight from the Force—but he suddenly knew one incontrovertible fact:

Anakin Skywalker was still alive.

five

Death came for her in the mining tunnels of Oovo 4.

Aurra Sing was working in one of the branch tunnels, a narrow fissure in the black rock, barely wide enough for her to stretch one arm straight from the shoulder. The vein of zenium she'd been following for the last three days was running dry; she estimated that in less than a meter it would diminish to the point that it would no longer be cost-effective to keep mining.

She lowered her protective faceplate. Except for the dark gray-black circles around her eyes that made them appear deeper than they were, the skin of her face and body were as pure white as the veined marble the miners occasionally encountered in their digging. The single thick shock of long reddish-brown hair gathered together by a band at the top of her skull was stunning by comparison.

She aimed the gasifier at the left side of the rock face, through which the lode of zenium stitched like a frozen bolt of purple electricity. The high-energy beam turned the rock into plasma almost instantaneously, and the incandescent gas was sucked away through a hose woven of carbonite nanofibers, to be vented through shafts that perforated the strata between where she stood and the surface.

Sing gasified the remaining rock that encased the zenium. She struck the exposed sheet—which, though only a couple of centimeters thick, was as tall as she was—with a small sonic tool, finding the cleavage lines with skill born of years of practice. The zenium fractured into several smaller, roughly hexagonal pieces. These she gathered up and stacked in the ore carrier. Disconnecting the gasifier line, she loaded it into the carrier as well, then stepped on the plate and activated the repulsor.

As the carrier zoomed soundlessly back toward the main shaft, passing through brief flickering pools of light cast by sconces that alternated with stretches of utter darkness, Sing wearily checked her rebreather's status. The filter's diffusion index was still green, she noted, although it had long since declined from optimal.

She tried to remember how the galaxy's Outer Rim had looked from the observation deck of the pirate ship, so long ago. It had been many years. How many, Sing herself wasn't sure. She wasn't sure of a great many things about herself, including her age and her species. She knew her mother had been human, but her father's ancestry was a mystery. Those she had worked for, including Wallanooga the Hutt, had speculated that he had been Qiraash, Rattataki, Umbaran, perhaps even Anzati. Never mind that none of these could interbreed with humans without a certain amount of genetic tinkering, and that none of those genomes could account for her longevity. So her origins remained a mystery, even to herself.

The past held no interest for Aurra Sing. All that mattered was the now.

Over the course of a long and eventful life Sing had learned to conserve energy and bide her time when the situation she happened to find herself in was less than satisfactory. In this respect her longevity served her well. She had survived onerous conditions before, and would again. If she could not shoot or fight her way out of a situation, then she would simply and patiently outlast it.

After all, one did not become known as a hunter of Jedi by being reckless.

It was hard to believe that she had once nearly embraced the Jedi Code. The Jedi Master known as the Dark Woman would never know how close she had come to converting her headstrong young Padawan. Had she not been kidnapped and taught the truth by the pirates—a rich irony, that—Aurra Sing might have been one of those sanctimonious wearers of sackcloth herself. And as a result, she might very well be dead now; just one more victim of Order Sixty-six, like the rest of the Jedi.

Well, good riddance to them. The only regret Sing had in that regard was that there were precious few left for her to hunt down and kill these days.

As she approached one of the ancillary shafts that connected with the surface, she began to see other beings. All were engaged in some aspects of zenium mining. An inescapable corollary of the activity was that none of them looked good. Even with the osmotic filters, zenium dust eventually found its way into respiratory systems—be they lungs, stomata, trachea, or whatever. Breathe it long enough and you came down with pyroliosis, or "firelung"—a condition that literally consumed you from the inside. In humanoids it ate up the aveoli like so much dry acid: an extremely painful way to die.

This was one reason only the most incorrigible criminals were sent to Oovo 4. Outside the occasional Podrace to blow off steam, the daily routine stopped only when the prisoner died.

Ironically, the mines on Oovo 4 were among the few labor camps in the galaxy in which organics actually outlasted droids. Despite shielding, the zenium dust affected droids' perceptor systems almost immediately, causing them to crash into the mining equipment and one another. In contrast, it took the more resilient organics several years to wear out. Their presence in the mines was a matter of cost-effectiveness, not ethics.

She saw Karundabar, an old Wookiee who had been down in the hole for so long he had forgotten the crime that had initially landed him here. He was nearly bald, his hair having fallen out over most of his body through the years. She watched him dump a pile of ore plates into a lift tube that would take it to Receiving on the surface. Almost blind, to judge by the cataracts that filmed his eyes, he had followed the route so often that he didn't need to see to do the job.

As Sing dumped her own load of plates into another tube, she kept her senses on full alert. Her connection to the Force would warn her of any imminent assault, sometimes even before it was initiated. That, and her deadly reputation, had kept her alive all these months in this rancor pit. Both would continue to do so.

Or so she thought . . .

The attack, when it came, was thus doubly surprising—first that anyone would dare attack her at all, and second because the Force had not warned her of it. Fortunately, that enigmatic energy was not her only ally. Even though the misbegotten Jedi flooz Aayla Secura had cut the antenna of her biocomputer implant, it still was capable of sensing danger at close range. That was what warned her now, barely in time, of the Trandoshan with the shiv who was lunging at her from behind.

Sing sidestepped, knowing from long practice just how much movement was necessary to allow the thrust to miss. The sonic blade slipped by less than a centimeter from her alabaster skin; she could feel the breeze it generated. As the big reptilian stumbled, thrown off-balance by missing his target, Sing caught him in an armlock and snapped his elbow.

True to his heritage, the scaly creature did not lose more jagannath points by screaming. Internalizing the pain, he hissed in anger. But he could not keep from gasping as Sing swung the broken arm up, dislocating his shoulder joint, and simultaneously used her leg to sweep her assailant off his feet. The Trandoshan hit the rocky floor of the shaft with a sickly thud. Snatching the shiv from his nerveless hand, Sing dropped to one knee beside him and prepared to drive the blade into his throat.

"Enough."

A life-sized three-dimensional image appeared before her. It was the projection of a human: a man sheathed in what appeared to be black armor, wearing a helmet of strange design and enfolded in a black cloak and tabard. At first sight Sing thought that everything about the image was unrelievedly black. Then she saw he wore a small chest panel with blinking red and green lights. Doubtless some form of biosystem monitor allowing for externalized connection to recharge critical life-support components.

She recognized the figure, of course. One could hardly live in the developed portion of the galaxy, or even on its fringes, and not have heard of Darth Vader, Dark Lord of the Sith. His origins were shrouded in mystery and rife with rumor: He was a centuries-old Sith Lord, reanimated by the sheer force of the Emperor's will; he was the last rogue Jedi; he was a genetically optimized clone, the ultimate warrior; he was a cyborg, some kind of specialized battle droid given human form.

Sing had no idea which if any of the rumors might be true, although Vader's alleged unequaled proficiency with a lightsaber would seem to argue for the first or second possibility. Her gaze automatically went to where the traditional Jedi weapon was attached to his belt. A sensible sentient would have been immediately intimidated by the Dark Lord's appearance. Aurra Sing smiled; a lazy, feral smile.

Vader's image regarded her in silence for a moment; then it spoke. The sound, like the image, was slightly distorted from its long journey through hyperspace.

"Your reflexes are quite impressive, bounty hunter. You have temporarily cost me the use of a trained assassin."

Sing spared a glance at the Trandoshan, still lying on the floor and whimpering softly as he tried to snap his broken arm back into its shoulder socket. Her gaze returned to the ebon image. "You set this one on me? Why?"

Vader nodded once. "Just so. I was curious to see if you were still at your peak after your time in the mines. I now—"

"You're wise," she interrupted the projection, "to stay in a safe haven parsecs away. This one"—she nudged the reptiloid with her foot—"just served to keep me from falling asleep after a day's work. Were you here in the flesh I'd—"

Vader raised a black-gloved hand, and Sing paused.

"I have a job for you," the Dark Lord continued. "Do it well, and I'll personally commute your sentence. Do it poorly, and you'll be back here breathing zenium dust until it eats you alive from the inside out. Are you interested?"

Sing was aware that the other prisoners nearby had halted their activities and were looking on in fascination. She also saw that three of her more brutish fellow miners were scowling in her direction. She could feel their resentment at this unexpected offer of clemency for her.

"You offer me a choice a fool could make."

"I didn't think you would require much convincing."

Their agreement concluded, at that point she expected the image to implode and vanish. She was somewhat surprised when it did not. Instead, the simulacrum stood silently, watching.

She turned to face the three prisoners she had noticed a moment earlier. Two were human; the third was a Shistavanen. All three continued to glare enviously at her, each waiting for one of the others to make the first move. Sing smiled. It was plain now why Vader had not ended the transmission.

The test wasn't over yet.

six

"Anakin Skywalker? *The* Anakin Skywalker? The Jedi hero of the Clone Wars?"

"You sound skeptical," Jax told Den.

"I am skeptical. In fact," Den added, "I'd say *skeptical* isn't nearly strong enough. I think I'll have to go with *incredulous*."

"I'm inclined to agree," Laranth put in from nearby. "All the Jedi—present company excepted—are dead."

Jax met her gaze evenly. "As you said, *present company excepted*. We've managed to stay alive all these months. Why couldn't he have as well?"

I-Five responded before the Twi'lek could. "Along with Obi-Wan Kenobi and Mace Windu, Anakin Skywalker was one of the most storied heroes of the Republic. Their battles and missions are the stuff of legend, or so my research would suggest. Ever since the end of the Clone Wars, there have been sightings of them reported from the Outer Rim all the way to the Tingel Arm. Not one has ever been confirmed."

Jax didn't reply immediately. He could certainly understand the others' reservations. He would have been equally dubious—had he not experienced the absolute certainty that often came with revelations granted by the Force. In this case, there was simply no room for doubt.

He told them as much. "There's no way I can convince you of it, I know. But knowledge gained through the Force can't be discounted. If I had to choose between the evidence of my senses and that which is revealed to me through my connection with the Force, I'd go with the Force every time."

Den shrugged. "Since I make it a point never to argue with zealots, let's just say I believe in your belief in it. But even assuming it to be true—and I say this with all due respect—so what? I mean, it would make an interesting ribbon for the holos, but since the only way you can prove the truth of it is to reveal yourself as a Jedi, it all strikes me as a little counterproductive."

"I'm not suggesting that. In fact, I'm not sure what I'm suggesting, if anything. It just hit me, just now. You couldn't say we were friends, since I don't think Anakin ever let anyone get close enough to justify the term. But he relied on me enough to trust me with something, once."

"A nugget of pyronium," Rhinann recalled. "You showed it to us before."

"Oh yeah," Den mused. "The rainbow rock. Goes through all the colors. Very nice. Does it do anything besides shine?"

"Indeed it does," I-Five said. "What makes refined pyronium so rare and valuable is that its ability to absorb energy of varying quanta is extraordinarily high. If left exposed to any frequency of electromagnetic radiation of sufficient intensity, its atomic structure stores it. It is theorized that when the quantum shells are filled, the additional energy is somehow shunted into a correlative hyperspatial lattice that . . ."

Jax, grinning, reached behind the droid's neck as if to flip the master deactivation toggle at the base of the latter's metal skull. The droid glared at him and stepped away. "My mistake," he said. "For a brief moment I was laboring under the delusion that I was dealing with beings possessing a sense of curiosity. How could I have been so naïve?"

"Don't get your circuits in a twist," Den chided his friend. "I was actually faintly interested in what you were saying." He returned his attention to Jax. "I can't help but wonder if this latest Force flash of yours isn't somehow connected to the Caamasi holocaust. Of course, you're the one with your veins all crammed full of little Force critters, so you'd know better than me."

Before Jax or I-Five could respond, Laranth, who had been standing by the door, turned suddenly toward it. One hand went to a pistol hilt as she said quietly, "We have a visitor."

Conversation ceased as everyone turned toward the door. They were in the front room of the domicile, from which the smaller separate sleeping quarters branched off. Jax edged quietly a step closer to the doorway, reaching out with the Force as he did so, letting its threads pass through walls and floors as easily as neutrinos through cosmic dust. Laranth was right: he could sense someone on the stairs. Female, advancing with a light, confident step. He wasn't able to ascertain if she was human, but she was definitely humanoid, and young.

He perceived no malice or hint of dangerous agenda in her purpose, but that was not conclusive proof of harmlessness. She might be very skilled at blocking her thoughts and feelings. He glanced at Laranth, received a slight nod that confirmed his assessment of the situation. Both relaxed slightly, and Jax activated the door panel. It slid open to reveal the figure of a young, humanoid female. She looked slightly startled as the portal hissed to one side without her having touched the external call pad. Jax stared. She was fully humanoid, all right.

She was also the most beautiful woman he had ever seen.

Her skin was cardinal red. Her thick, wavy hair was darker, a shade closer to burgundy. The irises of her wide-open eyes were a shocking scarlet. Not much shorter than him, she wore a one-piece garment that at its densest seemed to be about two molecules thick. Despite bordering on vapor, the material swirled and eddied with vivid colors.

Almost without his volition, the Force reached out and wrapped about her to sample her aura. What he felt was a sensation of rust, a dolorous mental shade very much at odds with her vibrant appearance. She peered into the room, and her tone was cautiously hopeful as she spoke.

"Please tell me one of you is Jax Pavan."

The Carrack light cruiser made a reasonably steady landing on the pad at Westport. Captain Typho was among the first to disembark. It would have been a pleasant enough voyage, with his rank in the Naboo military giving him preferential status in terms of accommodations and food, had he not been consumed with his mission. But despite the pleasures available to one of his rank on board ship, all he could think of was reaching Coruscant and pursuing the course that obsessed him. It had taken several months to clear up various obligations on Naboo so that he could proceed at his task totally unencumbered. Now he was finally here.

He had watched from the main viewport as the ship had descended. It had been hard, very hard, not to feel completely overwhelmed by the sight of the endless cityscape that stretched in all directions below him. As far as he could see, the snarl of streets, towers, plazas, stadiums, and countless other buildings and thoroughfares covered the surface, all of it stippled with flickering shadows thrown by the fast-moving repulsor-driven traffic above. Cosseted remnants of the original planetary biota, occasional patches of green and blue, peeped through the immense cityscape. But they were few and very far between.

It was nothing he hadn't seen before, of course. In his capacity as Padmé's bodyguard he had visited the city-planet several times previously. But on those occasions he hadn't been faced with the daunting task of tracking down a killer among the teeming trillions that populated the global labyrinth. It seemed utterly impossible, and Typho felt despair fill him. Where, in all this enormous endless urban sprawl, would he even begin to look for a surviving Jedi when so many believed all the Jedi were dead?

He squared his shoulders and set his jaw. No task was ever accomplished by cowering before it. If he continued to feel this way, he would be defeated before he had even begun. And Padmé Amidala would forever rest uneasily in her grave.

That could not be permitted.

A modest distance to the northeast of Westport lay the ruins of the Jedi Temple. Any investigation or exploration of them was forbidden by Imperial fiat. But such interdictions held little meaning for a soldier. Typho would begin his investigation with Anakin Skywalker, presumably the last Jedi to see Padmé alive. If he had survived Mustafar, some hint of his whereabouts might be found in the shattered remnants of his former sanctuary. And if such a clue existed, Typho would find it.

The captain set out upon his quest.

"I'm Jax Pavan."

The crimson woman looked relieved. It took Den a moment to identify her as a Zeltron. A small pang of worry rippled through him at this realization. Zeltrons, if he was remembering correctly, were exceptional representations of humanoid beauty, at least as far as other humans were concerned. In addition they, like the Falleen and some other mammalian species, shed pheromones that made them even more irresistible.

In short, not a species that made it easy to be objective.

The Sullustan cast a quick glance at Jax. Hard to tell what he was thinking. Den had become fairly adept at reading humans over the years—but not *that* good. Jax didn't look particularly smitten, however, even though the Zeltron seemed to be a prime example of human pulchritude. It was all academic to Den, of course. He took note of her beauty the same way he would recognize a thoroughbred of any sort.

"My name is Dejah Duare," the Zeltron said. "I've come to you for help."

Den watched his friends. Jax and Laranth glanced at each other, and the Sullustan guessed that they had both checked this visitor out through the Force. Whether she had passed or not remained to be seen. As for I-Five, though the mechanical was capable of projecting a surprising range of "expressions," he was now in full droid mode, pretending to be nothing more than a simple protocol unit. Rhinann showed little interest in the encounter. This wasn't unusual. These days the Elomin was pretty much in a perpetual funk.

Dejah was looking from Jax to Laranth as she spoke. "I've heard that you aid people who want to leave Coruscant. Is this true? I can pay you."

Considering that those last four words made up one of Den's favorite sentences, he felt impelled to speak up. "You heard right," he proclaimed briskly. "For the right price we can get you off this overpopulated rock and into a new life offworld that'll—"

Laranth silenced him with a look that stopped just short of singeing his eyebrows. Alternately mortified and irate, Den subsided.

"Payment isn't necessary. Tell us what you have in mind," Jax said. "How many people would be going?"

"Just two—my business partner, Ves Volette, and myself."

I-Five spoke up. "Your pardon, but would that be the famous Caamasi light sculptor of the same name?"

She looked startled. "Yes. He is—was—quite well known—on his homeworld." She was suddenly upset, so much so that she could hardly finish the sentence. It didn't take a brain the size of a planet to understand why. Even if Jax and Laranth had not just been front and center, metaphysically speaking, for the event, Caamas's shocking destruction had lately been the talk of the general media.

"You fear for his future," Laranth said, "and for your own, by association."

This was, as far as Den was concerned, an entirely reasonable concern. If the Emperor had gone to the trouble of destroying the Caamasi homeworld, for whatever reason, then it followed that he would take care to keep tabs on any survivors who might keep the issue alive by asking awkward questions. Already the general media was seeking them out. A small but vocal and active minority was an inconvenience someone like Palpatine would surely rather do without. Which no doubt meant anyone aiding such survivors would also come in for increased Imperial scrutiny. Den swallowed, running his finger around a suddenly too-tight collar. His initial enthusiasm for taking on this particular new client was fading fast.

"Yes, I do," the Zeltron said in belated response to Laranth's query. She gave Jax an imploring look. "Please help us. Ves isn't a coward, but like many artists he has little sense of the way galactic society works. I'm afraid he might do something reckless and vengeful, like producing a work deliberately insulting to the Emperor. That could get us both killed."

Her skin flushed an ever-so-slightly darker shade of red as she spoke. Den knew his eyes were probably the only ones in the room sharp enough to notice it, outside I-Five's photoreceptors. He had seen the Falleen Prince Xizor's skin darken the same way, and he suspected it was for similar reasons. This Duare person was in all likelihood pumping out some industrial-strength pheromones in an attempt to chemically sway Jax, and probably Laranth, too, to her side.

He was not sure if Twi'leks were immune to Zeltron pheromones. He recalled that the Paladin had been affected by Xizor's mesmerizing sweat, but that meant nothing here, of course. Duare was of a different species.

He realized that Duare was speaking again, and he listened intently. "I help Ves with his work," she was telling her audience. "You probably know that my kind are telempathic. It's an ability that comes in handy helping Ves get in the mood to do his best work."

I-Five must have seen Den's blank look. "Zeltrons can project and sense emotional states," the droid told him. "Think of it as telepathy with feelings instead of words." He addressed this explanation to his friend via a directional sonic pulse so that no one else could overhear it. Den was grateful for the information. He hadn't been aware of this last factoid. *Makes the whole pheromone thing seem kinda superfluous,* he mused.

He glanced again at Jax. The Jedi still seemed in complete control of himself, as did Laranth. Den wondered if the Force could somehow shield those who commanded it from the effect of both wafting chemicals and projected emotions. He wouldn't be surprised. To hear Jedi such as Barriss Offee and Jax talk, the Force could do just about anything. And Den had witnessed more than enough miracles carried out by its invocation not to doubt them.

Well, let's hope, he thought.

Jax cleared his throat. "There's been a lot of investigation by the regime into the activities of the Whiplash lately. They're especially interested in how renegades, radicals, and other dissenters are managing to flee offworld. Getting someone out has become even more dangerous than usual."

Den breathed a silent sigh of relief. He was glad to hear that, pheromone mist notwithstanding, his human friend was still thinking with his brain and not his glands.

"So," Jax continued, "we'll have to be extra careful getting you and your companion Volette out. But one way or another, we'll do it. I feel that we all owe it to the memory of the Caamasi." He smiled reassuringly at Dejah Duare, and the Zeltron smiled back.

Den clapped a hand to his forehead and groaned.

I-Five glanced at him. "Something wrong?" the droid asked.

"Headache," Den muttered. He left the room.

Se'lahn.

That was the word for it in the Sullust tongue. It meant disquietude, a sensation of unrest, a troubled heart. It was a word that described, with fair accuracy, Den Dhur's mental state these days.

It was a state well justified, he felt. After all, he had lobbied for some time without success for all of them, even the Elomin, to hit the outer plenum and get off Coruscant immediately, if not sooner. *Where* they went wasn't as important as *when*. The whole idea was to put as much empty space as they could between them and Lord Vader, since it was entirely possible that the Emperor's sinister adjutant was still interested in the whereabouts of Jax Pavan.

Den understood idealism and had even been known to get a little choked up himself on occasion. He had no difficulty with Jax devoting himself to Truth, Justice, and the Jedi Code. He did, however, have a big problem with doing so under the very nose of one of the most dangerous individuals in the galaxy.

And yet something was keeping Den on Coruscant. I-Five.

The protocol droid had accomplished a remarkable thing, Den reflected. The modified mechanical had become such a close friend that Den really couldn't imagine life without him.

I-Five had told Den that if Den felt he had to leave Coruscant, the droid would go with him even if Jax elected to stay. But I-Five had also promised the elder Pavan that he would watch over his son if Lorn died. The droid had taken this commitment very seriously, even though he had not been able to fulfill his former partner's request until Jax had become a grown man. Still, better late than never, and the droid's devotion to the task was intense, as if he intended to make up for those lost decades.

So if put to the test, would I-Five stay with Jax or go with Den?

The Sullustan wasn't sure he wanted to find out. And that was the crux of it. He, Den Dhur, crack reporter and professional cynic, had become as fond of I-Five as he might be of a sibling. Though they engaged in constant and sometimes acrimonious verbal sparring, Den had forged a bond with the droid that was stronger than any he had formed with any organic sentient.

Strong enough to keep him on a world he hated— or, rather, in the part of that world he hated. The Coruscant underworld: the slums comprising the lower fifty or so levels, the narrow, twisted surface streets and ramps, and the caverns and warrens that honeycombed the subsurface in so many places. The proliferation of buildings over the centuries had reached such a congested state that the sun could hardly ever be seen. And when it was visible, its light was strained through a veil of low-lying hydrocarbon smog that turned it blood red; an overly blatant metaphor, in Den's opinion, but nonetheless effective.

It might seem strange to someone with only a passing familiarity with Sullustans that Den should loathe the various underground neighborhoods so. After all, weren't his kind cave dwellers? Hadn't they adapted over the millennia to a life underground? So what was the problem?

In a word: *squalor.*

Coruscant—or Imperial Center, to use the approved nomenclature, not that he had ever heard anyone other than stormtroopers, mediacasters, and governmental shills do so—for the most part did a good job of hiding its seamy underside. Tourists, visiting dignitaries, merchants, and other intermittent travelers had little opportunity, and even less inclination, to peer too long and deep into the dark abysses that occupied the spaces between the cloudcutters and skytowers. Visitors usually came to the planet to catch glimpses of holoproj glitterati, to spend more on one meal than the average Ugnaught laborer made in a standard year, to gamble away piles of credits the size of monads without a second thought. They certainly did not come to be reminded of the filth and desperation of the conveniently concealed teeming masses who dwelled beneath the inversion layers that made many of the elegant taller structures look like they were floating on clouds. They most emphatically did not want to know that immigrants in search of the shiny dream life that escaped them on their homeworlds had been coming to Coruscant in droves since before the Clone Wars. Even though one of the first fiats issued by Palpatine had severely curtailed the flow, the ecumenopolis still processed more visas in an hour than most worlds beyond the Core systems did in a month.

All those questing, hopeful, desperate, frantic beings had to live somewhere.

Den was not speciesist. He had lived among too many different kinds of sentients to put any particular one above or below another. All he asked was to be left alone to go about his business. But it was hard, sometimes, not to feel alienated from the thousands of beings who endlessly roamed the congested streets.

Alienated, and somewhat superior, given the lack of personal hygiene that frequently seemed to characterize them.

Cave dwellers his kind might be, but it was absurd to compare the noctilucent beauty of an underground city like Pirin to these fetid warrens overrun with the dregs of every conceivable outworld society. The worst examples of Kubaz, Rodians, Ugnaughts, and myriad other species crowded the streets, the open-air markets and bazaars, the seedy entertainment districts, day and night, leaving, it often seemed, hardly room enough to breathe. It was a sad thing indeed when a Sullustan found himself claustrophobic.

And if all that weren't bad enough, there were the humans.

Everywhere you looked, humans walked the narrow, twisting avenues or piloted ground and hovercraft as if they had the whole planet to themselves.

Which they just might, and soon, if the worrying rumor that the reporter had recently heard carried the slightest bit of truth.

It had come from a fairly reliable and reputable source, at least for this kind of thing: Rhinann. The dour Elomin had told Den that a plan would soon be under way, if it had not already been implemented, to round up and quarantine as many nonhumans as possible, segregating them from the human population. Den had found this hard to believe. Even though humans by far outnumbered all other individual species on Coruscant, they were hardly dominant in the aggregate. From Anzati to Zeolosian, humanoid and nonhumanoid aliens made up the vast majority of the city-planet's population. Trying to segregate them all from humans seemed to Den to be just asking for an uprising that would make the final struggles between the Republic and the Separatists look tame.

And if that wasn't cause for *se'lahn*, he didn't know what was.

seven

Jax could sense the subtle but insistent tug of Dejah Duare's pheromones, the chemical call to come to her aid, the plea to do whatever was needed to help her and her comrade leave the city-planet. Before the urge could become strong enough to sway him he invoked the Force, warming the air molecules around him ever so slightly to create an adiabatic shield that deflected the biochemical entreaty.

It worked, of course. He could feel his full objectivity returning. He did not have to glance in Laranth's direction to know that she had resorted to the same tactic. He noticed that Dejah seemed slightly discomfited, as if she were aware that her aphrodisiacal scent was not having the desired effect. Jax thought none the less of her for trying it. It was natural for her to use everything in her physical and biochemical arsenal to persuade them to the greatest extent possible. Even though he had already agreed to help, she was just trying to finalize the deal.

After the near-disastrous episode with Prince Xizor, he had made a point of learning which sentients in the galaxy utilized pheromones to influence emotions and behavior. It had allowed him to anticipate the

Zeltron's effort. Forewarned was definitely forearmed in a situation like this. By the same token, he was not sure if her telempathic abilities were strong enough to project emotions into others' minds without their consent. But if such were the case, the Force would warn him of any attempts by Dejah to influence him that way as well.

"Well, then," he ventured, politely pretending not to notice her uncertainty, "let's get started." He turned to the Elomin, who huddled in a seat in a dark corner of the room. "Rhinann, you know who to contact at the ports. Start the process while I-Five and I go with Dejah to talk to her Caamasi friend. Laranth, you and Den—" He paused, looking around. "Hey, where is Den?"

"Here," came the Sullustan's voice as he stepped back into the room from the hallway. "Just needed some air."

There was something in his tone that didn't sound quite right to Jax. True, Den wasn't always the most enthusiastic of participants in their various undertakings, but if he had doubts about the advisability of taking on a client or a case he also wasn't reticent about letting his comrades know where he stood. Probing in the Sullustan's direction, Jax sensed dissatisfaction and annoyance. He couldn't tell what the source of the troubled emotions was, however, and didn't have time to probe deeper.

Well, he told himself, *if he's got a real problem, he'll mention it sooner or later.*

"You and Laranth hit the streets," he told Den. "You know what to look for."

"Right." Den sighed. Again he sounded uncharacteristically glum. Typically, Laranth said nothing, just nodded once and headed for the exit. Den trailed in her wake.

Jax glanced at I-Five as he and the droid accompanied Dejah out to her skimmer. Hard to tell what the droid might be thinking about Den's moodiness. Although I-Five was extremely good at simulating emotions and thoughts by subtly manipulating the angle and intensity of his photoreceptors, as well as uncannily mimicking human body language, his ability to project nuance and subtext could extend only so far.

According to the Jedi's chrono, it was just after sunset. For the most part the surface streets were already dark. Although the street sconces were designed to work for centuries, many had been in place for millennia and had either burned out, been broken, or been stolen. Most of what illumination there was came from glow rods carried by pedestrians or from fires in refuse barrels.

So much for the spread of advanced technology, he thought.

While the streets were dark, they certainly weren't quiet. The constant babble of thousands of beings speaking hundreds of languages, patois, pidgin, and favored dialects blended together to create a rich basilect brew. Cheunh, Durese, Bocce, Hapan, and multiphonic other voices not only made it impossible for Jax to hear himself think, it sometimes made it impossible even to be certain in which tongue he was trying to think.

Dejah Duare's skimmer had been parked three meters above the street, where it hovered, waiting for the return of its owner. Employing a secure remote, she brought it down within reach. The vehicle was an F-57 Nucleon, with inertial stabilizers and a Class Three repulsorlift drive. Its design was charmingly retro, with sweeping tail fins, a forward cab, and a one-piece windscreen. It was a deep maroon in color, accented with sweeping lines of chrome. Dejah looked like she had been born to fly it. Jax was properly impressed. It wasn't often one encountered a vehicle that had been tinted to match its owner.

Her nav comp found an insertion point in one of the traffic streams, and she took the vehicle up at the steepest angle allowed. They reentered the flow at Level 75, just below the cloud layer. Fifteen minutes later the skimmer was nestling neatly into a parking pod near the upper floors of an expensive resiplex.

"Does he know we're coming?" I-Five's sensors were alert as they entered the building. The gleaming metallic walls of the lobby were lit with subtle chromatics, providing an ambience of understated elegance. Jax was abruptly very much aware of the shabbiness of his apparel. The boots, trousers, bloused shirt, and sleeveless fleekskin vest, which had been exactly right to blend in with the riffraff downlevel, here looked distinctly out of place. He shrugged. So much for keeping a low profile.

He felt nervous, on edge. The Force was trying to tell him that something wasn't right. Something bad had happened in this building, not long ago. But just as the Force could be incredibly explicit with the visions and portents it sometimes granted, so, too, could it be maddeningly vague and inchoate, and this was one of the latter times.

"No," Dejah said, answering the droid's question. "I tried to comm him but there was no answer."

Jax looked at her. "You don't sound very worried about your partner."

She smiled thinly back at him as they walked. "That's because Ves is frequently incommunicado. When he doesn't reply I assume he's working. He always works obsessively when he's upset. It's his way of dealing with it. And," she finished, "sometimes the result is his best art."

They traversed a length of corridor, at the end of which was a portal to a resicube. As she put her palm on the identifier plate, Dejah continued, "He'll be in his studio. It's in the rear of the—"

She didn't finish the sentence. Instead, as the door slid open and she looked inside, she screamed.

The cube's interior was cream, pearl, and ivory, the furniture and finishings all in shades of white. Which made the bloodstains on the carpet next to Ves Volette's body stand out in stark and brilliant scarlet.

Prefect Pol Haus of the sector police was a Zabrak: a short and somewhat stocky humanoid whose stubby horns rose from his skull in an untidy arrangement with no discernible growth pattern. This undisciplined look was not confined to his head. Haus was a disreputable-looking specimen from head to toe. His rank was high enough that he no longer needed to wear a uniform, and his attire looked like it had been custom-tailored by a palsy-stricken Dug. Over his clothes he wore a duster afflicted with a profusion of pockets. These seemed able to produce just about anything necessary for investigating a crime scene. He sported no ritual tattoos—another rarity for a Zabrak—and his skin was an unhealthy hue that bespoke a persistent lack of exposure to natural light.

Watching the prefect as he went about his business, Jax didn't buy into the veneer of disorganization. One did not get to be an official in the planetary police by being lazy, slovenly, or both. The fact that Haus paid so little attention to his appearance suggested that he didn't have to. That was significant. The fact that Sector Command had sent somebody of his rank to investigate wasn't a good sign, either. Prefects didn't leave the station to personally check out routine homicides. Such unpleasantness was normally left to underlings.

Jax and his companions were in the hall outside the cube. The murder scene itself was swarming with forensics droids large and small, which were recording and cataloging everything in sight. Jax had some knowledge of the procedure. Everything that a killer might have come into contact with would be scanned and recorded down to the molecular level. Any conceivable trace evidence would be picked up, ranging from the obvious, fingerprints, hair, skin cells, and the like, to the not-so-obvious such as thermal traces and any remnants of exhaled gases. You could tell a lot about a being if you knew the percentage of carbon dioxide he breathed out. It was a very careful killer who did not leave behind some trace of him-, or her-, or itself behind.

Jax watched the forensics droids going about their business, admiring their efficiency. The smaller units hovered on repulsorlifts a few centimeters above the carpet, so as to avoid trampling its fibers with their shuffling gaits. He was impressed with their speed and thoroughness—impressed, and more than a bit apprehensive. They were the epitome of professionalism, and the last thing he wanted was to have that vaunted clarity, that merciless illuminating glare, turned upon himself and his cohorts.

Having concluded his cursory inspection of the room, the police prefect emerged to study those waiting outside. Jax could feel the official's disapproval. The biolight source in the hallway's ceiling was on the verge of final decay, and the illumination had grown unreasonably bright, like that of a star just before its death throes. The unit cast hard-edged shadows instead of bathing everything within its purview in a normal soft, diffuse glow. It gave the scene a stark, alien quality. Beneath it, even the beauteous if distraught Dejah looked cold.

Haus coughed softly. "Did any of you touch anything, other than the doorplate?"

Jax answered for the three of them. "No."

The prefect looked skeptical. "Not even the corpse? To see if he was still alive?" He looked at Dejah, who was sitting in a small hoverchair with a blanket draped over her shoulders. "You. He was your partner, and you didn't bother to check his vitals?"

Jax felt a small stab of irritation. While it was the prefect's job to ask questions, this one had been answered already. He was tempted to wonder aloud which part of *no* the Zabrak didn't understand, but he held his irritation in check. It was seldom a good idea to give in to easy emotion. Especially when being questioned in a homicide. Keeping his tone carefully neutral, he responded for Dejah.

"There was no need, Prefect. It was apparent he was dead."

Haus wore studied indifference like a mask. "You could tell that from across the room?"

"I could tell," Dejah mumbled lifelessly. "He had the death reek on him."

Not even the prefect saw fit to question this. A Zeltron could easily detect the scent of epinephrine and fear pheromones in the room, as well as the lack of empathic vibes from her erstwhile comrade. And the Force had made it unequivocally clear to Jax the moment the door had opened that the sculptor Volette was dead, but it wouldn't be even a remotely good idea to let Haus know that.

I-Five said, "Judging from the size of the bloodstain on the carpet, Prefect Haus, the proportions of the body, and the depth of the stab wound that killed him, the probability of him being anything other than dead was close to zero."

Haus regarded I-Five. "So now a *protocol* droid is offering me advice on what questions to ask? Had a lot of experience with murder victims, have you?"

I-Five was less than intimidated. "During the Clone Wars I was posted at a medical Rimsoo in a planetary war zone. I regret to say that my experience with organic exsanguination is rather more extensive than I would wish.

"Given the extent of the bloodstain and the thickness and easily discernible absorptive capacity of the carpet, a simple mathematical computation can determine the quantity of liquid necessary to provide such dispersal. The average humanoid adult has a blood volume of approximately four-point-nine liters, of which two-point-seven liters is plasma. Humanoid survival with an untreated Class Four blood loss— that is, greater than forty percent of total volume—is unlikely for more than a few minutes. The amount of blood soaked into this carpet is, I estimate, nearly three liters. Even if the deceased had recently spent some months at an altitude sufficient to have radically thickened his blood, his red cell count could not be sufficient to allow survival with such a volumetric loss. Quite easy to see from across the room." I-Five's tone was dry and matter-of-fact, but Jax caught the underlying sarcasm. He resisted the urge to smile.

The prefect looked at the droid, then at Jax. "You program this smart-mouth machine?"

Jax shook his head. "He came that way."

Haus made a rude, decidedly unprofessional sound. "Might want to have his head popped and a more polite template installed. Not all police are as easygoing as me." He turned back to the inconsolable Dejah. "So let me see if I have this right. The deceased was the Caamasi light sculptor Ves Volette, your partner. You were worried about his safety, and your own, and thus engaged this guy"—he nodded at Jax—"for protection."

This guy came out sounding quite a bit like *this amateur* to Jax. He silently counted to ten, first in Basic and again in Ugnaught pidgin. It was amazing the places and times where Jedi training could be put to use.

It was not really a question, but Dejah nodded assent. Before the cools had arrived, Jax had warned her about mentioning anything to do with fleeing the planet.

The prefect turned to Jax. "And it's your business to routinely provide this kind of security service?"

The hard-edged light illuminating the hall flickered; a quick, ghostly strobe, before shining even brighter than before. The scene became sharper, almost crystalline. The unit was definitely on the verge of critical failure, Jax decided.

"That's right," he said to Haus. "We—I'm licensed to do so. It's a new classification: Confidential Factfinder. Nonprofit."

"So the records seem to say. I have your time of arrival, and my docbot says the victim has been dead for two hours and fifteen minutes, give or take a few. I'll need statements from you as to where each of you was at that time."

Jax nodded, glad of the opportunity to agree. "Of course."

The Zabrak looked at Dejah again. "If you were worried that somebody might make an attempt to kill you or your partner, why didn't you call the proper authorities?"

She turned slightly and looked at the officer. The angle put half her face in deep shadow. "Ves's homeworld was recently destroyed by what rumor suggests was an action by the *proper* authorities. With all due respect to you personally, Prefect, my companion had reason not to trust anybody who represents the Empire in any form. Nor do I."

Haus turned contemplative. "I've heard about what happened to Caamas, of course. Everyone has.

But it was a military action." His tone sharpened. "The Imperial Sector Police is not political."

"Really?" Her words emerged steeped in bitterness. "Somebody should tell that to the Vesarian students at Imperial City University."

The prefect had the good grace to look embarrassed. "That incident was an aberration. As within any large organization there are, unfortunately, rogue elements. The centurion in charge of the unit in question was arrested and is awaiting trial."

"I'm sure that makes the parents of the dead students feel much better."

Haus made a dismissive gesture. "An officer will take your statements and will provide you two with locator rings." He gestured at I-Five. "And a locator plug will be flashed to your smart-mouth droid. Stay dirtside—we'll call you when we need to speak again."

He turned away, dismissing them as thoroughly as he would have any inorganic piece of evidence. Which was fine with Jax—he was perfectly content to be treated as part of the scenery.

A police droid rolled up. "This way, citizens."

Jax sighed. Hardly a great way to start one's day: hired to save a pair of clients, only to have one die before they even got to him. Now they were, at best, witnesses to the scene, at worst possible suspects. Affixed with police locator rings that could not be easily removed, they weren't likely to be leaving the planet anytime soon. Jax didn't much like the idea of the cools turning over the rocks under which he and his cohorts liked to operate, but that was going to happen now whether he wanted it to or not.

The best option for him and his friends was to figure out who killed the sculptor and present Haus with that information before the police came across something embarrassing or illegal, and there was plenty of both for them to find. Jax knew that a truth-scan required more than just suspicion of irregularity, which was why Haus hadn't ordered one on the spot. Also, the cools were not supposed to ask questions during a scan that touched on activities outside the direct scope of the crime under investigation. But such rules were seldom strictly enforced, particularly downlevel, and it wouldn't be the first time the authorities dug a bit deeper than allowed just to see what was there. A truth-scan would prove that neither he nor Dejah had killed the sculptor, but there were plenty of other things Jax did not want brought to light.

The Force could keep such things hidden, but if they pushed a scan too hard, he might suffer memory damage, or worse. A Jedi Master could resist a truth-scan in his sleep, but Jax knew his abilities did not begin to approach such a degree of control.

In short, the sooner the cools wrapped this up and went on to other crimes, the better for Jax and company. If Haus and his men didn't find the killer immediately, then Jax had better do so. Otherwise he and Laranth and the others would have the police in their hair until doomsday.

Aurra Sing exited the spaceport, having made her passage through Customs and Immigration with no trouble. The passport chip issued her by Lord Vader guaranteed her Prime Civilian Immunity status, the highest protection accorded someone who was neither in the military nor a member of royalty. She took a drop-tube down three levels to the commuter pad, where a chauffeured skylimo awaited her. As soon as she had boarded, it angled directly up into the highest traffic stratum, a rarefied lane reserved for governmental traffic only.

It had been some time since Sing had been on Coruscant—now Imperial Center—and she marveled at how quickly and thoroughly the destruction inflicted by the Separatists' carpet bombing had been either repaired or simply hidden from view. Rebuilding was still going on apace. From her privileged position above the general traffic flow she could see, near the horizon, one of the huge construction droids. As tall as a forty-story building, it was methodically masticating its way through a swath of condemned structures. She knew that the resulting rubble would be ground up and separated into component elements, to be reassembled by billions of nanodroids deep in the giant's metal-and-composite guts. The result would be excreted as pliable new material to be reshaped into whatever forms the architects and city planners decreed.

It was an impressive example of the power and achievements of the Empire. She did not spend too much time contemplating such things, however. Her focus was on learning one thing: whom she would have to hunt.

After all, one did not secure the release from prison of one of the galaxy's most feared and formidable bounty hunters in order to have floral arrangements designed.

For almost as long as Aurra Sing could remember it had been the thrill of the hunt that had kept her alive, that had given her a reason to progress from one day to the next. It was only when she relied solely on her own skills, her superb reflexes and unique training, that she felt anything even approaching a level of personal comfort. She had relied on nothing else for so long . . .

One of her earliest memories, from before she had even been capable of walking, was of her spice-addicted mother carrying her down the narrow, twisted, garbage-strewn streets of Nar Shaddaa. Being held safely in her mother's arms, she remembered it as being one of the very few times she had felt anything approaching security. The moment even approached that emotional state others called happiness.

For Aurra Sing, happiness remained as much theory and speculation as the origin of the universe.

That special, long-ago moment had seemed as if it would go on forever. Until Aunuanna, desperate for spice, had dropped her child to the slimy wet pavement as she raced to meet her dealer.

Left behind, forgotten, a lump of organic trash abandoned on the pavement, the child who would become Aurra Sing had cried alone for hours in terror and pain. Eventually, emotionally and physically exhausted, she had crept beneath some stinking rags at the side of the lane. There she had lain, whimpering. It had been nearly dawn before Aunuanna's dust-besotted brain had cleared enough for her to remember her abandoned child, and another hour before she managed to locate her.

Sing shook her head slightly, the movement

amounting to little more than a twitch of irritation. As a neglected child, she had felt terrified and alone on countless occasions. As an adult she had turned such memories into a perverse kind of gratitude. Without knowing it and certainly without intending to, the addict Aunuanna had taught her youngling the basic lesson of survival, and taught it well: *Trust no one, and look to no one but yourself for survival.*

Sing studied the endless streams of aerial traffic flowing below her. Vehicles crisscrossed, sank, and rose in a complex three-dimensional dance that, thanks to omnipresent navigational and speed control nodes, hardly ever resulted in a crash or spatial gridlock. It really didn't matter who her designated target would be. A Sakiyan warrior bound on redeeming his clan's honor, a Weequay on a blood quest, a Januul in a scalp-taking fury: nothing could be more debilitating than feeling her lungs being eaten away by zenium dust in the stone guts of a forgotten planetoid.

Nothing.

She leaned back into the soft luxury of the limo's seat, literal as well as metaphorical parsecs away from her former quarters, and smiled to herself.

Expecting to be taken to Imperial City for her meeting with Vader, she was somewhat surprised when the skylimo suddenly dipped down and exited the VIP lane without a government building in sight. The powerful craft went into a steep descent that plunged into a narrow abyss between equatorial cloudcutters. Overhead, it was early afternoon, with the sun still halfway between zenith and horizon. Down where she was being taken, it was night.

Down here, she knew, it was always night.

The unmarked limo came to a stop, hovering half a meter above a narrow, trash-strewn street. On either side, cyclopean towers rose from massive foundations sunk deep into the planet's crust, their flanks vanishing into the mist and gloom above. Her surroundings were eerily familiar; it was almost as if, after all these decades, she were back on Nar Shaddaa. She saw no entrances or windows and no signs of habitation. In fact, there was no indication of life at all—not even any vehicle or pedestrian traffic.

She stepped from the limo, which rose to hover perhaps a dozen meters overhead. The fire-blackened, gutted husk of a landspeeder rested where it had no doubt crashed against a huge ferrocrete block that formed part of a skytower's foundation. Save for the almost inaudible thrum of the limo's repulsors, the silence was complete.

No, she realized—not complete. There was another sound, a sound she had never heard before, yet one that struck her as oddly familiar. A regular, measured susurration, growing gradually louder.

Whipping her lightsaber from its hook and activating it in a single movement, she whirled. The red glow of the shaft illuminated an alcove in the base of the building closest to her, and illuminated as well the tall, black-clad figure that emerged from it.

Before she could determine whether his intentions were malign or benign, he extended one black-gloved hand toward her. Her lightsaber leapt from her grasp, its fire extinguishing as it did so. It flew across the intervening space and slapped into Vader's hand.

He had been quick enough and powerful enough to

take her primary weapon from her before she had even realized she was in danger of losing it. A striking display of mastery over the Force, Sing had to admit to herself. But surely he didn't consider her helpless just because he had relieved her of one part of her arsenal.

As she dropped into a low fighting crouch, both hands seized the twin r'rüker'at knives secured at her waist. Her blasters would be futile, she knew; he could easily deflect the bolts with the lightsaber. Her only chance was to do the unexpected, and that meant getting in close enough for blade work. Forged by Alwari smiths in the jungles of Ansion, the knives were designed to be hidden in plain sight as part of the complex intaglio carved into her belt. Four rings allowed four fingers an unbreakable grip on each, and she had never let go before until the blades had finished their work.

Instead of following up his first move with a direct assault, however, Vader did something completely unexpected. He just stood there, ignoring her as casually as if she didn't exist. As she stared, he inspected her lightsaber thoughtfully; then, holding it out at arm's length, he reactivated it. The crimson spire of destructive energy pointed straight up from his gloved fist. At first, nothing seemed to be happening. Then Sing realized that the shaft was getting brighter. Its brilliance intensified until she had to raise a hand to shield her eyes from the all-but-blinding scarlet radiance. The refulgence dazzled her eyes, overwhelming everything else; the street, the buildings, the wrecked landspeeder. Only Vader remained somehow visible; standing there, holding the weapon easily, seemingly unaffected by the blade's terrible radiance. The familiar deep hum that was the weapon's identifying sound rose in pitch, higher and higher, until it tore at her hearing. And then, in a final burst of screaming incandescence, the lightsaber's shaft *vanished*.

Sing stared in sheer disbelief. Her eyes were capable of adapting much more rapidly to changes in ambient light than were a human's. A couple of blinks and the afterimages cleared, normal vision returning almost immediately. Vader stood motionless, the weapon's hilt still gripped in his outstretched fist. She could see a tiny wisp of smoke curling from the emitter.

He had *overloaded* the lightsaber's energy crystal through the Force. Sing prided herself on her knowledge of weaponry and their individual strengths and weaknesses. It was her profession, after all. But she had never seen or heard of such a thing before.

The Dark Lord opened his hand. Reduced to a cylinder of useless metal, composites, and components, the now harmless weapon clattered onto the pavement.

"As I told you back on Oovo Four," he said, "I have a job for you. Take up a weapon against me again, even reflexively, and I'll have you on the next prison barge offworld. Do I make myself clear?"

Slowly Sing returned the knives to her belt, folded her arms, and regarded him levelly. "I'm listening," she said.

The cul-de-sac known as Poloda Place was one of the few locations downlevel that still retained a glimmer of respectability. The buildings, rococo resiblocks for the most part, were packed close together. What narrow, winding passageways once connected the plaza with the rest of the underground had long ago been mortared up or otherwise sealed off. The only means of ingress or egress was a serpentine lane with the picturesque, not to mention evocative, name of Snowblind Mews. Den had wondered more than once how it had come to be named that, since snow had not fallen anywhere on Coruscant save in recreational areas specified by WeatherNet for many thousands of years.

Due to the combination of cheap rent, spacious living areas, and a spurious sense of safety, Poloda Place had acquired something of a reputation as an artists' colony. It was here, over twenty years earlier, that the novelist Kai Konnik had written his award-winning tale *Beach of Stars*. The Fondorian composer Metrisse had crafted his famous *Études of Time and Space* while sojourning there, and the notoriously decadent Twi'lek Dreamdancer Nar Chan had held her infamous, weeklong bacchanals in the court.

Those were indeed the days, Den reflected, hurrying to keep up with Laranth as she crossed the flagstones and made her way through the exit.

"Slow down!" he complained. "Not every species has grotesquely long legs, y'know."

The Twi'lek glanced back over her shoulder without slowing her pace. "Then stretch yours."

Swearing under his breath, Den broke into a trot. "I gotta tell you," he muttered as he caught up to her, "this whole fatal fem thing is getting old. You know you're hard, I know you're hard. Anyone around you for more than five minutes who doesn't know that you're hard isn't operating in the same sensory framework. So as a personal favor, why don't you lighten up?"

Laranth halted sharply and looked down at him. "What makes you think I have a choice?"

This was not the response Den had expected. Not that he'd had any particular rejoinder in mind. He came to a stop as well, thankful for the respite. Gazing up at the unsmiling Twi'lek Paladin, he observed how the various krypton, argon, and neon spectra from a nearby floating advert-sphere shone off the glossy scar tissue of her face. He noticed as well something he hadn't seen before in her eyes. Instead of the usual bleak mixture of determination and resignation, Den was surprised to see a flash of hurt—hurt, and an infinite weariness. It vanished quickly; so quickly that anyone else might have wondered if there had really been anything there at all. But Den was, above all, a reporter, and he trusted his perception. Not every insight came through utilization of the Force. He knew he had just gotten a glimpse of some very real and very old scars.

"Sorry," he mumbled, abashed. "Didn't mean to—"

She interrupted him with a shrug as she turned away. "Forget it." She was in motion again, strong legs striding. After a moment, he followed.

As he hurried to keep up with her he found himself turning over in his mind what he knew about Laranth Tarak. There wasn't much. He knew that she had been a Gray Paladin, a member of the renegade group that had splintered from the Jedi mainstream. He didn't know much about them, save that they were dedicated to the Jedi Code but considerably more

militaristic than the Order itself. Since the Jedi
Knights weren't exactly mantra-chanting pacifists to
begin with, this suggested that the Gray Paladins
were capable of some serious butt kicking. Den knew
this to be true from experience and not just anecdote,
as he'd had the privilege of seeing Laranth in action.
The Twi'lek's weapons of choice were the twin DL-44
blasters he had rarely seen her without, and her skill
and accuracy with them were uncanny. Aided by the
Force, she was good enough to block enemy fire with
her own blasts. It was not quite the same as parrying
shots with a lightsaber, but it was still impressive.

That was pretty much all he knew about the Gray
Paladins. Little as it was, it was more than he knew
about Laranth herself. This despite the occasional research he had carried out employing his reportorial
skills. Laranth Tarak had dropped off the grid of the
knowable a long time ago. He knew that she and Jax
had first encountered each other during the slaughter
of innocents known as Flame Night, a nocturnal mas-
sacre of Force-sensitives designed to rid the Empire of
potential future threats as well as to draw any remaining Jedi out of hiding. It had been one of the first
actions taken by the newly formed Inquisitorius. By
the standards of that formidable and menacing body,
the operation had been a great success, winning high
praise from the Emperor himself.

By combining forces, Jax and Laranth had managed to barely escape from the ambush, although
Laranth had not emerged unscathed. Den didn't
know if the Paladin's grim nature had always been a
part of her personality, or if it had been annealed that
night by the blasterfire that had truncated a lekku and

seared one side of her face. It didn't really matter. Whoever Laranth Tarak had been before had been thoroughly purged by the horrors of Flame Night.

Inquisitors, those "truth officers" steeped in the dark side, still prowled the multifarious sectors of Imperial Center, albeit in fewer numbers. The majority of them had been dispatched to the Outer Rim Territories and similar galactic backplanets to sniff out illegal Force activity. But the ones who remained were still to be feared. Den had heard that some were capable of isolating a lone Force-sensitive, nascent or otherwise, out of a population of millions. The chances of discovery were still astronomically slim—nevertheless, the Sullustan sweated every time Jax or Laranth made use of the Force.

Laranth had never been deliberately unkind to him. But even though she had saved his life on more than one occasion, Den still at times felt a small knot of uneasiness in his gut whenever he had to deal with her. She was so unremittingly *gloomy*. Not once could he recall seeing her smile.

Probably a good thing, he thought. *Might crack that scar tissue wide open.*

In any event, now was not the time to be wondering about Laranth's past. Jax had given them an assignment, which was to check the availability of possible UML routes and determine the quickest and safest way to get the Caamasi and his girlfriend offworld. For unavoidable security reasons this had to be done in person and not via electronic means of communication that could be intercepted or traced.

There were a number of Whiplash outpost agents in this sector. Each of these operatives was assigned to a certain section of a route. None knew any of the others. All operated on a strict need-to-know basis, and the order in which they were approached was chosen at random.

"So who's up in rotation this time?" he asked Laranth.

She hesitated a moment, then said, "The Cephalon."

Den smacked a hand to his forehead. "Sweet Sookie's maiden aunt," he groaned. "Do we have to deal with that *thing* again? He—it—they—I don't even know what pronoun to use, but it gives me the creeps."

"I sympathize," Laranth replied, "but that's who we're seeing. Come on—let's get it over with." She increased her pace, striding swiftly down the litter-strewn street that was becoming more crowded as the day progressed.

Den groaned again and hurried after. "I don't suppose it would do any good to say that I've got a bad feeling about this."

"Consider it indigestion," she replied curtly, "and deal with it."

eight

There were in the galaxy two main types of intelligence: chordate and ganglionic. Evolution, by panspermic and convergent means, had mandated that the vast majority of sentient beings be of the former design: creatures with a rod of cartilage or bone running the length of their bodies from which a skeleton could be hung and atop which a lump of cortical tissue could, in some cases, eventually grow into a self-aware brain. There were exceptions, of course. The Hutts, for example, were essentially giant invertebrate mollusks, their decentralized brains composed of billions of concatenated subneural chains integrated into their flesh. For the most part, however, intelligence had evolved through building notochords and parking gray matter atop them. This generally resulted in one consciousness per body, which seemed to Den a sensible way to arrange things.

Ganglionic intelligence was quite different. Most thought the term referred to a collective sentience, or hive-mind: the sum of many individual brains working in concert toward a common end, such as the bafforr trees of Iffor or the bivalves of Mon Calamari's

Knowledge Bank. Den had thought so as well, until I-Five had set him straight:

"What you're thinking of is symbiotic intelligence. Aggregated consciousness. Ganglionic intelligence is another thing entirely. Almost the opposite, in fact. It's *compartmentalized* consciousness. Try to envision your arms and legs having minds of their own, as the saying goes."

Den tried to imagine such a thing, and failed utterly. "It makes no sense," he argued. "Actually, it's even worse than that. It makes *anti*-sense."

I-Five sighed. He was capable of giving the sound a remarkably human resonance, given that he didn't breathe and had to synthesize it mechanically. "Take my word for it, then."

"I guess I'll have to. So you're saying that this—this—what do they call themselves again?"

"They don't. Humans and other species usually refer to them as Cephalons, which just means 'head' in Oldspeak Basic. They see no need for names, as their consciousness apparently exists in and perceives four dimensions."

"That sounds like a cosmic non sequitur to me," Den said. "But setting that aside . . ."

The droid anticipated his next question. "They 'see' time the way we see space."

"Uhh . . ."

I-Five projected the near-infinite patience of a parent trying to explain a difficult concept to a child. "The theory is that they're not limited to a linear one-way perception of time as most sentients are. They perceive temporal events the same way you're cognizant of items in spatial relation to where you are. See that landspeeder parked behind you?"

Den looked behind him. "Yes."

"Call it the past."

The Sullustan frowned. "Why?"

"Because it's behind you. See that trash bin ahead of you? That's the future."

"For you, maybe. I try to be more optimistic."

"How fortunate for me my chassis is made of sealed metal. Otherwise I might split my sides from laughter." I-Five took Den by the shoulders and turned him around. "Work with me on this." He pointed at the landspeeder. "Now *that's* the future, and the trash bin is the past. See? They conceptualize space and time as a four-dimensional hypermanifold. Simple, really."

"Why do you hate me?"

The Sullustan had tried to wrap his head around it, he really had, but it was just too bizarre. The Cephalon was easily the most alien of alien beings he had ever encountered, and for someone who had spent as much time as he had in a front-line Rimsoo, seeing in a week more xenomorphs, both inside and out, than most people did in a year, that was saying something.

But there did seem to be one small plot of common ground, and that was the Cephalon's willingness to aid other beings in escaping repression. Which meant that, every now and then, it had to be dealt with.

But that didn't mean Den had to like it.

Such a pathetic state of affairs, Haninum Tyk Rhinann told himself. How sad that he had come to this lowly state. It was undignified enough to be dependent on a human benefactor such as Jax Pavan, but it was much, much worse to actually be *envious* of him. His bauth—an Elomin concept largely untranslatable in Basic, indicating a combination of unshakable poise, brazen effrontery, and a touch of aloof amusement—which had once encased his soul in impenetrable armor, now hung in tatters. He had no individual future, no course, no star by which to steer. He had been cast down.

No, it was worse than that: he had cast *himself* down.

It hadn't always been thus. Once, not long ago, Rhinann had been puissant indeed. His word had been powerful enough to open doors and to close them as well, locking away behind them the enemies of his master. Perhaps it was true enough what his critics had said: that he had held no real power of his own, but instead had been merely a pale reflection of his master's glory, like a planet throwing back the light of its star. Perhaps. But there were worlds that reflected the dim ruddiness of red dwarves, and there were worlds that reflected the blinding azure of giant blue-white stellar furnaces. And save for Palpatine himself, no star burned more brightly in the firmament of the Empire than that of Lord Darth Vader.

It had been a heady draft of power, at first. Rhinann had been Vader's aide-de-camp, his personal adjutant and factotum, and as such the flail the Elomin had swung had been heavy. Given such a position one could ask, with perfect justification, why he had sought exile voluntarily.

On the surface of it he had had a most excellent

motivation: survival. His master had at last run the
rogue Jedi Pavan to ground, it was true. Unfortunately, that location had also been ground zero for an
imminent overload, initiated by Pavan in an underground reactor in the Factory Works, that grim an-
tipodean no-being's-land populated solely by feral
droids. The Imperial *Lambda*-class shuttle's stabilizer
vanes had been disabled by Pavan's lightwhip, whereupon the Elomin had acted out of sheer instinct for
perhaps the only time in his otherwise wholly rational
life: he had abandoned the un-airworthy ship and, in
so doing, abandoned his lord and master as well. As
a consequence, he had been left with little choice
but to throw in his lot with Pavan and his group of
motley companions.

Such disloyalty to the Empire could not be for-
given, even if his only alternative had been being reduced to a wisp of radioactive gas drifting forlornly
across the devastated landscape.

His plight might not have been so bad, his eventual
fate not as certain, had Vader been transformed into
free-floating ions like the rest of the Lambda's crew.
But Rhinann had seen the telltale footage captured by
the *Far Ranger*'s rear cameras, the instant in which a
life pod had jettisoned from the shuttle at maximum
speed. He hadn't needed the calculations quickly performed by I-Five, which had given the occupant of
that life pod a one-in-eight chance of escaping the immediate area and finding adequate shelter among the
deserted protective husks of buildings farther from
the blast site. The odds, the droid had hypothesized,
would be improved to an unknown degree should the
pod's passenger happen to be a master of the Force.

Rhinann had believed then what he knew now to be true—that this was precisely what had happened. After all, this was Darth Vader. The monster was all but indestructible. Of that Rhinann was convinced, and knew he was far from alone in his judgment. Because, in addition to his augmented strength and reflexes, Vader seemed to be more powerful than anyone in that most mysterious and wonderful of intangibles: the Force.

The Force captivated Rhinann. He had devoured every scrap of information on it he could find—no easy feat, given Emperor Palpatine's galactic ban on any and all hard data concerning the Force. After years of cautious study, the fascinated Elomin still had little idea of what it truly was. Most savants dismissed it out of hand, calling it a legend, a myth, a throwback to the sort of primitive religions that thankfully had all but died out in this modern, more enlightened era. Of course, none of them had felt an invisible noose tighten around their necks in concert with Vader's slowly contracting fist. But Rhinann had, and he knew that, whatever else it might be, the Force was no myth.

According to the lore, both ancient and modern, that he had assimilated, the Force was a form of energy that could be controlled and manipulated by conscious will. There were two theories as to how this was possible, which Rhinann felt were not necessarily mutually exclusive. One was that the ability to access the Force was based on a kind of apperception precipitated and augmented by endosymbiotic cellular organelles called midi-chlorians. The other theory held that the Force itself somehow brought into being those same midi-chlorians in order to facilitate its connection and thus manifest itself to varying degrees of potency in various species and individuals. There was also evidence that it was hereditary, although a wide gene pool seemed to be required for it to flourish. Nick Rostu, a native of Haruun Kal, was supposedly descended, along with all the other Korunnai, from a seed population of Jedi shipwrecked there centuries ago. Yet that soldier's connection with the Force had been weak. It would seem that midi-chlorians, and their resulting Force manifestation, did not increase their potency through inbreeding.

With great caution and stealth Rhinann had recently arranged to have his own midi-chlorian count tested. The results, carefully shunted and sliced through a plethora of servers and screens around the galactic information hyperlane, had at last come into his possession. As he had suspected, the number was pitifully low: a mere two thousand per cell on average. No one with such a low reading would ever feel the Force flowing through them. Although this merely confirmed his suspicions, he still found it disappointing.

Rhinann sighed, his nose tusks vibrating in high C. He'd reluctantly come to the conclusion that he had spent enough time on this quixotic quest for his own mastery of the Force. Better to concentrate on the far more mundane but realizable task at hand. He was supposed to be searching for lightsaber components. Trying to be something he was not was utter foolishness, and unworthy of whatever meager pride he had left.

He gestured at the holoproj, intending to change

sources, when he noticed a blinking node signifying a datum of possible interest that fell within his search parameters. It was dated nearly twenty standard years ago, and appeared to be a transmission from one of the outlying planetary fronts during the waning years of the Clone Wars. An odd sort of communication to stumble across.

Intrigued, he investigated further. Careful probing revealed what likely had been an obvious attempt to scour the item from the data banks, because it existed now only as an endstate echo, a digital reverberation of the original. Twenty years of quantum flux had resulted in considerable degradation. But Rhinann was an excellent slicer. With patience and skill he extracted what data he could from the various shells.

Interesting . . .

What he had found appeared to be a report from the world of Drongar, composed by the Jedi Padawan Barriss Offee to her Master Luminara Unduli concerning a native adaptogenic plant called bota. The Jedi Offee had apparently—whether by accident or design was not clear—taken an injection of the plant's distillate. The result apparently was a considerable increase in the Force's potency within her. Offee went on to say that she was sending a vial of bota serum to the Temple for further research. How this was to be accomplished was too corrupted for Rhinann to decipher. Her report went on to note that the plant's effects were opportunistic and varied widely from species to species. Given the potential ramifications of her discovery she strongly recommended that . . .

Rhinann's frustration knew no bounds: despite his

best efforts, the rest of the message proved unreadable.

He felt his ear hairs quivering with excitement. While by no means certain, could this forgotten discovery by a now deceased Jedi be the "magic slug" that might enable him to experience the Force?

He had, of course, heard of Bariss Offee and Drongar. Den Dhur and I-Five had spoken often of their sojourn on that pestiferous jungle world, as well as of their comrades in arms there. He could not recall hearing them mention anything about plant derivatives, much less bota distillate, but surely there should be a way to find out more about it.

He would have to be circumspect in his seeking, he knew. He had observed that Jedi were protective of their connection to the Force. If Offee's finding was authentic, and if Pavan and Tarak were at all familiar with it, they would no doubt be reluctant to share such information, especially with someone not of their clique. Haninum Tyk Rhinann was not a foolish or reckless being. Proof of this lay in his continued survival despite the often threatening circumstances in which he found himself. He would proceed cautiously.

And if it was true—if this reputed botanical enhancement could still be found, and if it could somehow facilitate a connection between him and the Force—well then, those who had taken advantage of his new miserable station in life would have ample cause to regret it.

nine

Night had overtaken much of Imperial Center by the time Typho came to the reluctant conclusion that his search through the ruins of the Jedi Temple had been futile. The vast repositories of the library had been stripped of most archival material, electronic as well as physical. No matter how skillful and experienced a slicer he was, what remained was still far too much for one being to sift through. The library wing had once been the repository for a thousand worlds' histories, cultures, bestiaries, and countless other data. What was left had been thoroughly disrupted by wave after wave of barbaric vandalism and looting. Entire files, together with their multiple backups, had been defaced or deleted, seemingly for the sheer pleasure of the destruction. He realized he would find nothing here to aid him in his quest.

He was standing in what had once been a long curving corridor lined with different forms of information storage: datasticks, memory chips, holoproj activators, and even a few ancient records created by layering dark images on dried plant pulp. He was holding a datastick in his hand. Its contents had been scrambled so that anyone attempting to read the contents would find themselves presented with gibberish.

Angry, he hurled it to the tessellated floor. It shattered with a flash of light as the residual electron storage lattice disintegrated, sounding in the stillness like a glass globe being crunched underfoot.

Pointless. Hopeless. He could easily spend a year or more searching the remnants of this one ruined library. It would take him the rest of his life to investigate the cubic kilometer of buildings, streets, stores, and various other institutions that surrounded him and had been associated with the Order. Was it really worth it?

Unbidden, the image of Padmé's face rose before him. Soft, sensual, intelligent, and caring.

Yes, he told himself. Yes, it was worth it. He was prepared to sacrifice his life. He could certainly sacrifice his time.

He knew what his next step had to be, the next question that had to be answered. Had Anakin Skywalker, who had been the last person to see Padmé alive and thus topped his suspect list, really died on Mustafar? Or had he somehow escaped?

He was uncertain where to go to find the answer. But it was clear now that it was unlikely to be here. He turned to go—and froze as his ears registered a sound.

The interminable cityscape was rarely silent, even in these huge and deserted ruins. There was the Dopplering buzz of the traffic, both above and below, the distant whine of repulsors lifting larger vessels into orbit from the nearby spaceport, and the thousands of small seismic creaks and groans of contraction and settling as the huge structures all about him reluctantly gave up the day's heat. These were noises so omnipresent that they had long ago faded into the background. They were the soundscape of the city-planet.

But this was different. It was the stealthy crunch of footsteps upon the debris that coated the floor. A sound that instantly alerted the soldier within Typho. Before he knew it his blaster was in his hand and he was pressing his back against the end of a storage bin.

He didn't have to wait long. From around one of the huge shattered columns appeared a female humanoid of most striking appearance. Her skin was as white as alabaster. It gleamed coldly in the starlight that poured down through the shattered ceiling. She was bald save for a hank of dark red hair that rose from the top of her head like a magmatic eruption. The tight-fitting jumpsuit she wore was tinted a similar shade. He was able to make out the stub of some kind of biocomputer device protruding from her skull as well.

Even in the dim light Typho could see that she was heavily armed. A long-bore slugthrower was sheathed across her back, and twin holstered blasters rode low on her hips. But it was the weapon she held in her right hand that he found most intriguing. Unless he was greatly mistaken, it was the dormant hilt of a lightsaber.

It took a moment longer for him to realize who she was. He blinked in silent surprise. He had pegged her occupation almost immediately; few save bounty hunters went about in public so well protected. Some had acquired reputations that extended beyond their immediate and specialized field of work, and were recognizable on multiple worlds. Certainly none was better known than the woman he was now staring at: the mysterious Nar Shaddaan called Aurra Sing.

As a military professional it was part of Typho's job to familiarize himself with the most dangerous outlaws and renegades, on the off-chance that he might one day be required to confront such reprobates. None qualified more than Sing. Born into unknown circumstances in the benighted urban jungles of the Smugglers' Moon and eventually raised by Jedi who had sought to develop her nascent Force potential as an instrument of good, she had been kidnapped by pirates who had turned her against her benefactors. Aurra Sing was notorious the length and breadth of the Empire. He had heard that she had the death mark on her in more than a dozen systems. It was also rumored that she had been working for Count Dooku during the Clone Wars but had disappeared shortly after his death.

And now here she was, rooting around in the ruins of the Jedi Temple even as he was, looking for—what?

He decided that unless there was evidence to the contrary, the notorious Aurra Sing's preoccupations were none of his business. He was not on Imperial Center in any official capacity, far less that of a military officer. He had come here on a purely personal matter. To assume that the doings of the outlaw Sing had anything to do with his work was too fantastic to contemplate. Best, then, that he simply slip away, unnoticed, into the night to resume his own quest, and leave the fabled and feared bounty hunter to hers.

There was a problem with doing that, however. The floor all about him and Sing was littered with the debris and impedimenta of the library that before the Jedi Purge had been arranged in a neat and orderly fashion. It was impossible to make the slightest move without disturbing this technological regolith. Typho had no doubt that any resulting noise would immediately alert Sing to his presence. He had been exceptionally fortunate to have heard her before she had taken notice of him.

Given their mutual isolation and unpopulated nocturnal surroundings, he doubted she was likely to stop and listen to an explanation of his presence, however brief he might try to make it. Based on her reputation, she was far more likely to shoot first and ask questions later.

Typho was by no means a coward, but one did not pursue a successful military career without learning caution. It would serve no useful purpose to engage the bounty hunter in combat, and could very well prove catastrophic. Glancing warily about while keeping Sing in view, he noticed another datastick located at eye level on a shelf opposite. Careful not to make the slightest noise as he moved, he reached for it. Hefting it firmly, he prepared to toss it far across the open floor, hoping that the flash and bang it would make on impact would give him time to . . .

She moved almost too fast for him to see; in an instant her lightsaber was activated. Part of him noted almost academically that the ignited shaft was almost the same color as her hair and jumpsuit. He had ample opportunity to appraise its exact hue because the incandescent tip now hovered entirely too close to his throat as it backed him up against the shelves behind him.

Typho realized he had made a foolish and possibly fatal mistake. He had neglected to take into account Sing's storied connection with the Force. Unrefined and untrained though it might be, it had obviously been strong enough to alert her to his presence.

"Who are you?" Her voice was as cold and hard as the alabaster her skin resembled. The lightsaber that threatened his throat was as steady as if held by a droid. "More importantly," she continued, "who sent you?"

"No one sent me." Typho did his best to stay calm. His tone was as unthreatening as possible. "I am Captain Typho of Naboo, formerly of the Senate Security Council. I am here on my own. No agency or individual has sanctioned my undertaking."

Sing's eyes were red with the light of the shifting, scarlet shaft, as if they could suck up its energy through the sheer force of will that was contained behind them. "Why don't I believe you?"

Typho realized that he had only moments left in which to save himself. If the gleam that danced in the bounty hunter's eyes wasn't madness, it was still borderline homicidal. This was not someone who would choose to engage in extended conversation in the ruins of a dark and deserted building in the middle of the night. Rather than spend the time to establish whether or not he posed any threat, she would simply kill him and be done with it.

Unless . . .

He still held the damaged datastick in his gloved hand. Without thinking and trying not to give any mental foreshadowing of his intention, he closed his eyes and squeezed his hand into a fist. As the storage device shattered, it released a burst of eye-smiting light and a sound like the bass *thump!* of heavy artillery being fired.

His glove was sufficient to protect him from the burst of heat that resulted from the globe's destruction. And his action had the desired effect. With a surprised cry Sing staggered back, momentarily blinded. Typho moved quickly, knowing he had only one chance. He kicked upward, the toe of his boot slamming into Sing's wrist. The lightsaber fell from her stunned fingers, its shaft shutting down automatically. Typho caught it.

In the course of his tour of duty on Coruscant, Typho had handled lightsabers under the supervision of Qui-Gon Jinn and Mace Windu. As a result, he was far more familiar with them and their capabilities than was the average Naboo officer. Even though all lightsabers were slightly different, the construction of each having been finalized by the Jedi who owned it, there were certain design characteristics that were of necessity common to all. Most crucially, given his present situation, the activator stud was nearly always positioned so that it would fall under the thumb of a gripping right hand.

Typho thumbed the stud and felt the vibration surge up his arm as the unit powered up. The deep hum changed pitch as he moved the blade. If Sing pulled a blaster on him, he was as good as cooked, since he didn't have access to the Force to warn him of incoming fire.

Instead she did something entirely unexpected; reaching down to her waist, she pulled another lightsaber from her belt and activated it. A second shaft of deadly energy, this one emerald in hue, sizzled into being.

"This is wonderful!" Sing declared. Her eyes were shining, her expression alive with cruel delight—and Typho decided, more than a touch of madness. "It's been ages since I've had a decent lightsaber workout." Stepping back, she assumed a defensive stance. The glow from her weapon bathed her white skin and pitiless smile in an unholy viridian light. "You know how to activate one. I hope you can handle it well enough to put up something of a fight."

And so saying she leapt forward, the glowing length of lethal energy upraised to strike.

Typho had no choice but to fall back, swinging wildly in the hope of warding off his attacker. A few hours of desultory practice with the weapon had in no way taught him how to handle himself against a master of the art. Lightsaber combat was quite different from traditional sword fighting in a number of ways, not the least of which was that the lightsaber's weight was all in its hilt, yet a firm two-handed grip was still needed because of the gyroscopic precession effect that gave the weapon a sense of mass.

He managed to block Sing's first two attacks. His success was due as much to luck and frantic energy as to any limited skill. He didn't fool himself into believing that his temporary reprieve was likely to last much longer. His fighting ability was further lessened by a lack of depth perception caused by the past loss of one eye. Not for the first time he found himself wishing that an accident of genetic programming had not rendered him immunodeficient to transplants cloned from his own organs.

Despite all his energy and efforts, he was quickly driven back across the broken remnants of the library aisle. Another moment and he found himself with his back up against the base of a shattered column. Grinning humorlessly, Sing raised her blade.

"On behalf of Lord Vader I was hoping to find evidence here of a Jedi named Jax Pavan," she said. "If you have any knowledge of his whereabouts, you may continue to live for a few more seconds. No? Pity. Well, then—"

She was preparing to lunge, Typho knew. A surprise attack was his only chance. He hurled himself forward, under the humming shaft of her weapon but intentionally aiming his thrust high, as if still unfamiliar with the lightness of the bound arc wave. Her countering slash missed him by the thickness of a nexu's whisker. He felt the heat as the light wave whizzed by just above his back.

Her following move was just what he expected— and had hoped for. She chose the easiest way to avoid the thrust, which was simply to duck and allow his clumsy attack to pass over her head and hair. An instant later her triumphant grin turned into a rictus of agony. Spasming once, she collapsed to the littered floor and lay there unmoving. She was either unconscious or dead; Typho couldn't tell which, and did not particularly care. Her weapon extinguished itself as her grip went slack. He staggered back, looking at the supine form. In the dim light he could barely see the tiny wisp of smoke that curled from the blackened tip of her biocomp antenna where he had grazed it with the lightsaber. The resulting biofeedback shock had done the rest.

Peering harder, he could make out the slight puffs of fog caused by her breath meeting the cold night air. Not dead then. Only unconscious. He had no desire to still be in her vicinity when she recovered from the shock. Already her lithe body was starting to twitch with the beginnings of a return to awareness. And, he told himself, it could all be a sham. She could be playing half dead, her intent being to lure him close.

Of course, the sensible thing to do would have been to run her through while she was on the ground, but he could not bring himself to do it. His uncle Panaka, who had been Padmé's bodyguard when she was Queen, had taught him to show mercy whenever possible. To do less, Panaka had warned, was to risk becoming a monster like the ones often faced in the line of duty.

Typho could not have that. His intent, his desire, his mission, was to avenge Padmé, but not at the expense of a blot on her memory. Criminal though she might be, slaughtering the woman now lying stunned would do his cause no honor. His probity was on shaky ground as it was. He was here in this place under false pretenses, had come with vigilante justice on his mind and dominating his thoughts. Under such circumstances, it could be argued that he had more in common with the bounty hunter than with the strict military code of Naboo. She sought money, he sought revenge. Who could say which, in the end, was the more honorable? Surely he, in his current state of mind, was not one to render such a judgment.

Her purpose in stalking the heart of the Temple had been to find a Jedi named Jax Pavan. It had not been to challenge the wandering Captain Typho. Were that the case, he was certain she would have said so. They had met by chance; now they would part in equal ignorance.

And so he left Aurra Sing lying unconscious in the rubble of the Jedi Temple, and continued onward into the night in his quest to determine if the Jedi Anakin Skywalker still lived.

ten

—*Servant. Aide?*

As usual, the polite brevity of the Cephalon's question took Den by surprise. The Standardized Basic translations that appeared on the monitor screens next to the tank showed its sub-brains all quietly humming away like banks of compartmentalized computers, each busily parsing its particular outlook on reality. Somehow these various disparate takes were codified into coherent thought—or what seemed to be to the Cephalon coherent thought—and used by the central brain, the one that was capable of abstract conceptualizing. Den did not pretend to understand how it worked. He had enough problems trying to make the single brain he'd been born with operate. The thought of having to handle input from various semi-autonomous sub-brains made him dizzy.

But such concepts and imaginings were at worst merely confusing and irritating compared with the Cephalon's appearance. It loomed hideously out of the sulfate-laden cloud in the tank, its great sessile mass distorted by the thick transparent barrier that contained its poisonous environment. It was tethered to a coral accretion in the cheap downlevel habitat that formed its home. Or its office, or embassy; Den was not sure which of those identifiers, if any, applied.

The Sullustan could barely keep from recoiling every time he saw it. The Cephalon's skin was the mottled flat gray of long-dead flesh, its shape an undulating oblate globe, festooned apparently at random with tentacles, antennae, feelers, and chelae. It had no eyes or other sensory organs that Den could see. According to I-Five, it perceived its external environment by means of electroceptive matrices, whatever those were. Its mouth was a baleen plate that sieved extremophile microorganisms from the dense, primarily methane atmosphere that sustained it.

The Cephalon was surely one of the most bizarre species in the entire galaxy. Its inner thoughts were as unknowable as nearly everything else about it. Working with a Force-sensitive Inquisitor, Imperial scientists had managed to identify nine distinct emotional states, of which only three bore even a faint resemblance to the sentiments that most humanoids experienced. There might be more, but it was rumored that the Inquisitor himself had gone mad from trying to wrap his own mind around the varying states of the Cephalon's four-dimensional consciousness.

There's a comforting image with which to open a negotiation, Den thought. Aloud, he began, "We, uh, we have two sentients on the UML who, uh, need . . ."

—Elaboration is/was/will be unnecessary. This was another eerie thing about the Cephalon. Since it could "observe" happenings in time as clearly as Den could see objects in three dimensions, it always knew what he

was about to say. The Cephalon was not omniscient—
it couldn't conceptualize every incident in the fourth
dimension any more than most beings could see
everything in all three spatial directions from any single vantage point. But it seemed to know enough
about the immediate future to be able to make predic-
tions with unsettling accuracy.

    *—Sentients are/have been/shall be non-united. Point-
pattern at now contingent modalities nonviable. As
yet point-pattern in noncollapsed state,* it told them.
*—Probability matrices undefined. I/we apperceive
discontinuity. Suggest cautious/passive/observational
mode.*

This was one of the biggest problems in attempted
communication with a nonlinear being, as far as Den
was concerned. The translation did its best to keep up
with the Cephalon's erratic and seemingly irrational
changes between tenses and personae, as well as
struggling to fit its static perception of the time-
stream into terms of past, present, and future. The result was often a translation that usually seemed right
on the verge of making sense. The Sullustan sometimes felt that he actually might be able to understand
it, if he only had an extra lobe or two with which to
process the mishmash. Usually, however, it was as far
over his head as a skyhook penthouse.

    Which was the case this time. At wit's end in time
as well as space, he glanced helplessly at Laranth.
"Any idea what all this probability poodoo is
about?"

    She shook her head. "I have the impression it's in-
decisive. Basically, it's advising us to wait and see."
She turned to exit the habitat chamber.

He gaped at her retreating back. "That's it? We come all this way . . . ?"

"It was three blocks, Den."

"That's not the point. The Cephalon's supposed to give us tips on the best UML routes, the right officers to bribe, that sort of stuff. He—excuse me, it—is our go-to guy in the prognostication department. I could get better advice from a Mon Cal kismet biscuit."

Laranth did not reply. Den sighed and started to follow, when from the corner of his eye he caught a glimpse of more words forming on the monitors. Scowling, he turned back. *You'd think the thing could at least afford a vocabulator,* he thought as he read the creature's latest words.

—Vulnerability apperceived in alternate probability. Extreme discontinuity in Force convergent. Prioritize discreet vigilance anent fugitive recovery operation.

"Okay," Den said. "That's cryptic even for a giant floating four-dimensional sack of brains." Glancing toward Laranth, he saw that she had read the Cephalon's words as well. "Think you can translate the translation?" he asked.

She shook her head. "Let's worry about one thing at a time. I have a feeling that this job isn't going to be easy."

Den sighed as he followed her out the door. "Are they ever?"

"Let's review what we know," Jax suggested.

"Easily done," I-Five responded, "since at this point we know practically nothing."

The droid, the Jedi, and the Zeltron were sitting in a Southern Underground saloon called the Dizzy

Dewback Cantina. Actually, Jax and Dejah were sitting and I-Five was standing close to Jax, so as to better maintain the illusion of a properly servile droid. Jax knew it made no difference in terms of wear and tear on I-Five's chassis whether he stood or sat. He could have held an erect posture until the building crumbled around him. But it was galling to the modified droid's pride to have to subscribe to an inferior status, and the Jedi found it difficult to resist a grin.

Jax had come to this serviceable haunt more than a few times over the last several months. It was a good place to relax while plotting strategy: reasonably quiet and out of the way, plus the food was tolerable and the drinks cheap. Of course, having been raised a Jedi he had never really developed a taste for alcohol or similar ingestible stimulants, which was why he was currently nursing a cold slush of ice flavored with various exotic fruit juices mixed with supposedly healthy items such as powdered guroot and desiccated Kaminoan sponge. It wasn't as palatable as it sounded, and it didn't sound all that palatable to begin with.

Dejah, on the other hand, was staring moodily into the depths of a half-empty Arboite Twister. This was not the sort of liquid concoction one expected to see a refined creature such as her imbibing. Jax had once seen a couple of downed twisters almost embalm a two-meter-tall Weequay. The mere scent of the potion wafting across a room could make a Troig bang its heads together until binary unconsciousness resulted. He'd heard somewhere that Zeltrons had two livers. *She'll need them,* he thought as he watched her drain the last of the high-octane blend.

He didn't blame her, of course. From the little she had said before the discovery of her dead partner, it was apparent to anyone that Dejah had been, at the very least, deeply fond of the Caamasi. Jax didn't get the feeling that their relationship had involved romance, but it didn't have to for her to feel keenly the sting of his death. Zeltrons were flagrant in their passions; they seemed incapable of entering into any relationship, be it carnal or casual, with anything less than wholehearted fervor and abandon—a consequence due at least in part to their powerful empathic abilities. When tragedies happened, they felt all the searing pain that a sentient was capable of feeling.

Of course, the reverse could just as easily be true. Fiery love could transmute into icy hatred in the blink of an eye.

He abruptly realized that I-Five had just said something and was now waiting for a reply. The droid was projecting an attitude of patience mixed with slight resignation, as if he had expected having to wait for the Jedi to rouse from his quiet reverie.

"I'm sorry," Jax murmured. "What?"

In the absence of having a throat to clear, I-Five emitted a terse electrical crackle. "To reiterate—if I may. Prefect Haus's men have not found the murder weapon yet. I venture that its discovery may shed more light on this mystery."

"It's been three hours since we left the resiplex," Jax pointed out. "How do you know the forensics droids haven't turned it up by now?"

"Because," the droid replied, "I'm monitoring the wavelengths reserved for sector law enforcement transmissions. There has been no mention of such a finding."

Jax slowly shook his head in disbelief. "One of these days they're going to home in on that illegal slicing you do and hit you with an echo pulse that'll leave you about as self-aware as a crisper."

"Something to look forward to, given the level of intellectual simulation around here," the droid shot back. "Now, having disposed of the requisite badinage, perhaps we could return to the subject at hand?"

"By all means." Jax stole another glance at Dejah. She was slumped in her chair, her eyelids fluttering and her breathing much heavier than what was required to keep her lungs expanded. "You might want to keep your voice down, though it doesn't look like she's all that aware right now."

"She's not," I-Five confirmed. "My olfactory subprocessor has calculated the volume of alcohol in her blood. Adjusting for species-specificity, I estimate that she will shortly lapse into and then remain in a near-comatose state at least until dawn. Even her pheromone discharges are about twenty proof."

Jax stuffed a cushion behind Dejah's head, then leaned forward in his chair. With a hand he waved away a cloud of stimstick smoke that had drifted over from a nearby table full of raucous Kubaz.

"We know that Volette died of a single stab wound to the celiac plexus." The Jedi stared into the distance. "If I remember my xenobiology classes back in the Temple, that's the anterior part of the autonomous system node, right?"

"In most hirsute mesomorphic humanoids, such as

Caamasi and Equani, yes. A puncture wound of any size there is almost certain to be fatal, much as a wound to the heart is to humans. According to the planetary police 'casts, they've hypothesized the murder weapon as a short-edged passive instrument."

Jax nodded. In the context of the police report, *passive* meant something other than a vibroblade or other energized weapon. "Then Volette was killed by an extremely primitive knife or its equivalent," he said. "Which leads us to ask, how was the act performed? If the police theorizing is accurate, something easily concealed but having to be used at close range seems most likely."

"Which inversely presupposes someone of considerable strength. The anterior region of a Caamasi is protected by a layer of thick cartilage." The droid gestured at Dejah. "That would seem to exclude her as a suspect."

Jax nodded. It was certainly true that Dejah could have approached her partner Volette closely without arousing his suspicions, but there was no way she could have stabbed him hard enough to penetrate the protective carapace, especially with a nonvibrating weapon. The Zeltron simply did not possess sufficient musculature.

He realized he felt relief to know that Dejah was not a viable suspect. Had some of those pheromones slipped through to affect his wariness? He hoped not. Life was complex enough already. But even if Dejah Duare could be ruled out, she was only one suspect out of billions. They still had quite a way to go.

"There's no escaping it, I-Five. We have to find the killer before the prefect's investigation decides to focus on us. If the cools ever suspect we're linked to the Whiplash, we're plasma. They'll lock us on a moon and throw away the moon." Jax held up his right hand, showing the sparkling arc of the locator ring that banded his middle finger. "And there's no way Duare or I can take this police jewelry off or deactivate it without the inbuilt circuitry paralyzing our motor responses while simultaneously communicating our whereabouts to the local cools."

"Good point, if obvious," the droid concurred.

"Don't be so smug. As long as you're wearing that bolt, you're just as stuck as—" Jax stopped in midsentence and stared openmouthed as I-Five held up the restraint plug that the police droid had just recently flash-welded to his chassis. The Jedi's mouth collapsed into a grin as he shook his head. "Is there anything you can't do?"

"Yes," I-Five replied. "Dance."

Jax took the restraining bolt and examined it. "You never told me you've had bootleg anti-restraint programming installed."

The droid shrugged metal shoulders. "What's the point of being sentient if you can't cultivate an air of mystery?"

Jax tossed the bolt back to the droid. I-Five caught it easily without looking in its direction. "And when they try to track you?"

"They'll find themselves following an ouroboros circuit with which they'll never quite catch up." The droid put the bolt on the floor, aimed an index finger at it, and melted it into unrecognizable slag. Then he turned to gaze speculatively at the unconscious

Dejah. "It would appear that her plans to leave Coruscant will have to be postponed."

"It's Imperial Center now, remember?"

I-Five's vocabulator produced a sound remarkably like a disdainful sniff. "I'm a droid. I don't make mistakes."

"I doubt any passing stormtroopers or Inquisitors would agree."

"As your father once said: no matter what they call it, it's still just an overbuilt, overpriced ball of rock."

Jax went quiet, the mention of his father turning him suddenly introspective. After a while, I-Five was moved to ask, "Does it upset you when your father is mentioned?"

"No. But it does make me wonder at times how he would react to my choice of lifestyle. To the decisions I've made."

The droid moved a little closer. "All too many of those choices and decisions have been foisted on you, Jax. I knew Lorn Pavan better than anyone, and I think he would have been quite proud of you."

Jax looked up. "I thought he hated the Jedi."

"He did. But only because they took you from him. He wouldn't have hated you for becoming one. I think he would have approved of the choices you've made—most of them, anyway. Especially your decision to stay here and aid the Whiplash. Lorn admired courage. Particularly the courage to stand up for one's convictions."

Jax's expression was unreadable. "I almost quit, you know."

I-Five projected mild surprise.

"It was months ago. I was packing my kit, ready to

dust. Then Nick Rostu told me about what happened to Master Piell." He shrugged. "I couldn't leave after hearing that. Certainly not until I'd completed his last mission."

"Which you did, to the best of your ability. So tell me: what's stopping you from leaving now?"

"It will never be finished," Jax told him. "Defeat the Emperor and Vader, and liberate the galaxy? The idea defines craziness. I should get out now, while there's still a transport berth with my name on it."

"I believe Den would agree with you," the droid replied. "Vociferously."

"No doubt." Jax sighed. "And yet . . ."

"You can't."

"You know me so well."

"I know humans so well. I know your kind with an intimacy that only an outsider can achieve. I've seen humanity at its most selfless and noble—and at its most base and ignoble. It can be quite a range. That's why it doesn't surprise me at all that you remain here to continue the fight for what you insist is a lost cause. If presented with that choice, I knew from the day I met you which one you would make."

"Is that so?" Jax looked about him; at the garish holo-ads on the walls and the various species toking, imbibing, or otherwise altering their brain chemistry in pursuit of congenial oblivion. He suddenly felt very tired. "Which choice was that?"

"The right one," the droid said.

Aurra Sing awoke disoriented, angry, and possessed of a throbbing headache in the ruins of the Jedi Temple. Her baffling opponent was long gone, which was no surprise. What was surprising was that she was still alive.

A guarded inspection of her immediate surroundings confirmed that she was indeed alone. Her opponent, Captain Typho of Naboo, had no doubt fled, taking with him one of her lightsabers. Even in the throes of her fury, Sing had to admit that she was impressed. He had tricked her most cleverly, lulling her into vulnerability and then using her own prosthetic against her. She had briefly succumbed to the worst enemy someone in her profession could face: overconfidence. That accepted, she still had to give the man his due. He was resourceful as well as skilled.

Good. A challenging enemy was a worthwhile enemy. She would enjoy tracking him down.

But such enjoyment would have to wait until she first completed her primary task: the capture of Jax Pavan for Lord Vader. She had no intention of going back to Oovo 4, and the easiest way to ensure that she never saw that hated place again was to fulfill the assignment she had been handed. Not that she had any intention of doing otherwise, even if she could have figured a way out of it. She would have paid Vader for the opportunity to stalk one of the last Jedi.

The night was quiet, save for the eerie whistling of a breeze through the columns and rooms of the ruined Temple. Except for the endless stream of air traffic high overhead there was no movement. All seemed calm again, but Sing did not relax. She could no more stand down from her state of habitual alert than she could stop breathing.

A slight movement behind her . . .

In the space of a breath Sing's lightsaber was lit.

The bounty hunter swung it in a deadly arc behind her, spinning about as she struck to face whatever foe might be lurking there.

Its body cut neatly in half, a large armored rat writhed momentarily on the ground before her. It shuddered briefly and then lay still.

With a grunt, Aurra Sing deactivated her weapon, clipped it to her belt, and strode off to resume her search for Jax Pavan.

"Extreme discontinuity in Force convergent." Jax repeated the phrase to himself, then looked at Den and the Paladin. "Any idea what it means?"

"Well," the Sullustan replied, "I've given it a lot of thought, and I'm fairly certain that I have no karking idea whatsoever."

"You're a lot of help." Jax turned to Laranth. "I hope you've got something more substantive."

The Twi'lek shook her head. "I wish I did. Unfortunately, I'm just as baffled as Den."

Jax looked around the room. Present were Laranth, Den, and I-Five. Missing were Rhinann and Dejah. Jax didn't know where the Elomin was. The Zeltron was in one of the bedchambers sleeping off her concussive hangover. He sighed. "Anyone else care to venture a guess?"

I-Five spoke up. "Obviously the concept that is being communicated has something to do with four-dimensional perception. We know that the Cephalon can to a certain extent see into the future the way we can see down a path. Unfortunately, it's a winding path that seems to meander through mist and clouds, rendering the final picture inconclusive."

Den raised a brow. "Wow, that was almost poetical. Almost."

The droid peered down at his companion. "This from a representative of a culture whose crowning artistic achievement is a paean to the military-industrial complex." I-Five addressed his next remark to Jax. "It's clear that the Cephalon was trying to apprise us of some future event. It is up to us to figure out its meaning."

Den rolled his eyes, the result being quite impressive. "Why, why, *why* do these sort of hints have to be all roundabout and mysterious? Why can't we for once run into a fortune-teller who's clear and up front about things? *A week from now the Festering Plague will break out in the Blackpit Slums. Wear gloves.* Like that."

"I doubt that the Cephalon was striving to be oracular just for effect," the droid replied. "Attempts to reduce a four-dimensional tense into Basic are frequently less than completely successful."

Jax was about to comment when a bulky shadow filled the doorway. It was Rhinann. His gaze swept over the others with monumental detachment and disinterest, to drop anchor upon reaching Jax.

"There are, as far as I have been able to determine," he said lugubriously, "no lightsabers or components thereof remaining on Coruscant."

"You're sure?" Den asked. "Did you look behind the couch?"

Rhinann ignored this. "My investigation into the matter has been thorough and exhaustive. It is, of course, entirely possible that in a city covering five-point-one times one hundred and eight kilometers squared, a weapon approximately one meter long when activated and rather less when not just might have escaped my notice. If you suspect that to be the case, I urge you to continue your own search."

"What about crystals?" Jax asked.

"No traceable signs of Adegan, Ilum, or Dantooine crystals, either. Again," Rhinann added, "I cannot guarantee that someone somewhere doesn't have one sitting on their mantel as a curiosity. There is simply no way to trace such a thing."

Jax nodded, thinking. Though the majority of Jedi had been slaughtered by the clones offworld, there had still been a respectable garrison at the Temple when Anakin Skywalker had initiated his one-man pogrom. Furthermore, Jax knew that Palpatine had ordered their weapons destroyed. If Rhinann was right, the troopers had been most thorough.

Laranth said to the Elomin, "You're patently wrong in one instance. Darth Vader still carries one."

"Vader's a Sith," Jax said before the Elomin could respond. "Or so gossip has it. I think it's true. It's the only way to explain his proficiency with both the lightsaber and the Force." His expression fell. "It would appear that you all were right. I'm not meant to have one."

"Being a Jedi is more than just having a lightsaber," Laranth pointed out. "Through the use of the Force one can become proficient in other modes of fighting that are almost as effective."

"I know." Jax looked away. "It's just that I never really had a choice. I had only just graduated to full-fledged Jedi Knighthood when Order Sixty-six was implemented. After that, my life was all about survival. A big part of that was keeping my head down and not using the Force." He offered a wry smile. "I've really only had the opportunity to use it once in a life-or-death battle, against Prince Xizor. And the irony is that *he* had the lightsaber and I was reduced to using a lightwhip."

"Not to mention a somewhat sputtery connection to the Force," Den added.

"Unless you have some reason for my continuing to pursue this chimerical task, I shall consider it settled. I have other matters to which I must attend." The Elomin's sepulchral voice said quite clearly that, as far as he was concerned, the subject was closed.

Then to his surprise, Jax heard Den say, "Wait a minute."

As he listened to his own mouth forming words seemingly independent of his brain, Den was somewhat taken aback by what he found himself saying. He was also a little nervous. It had happened before, this disconnect between his tongue and his head. It was as if the former was ruled by a semi-autonomous sub-brain, like one of the Cephalon's appendages. The results were seldom good.

"Wait a minute," he heard himself saying. "I'm sure Rhinann has done an exemplary job trying to locate a lightsaber. But there's more than one way to gut a gokob."

"How colorful," I-Five said.

Den ignored him. "I was a reporter once, remember? A good one, back in the day. I can track a story over bare rock in a monsoon."

The droid clicked two metal fingers together.

"There is a point to all this, I presume? The organics in the room aren't getting any younger."

"Neither is your humor." Den looked at Jax. "If you really feel that getting your own lightsaber will help you function more effectively, then let me see what I can find out."

Rhinann gave him an opaque stare. "What makes you think that you can succeed where I did not?"

Den raised pacifying hands. "Hey, no offense, but I just have a feeling about this, y'know? Maybe it'll lead to something, maybe not. Either way, it's no hair off your ears."

"That's enough," Jax interrupted. "Den, if you're serious about this, you're welcome to have a crack at it, but in your spare time. Our first priority is finding Volette's killer, and I need your fabled search-and-find abilities working on that foremost."

"Whatever you say, boss." Den settled back in his chair. He still wasn't quite certain why he had volunteered to take on this extra task, although one reason was self-evident: he didn't like Rhinann. The tall, saturnine biped could bring the mood of any group crashing down faster than the gravity well of a neutron star. Besides, he hadn't flexed that particular set of muscles in quite a while. It would be a worthwhile diversion.

As long as he didn't let his inquiries bring him too close to Vader's orbit. . .

"We had no real friends," the sad-eyed Zeltron was saying. "Just acquaintances and professional associates. We hadn't been on Coruscant all that long. A little over two months, and most of that time was spent in making contacts that were invariably more business than social. We were . . ."

Dejah paused, setting her jaw momentarily, and Jax was surprised to see that she was overcoming the urge to cry. He had heard that, overall, the defining characteristic of the Zeltron species was that of hedonism. That they tended to be industrious and productive only with an eye toward that end, and were unwilling or unable to deal with negative emotions. Dejah, in contrast, seemed to be made of somewhat sterner stuff.

She continued. "So you see that we were rather isolated. Save for Baron Umber, whom we saw quite frequently."

Jax, Dejah, and I-Five were sitting in the bleachers of a local recreational park, watching a game of shock-ball being played between two young groups—mostly Rodians versus Haserians. The crowd was following the sport enthusiastically, providing plenty of ambient noise as cover for their conversation.

I-Five pondered briefly. "The identifier *Baron Umber* is unfamiliar to me. The title naturally indicates a person of importance. Perhaps you could elaborate?"

"I'm sorry," she replied. "I assumed most people around here were familiar with the name. He's a Vindalian. I understand that not too much is known about them. We heard that they're rather secretive. One thing that is known is that they tend to be great art fanciers. Certainly the Baron was no exception. He bought a great many of Ves's best light sculptures." She blinked in sudden realization. "I don't know if he's been made aware yet. Keeping to themselves, Vindalians pay less attention to what's called the 'common' news than do many species. If he doesn't know, this is going to hit him quite hard."

"I'm sure the sector police have notified him," Jax pointed out.

Her lips compressed into a thin scarlet line. "That's right, of course." Her tone was bitter. "No doubt they delivered the information with all their customary tact."

"My impression is that Pol Haus is a pretty good cool," Jax told her. "Which is one way of saying that you can trust him as long as you don't cross him. But like anyone in his position he's not immune to either politics or pressure. He won't let anyone or anything jeopardize his job. My take is that he's only investigating Volette's death because your partner was a minor celebrity. I wouldn't be surprised if there's pressure on him already to wrap it up fast, stick any results in a tube, and bury it. He'll take any solution that seems reasonable and that answers most of the questions. I'm sure that his higher-ups don't want a big deal made out of a Caamasi case. Not when Palpatine took the political risk of having Caamas destroyed. If indeed he was ultimately responsible."

Dejah looked grim. "So you would advise me to leave sleeping akks lie?"

"It would seem the safest course, if we're to get you offworld," I-Five said.

Turning away from them, she watched the game for a few minutes. One of the Rodians scored, and the crowd went wild. Finally she said, with more assurance than she had exhibited in some time, "No. Ves wouldn't abjure justice for me if the situation were reversed. I can't leave this place until I'm convinced that everything possible has been done to find his murderer."

Jax took a deep breath. "Well, I admire your determination, if not the decision." He looked at I-Five. "Next move: I suggest we find this Baron Umber and have a chat with him." He smiled thinly. "We can talk about art."

"His conapt is located at Seventeen Gallifrey Lane, Sector One-Oh-One-Seven in Manarai Hills," I-Five replied immediately.

Dejah looked surprised. "That's his private address. It's unlisted. How did you . . . ?"

The droid tapped the side of his head with a metal finger. "Connections."

eleven

The Manarai Hills district was one of the posher neighborhoods on Imperial Center, which was saying something. An eclectic combination of architectural styles, the luxury conapts that made up the majority of its domiciles had been designed by the renowned Benits Stinex, one of the galaxy's premier architects. The building Umber lived in was semi-autonomous, its exterior accented with smooth, streamlined chevrons and towers. Once again, Jax felt profoundly out of place.

The melded chimes that made up the door were answered by a 3PO protocol droid, its silver chassis burnished to a high gleam. After an unmistakably disapproving glance in the direction of I-Five, it acknowledged Dejah immediately.

"Please come in. My master will be most happy to see you." It ushered Dejah through the foyer as Jax and I-Five followed.

"Please, rest comfortably," the droid insisted. "May I offer you beverages? No? Then I will inform the Baron of your unexpected and extremely welcome visit." It shuffled away across a vast expanse of burgundy carpet, leaving a flattened trail of scuffed carpet in its wake, and disappeared through an arch.

Jax studied his surroundings. They were expansive, with curved walls dimpled and folded to allow more space for the exhibition of paintings, friezes, ceramic floats, and other artwork. Tastefully displayed on slowly moving pedestals scattered around the floor were several examples of art that had to be the work of the late Ves Volette. Sculptures formed of animate light, they writhed and undulated hypnotically within their individual containment fields. As he looked on, they shifted spectra according to how they had been woven, cycling through various hues and patterns. Each was uniformly delicate, ethereal, and utterly beautiful.

He glanced at Dejah. The Zeltron was looking at the sculptures as well, her expression forlorn.

Approaching one of the sculptures, I-Five examined its undulant prismatic form closely. "Most intriguing. The energy signature is quite similar to the arc wave of a lightsaber. I would hazard a guess that its energetic source is a crystal—Adegan, Luxum, or something similar."

Jax raised an eyebrow. "The same kind of crystals used to drive a lightsaber."

"Quite right," said a new and commanding voice.

Jax turned about to see a bipedal figure standing in the archway. He was tall and slender to the point of anorexia, dressed in flowing robes of shimmersilk. His features seemed quite human, although something about the shape of the face and the ears gave a subtle vulpine cast to his appearance. As he came toward them he made straight for the Zeltron.

"My dear Dejah." His voice was warm and buttery with compassion. "Such a shock. I was told of Ves's fate not two hours ago by that thuggish police prefect." Reaching out, he took her hands and held them in both of his. "You must be devastated. I tried to comm you as soon as I was informed."

"I turned my link off," she whispered.

"Perfectly natural, and who could blame you? If there is anything you need, anything at all, you have only to ask." Looking to the side, he took note of Jax and I-Five, his gaze sharply appraising. "I see you've brought a friend." I-Five stiffened at the cavalier omission but said nothing.

"I'm sorry," Dejah said. "Where are my manners? Baron Umber, Jax Pavan, captain of the merchant ship *Far Ranger*. Jax, this is Baron Vlaçan Umber of Flavin Hold, Vindalia."

In his all-too-brief tenure as a Jedi Knight, Jax had learned the Galactic Standard protocol for addressing nobility of various species. He inclined his head and made the proper hand gesture. "An honor, Baron." He saw Umber's eyes widen slightly in surprise, and realized that his studied courtliness must seem incongruous coming from someone dressed so shabbily.

"The honor is mine," the Baron replied, making the requisite response motion. He glanced briefly at I-Five, who stood in formal posture beside Jax, looking every centimeter the proper protocol droid. "One of the Orbots line," the Baron commented. "Something of a collector's novelty these days. Nicely restored." Jax repressed a smile as he thought of the acidic response that was no doubt crackling through the droid's positronic brain.

"Baron," the Jedi ventured, "if you don't mind, I have a few questions I'd like to ask. They concern your relationship with Ves Volette."

Once again Umber could not quite conceal his surprise. He looked questioningly at Dejah, who nodded reassuringly. "It's all right, Vlaçan. You can trust this one. He's bound himself to help me find Ves's killer."

"I—see." Despite the Zeltron's assurance, the Vindalian's skepticism was obvious. He looked at Jax again, his gaze much more critical this time. "Are you—affiliated with the sector police?"

Jax found himself more amused than irritated by the Baron's obvious disdain. "I'm an independent investigative agent. Dejah asked me to pursue this matter through unofficial channels."

Keeping his eyes on Jax, Umber addressed his next question to the Zeltron. "Are you sure this is wise, Dejah? For one thing, I strongly doubt that any facts or evidence uncovered by this method will be considered admissible in a tribunal."

It was I-Five who responded to that. "Actually, the law admits evidence submitted by outside sources on deontological grounds."

The Vindalian's gaze narrowed as he regarded the mechanical. "I don't recall anyone giving you permission to speak, droid. Nor do I require instruction in legal proceedings from a nonspecialist device."

"A knowledge of the law, especially as it relates to Imperial dictates, is an important facet of protocol," I-Five said. "You must admit that these days, with new laws being promulgated every day and old ones revised or eliminated, it is next to impossible even for specialists in such matters to keep up. You need not be embarrassed to confess ignorance in such matters."

The Baron seemed on the verge of apoplexy. "I was not confessing anything!" he sputtered. "Least of all ignorance! Of all the—"

Reaching out, Dejah put a hand on his arm. The Zeltron touch was enough to calm their host somewhat. He was by no means pacified, however. He stared hard at I-Five. "You're right, however. Today's statute is tomorrow's misdemeanor, so to speak. None of which addresses the matter of you speaking unbidden."

Jax hastened to interpose himself between the two. "I-Five's encoding has been modified. He doesn't always react like your standard protocol model." The Jedi glanced warningly at the droid. "Sometimes he suffers from an intermittent glitch known as Big Mouth Syndrome."

I-Five projected annoyance. "The dimensions of my verbal simulation orifice are absolutely factory-standard."

"Maybe," Jax said, "but the brain behind it sure isn't. You will show our host proper respect."

A moment of uncomfortable silence ensued as the Jedi glared at the droid. Then I-Five turned to face Baron Umber and bowed slightly from the waist.

"My sincere apologies, sir, if I have inadvertently offended you."

"And . . . ?" Jax prompted him.

I-Five's immobile metal countenance somehow managed to look disdainful—or perhaps Jax was reading too much into it. He hoped so, at any rate. "I also regret speaking out of turn," the droid continued.

Umber was mollified. "Well, no harm done, no insult intended. Especially if, as you say, this model's programming has been clumsily personalized."

"Clumsily?" I-Five echoed. "May I just point out that—"

"—our questions will be concise and our time here brief," Jax hastily concluded for the droid, punctuating his assurance with a glare in I-Five's direction that fell just short of melting several of the softer alloys. He stepped between the droid and their host, blocking the former's view from the latter. "Dejah tells me," he continued, "that you're a longtime collector of the late Ves Volette's work."

Umber gestured assent. Turning, he indicated the alcoves where many of the artist's finest creations twirled and flashed in syncopated brilliance. By themselves, they provided more than enough light to illuminate the end of the room in which they were displayed.

"From the moment I encountered his works I knew I had to have one," the Baron said. "The first led to a second, the second demanded a third to offset its shape and style, and by the time I determined to purchase a fourth and fifth, I counted myself not merely a patron of Ves Volette, but his friend." He looked to where Dejah sat quietly on a couch. "And his companion's friend as well."

She smiled. "Ves abhorred the formal art scene on Coruscant, where creators are expected to mingle with potential buyers, flatter their usually nonexistent taste, and offer discounts. He was a true artist. If you liked his work, fine. If not, he dismissed you, but without anger or prejudice. He recognized that tastes differ, or all art would be the same."

Umber nodded solemnly. "That was one of the things that made Ves and his work so special. He was entirely independent of the commercial art arena. He did what he wanted, the way he wanted."

Dejah was obviously thinking back to happier times. "I remember once when a Senator from a wealthy world approached Ves about one of his pieces." She smiled. "He asked if Ves would alter the main spectral current so that the result would match the décor of the Senator's sleeping chamber. The asking price for the work was high, and Ves could have pocketed substantial credits. He simply refused, quietly and without rancor. 'This is the color scheme that coalesced in my mind,' he told the Senator. 'This is the pattern the color took. It is what it is—just as are you and I.'" She looked up at Jax. "That was Ves. He was as straightforward as his art."

"*Straightforward* is another word for *blunt*," Jax said. "And bluntness could be misconstrued as arrogance."

The Baron hid a smile. Jax looked at him. "Are you amused, Baron?"

"My apologies. But had you known Ves even for a short time, you would realize the absurdity of your suggestion. He never meant to hurt anyone's feelings."

"But he sometimes did?" Jax glanced at Dejah, who nodded slowly.

"Most people excused it on the grounds that he was an artist. Just being creative seems to excuse a multitude of offenses that would get ordinary folk thrown out of a party."

"Or killed," I-Five said. This time Umber did not upbraid the droid for speaking without permission.

Jax turned back to their host. "Did he ever offend you, Baron?"

Umber looked startled. "No, never. I understood his art, therefore I understood him. We always got on well, and there was never a time when I was displeased to see him. We held differing political opinions, of course, and discussion of them sometimes led to raised voices and sharp gestures, but never to hostility." He paused, then asked, "You're not suggesting that *I* had anything to do with his death?"

"Of course not," Jax replied immediately, though that was exactly what he was thinking. As a Jedi, he was sworn never to lie. Occasional misdirection in the service of the greater good was, however, permissible. "I'm just trying to build a picture of your relationship with Volette in order to get a better idea of what he was like, what his social life was like, and through that maybe a hint or two of the kind of individual who might have wanted him dead."

"For example," I-Five suggested, "someone who owned a surfeit of an artist's work would stand to profit substantially by his death, if his passing subsequently raised the value of that individual's work."

Jax contemplated deactivating his outspoken mechanical companion. What he really wanted to do at that moment was use the Velmorian energy sword sheathed at his waist to seal the droid's mouth shut.

To his credit, however, and somewhat to Jax's surprise, the Baron took no visible offense; instead he simply nodded thoughtfully. "That certainly might be so. In the case of Ves's work, however, he has not been dead long enough for the market to be thus affected. And I treasure even the least of his pieces in my possession and have not the slightest intention of selling any of them, so their monetary value is of only peripheral concern to me." Spreading his arms wide to encompass their elegant surroundings, he added, "As you can see, my position and personal resources are adequate to allow me to comfortably maintain a certain lifestyle without the need to—I believe the Basic term is *hock*—any of my property. Even if such a necessity should occur, my Volettes would be the last assets I would part with."

Dejah managed an approving smile. "Of all Ves's clients, Baron Umber more than anyone deserves the honorific title of *patron*. Ves knew it, too."

Their host performed an odd little sideways bow in her direction. "You honor me with your confidence, my dear." Straightening, he looked back at Jax. "You have other questions? Perhaps you would like to search my domicile for a murder weapon, or signs of Ves's DNA?"

"No, no." Jax waved a hand. "I believe what you've told us." He looked toward the couch. "Even more, I believe what Dejah has said about you. Coming here, meeting you in person, seeing how you feel about the artist's work, I'm confident you had nothing to do with his demise." Leaning slightly to his right, he peered past their host. "You're not alone here, are you?"

Pivoting, Umber gestured to where a figure stood

behind a fold of arch. "Come out, my dear, and meet our guests. Dejah is here."

The Vindalian female was notably larger than her mate, though not unattractive. While sexual dimorphism was common among humanoid species, it was usually the male who was larger. Usually, but not always. In this case, the female who emerged from concealment not only massed more than the Baron, she was half a dozen centimeters taller as well.

"This is Kirma, my wife," the Baron informed the visitors.

The Baroness was casually dressed in a sweeping spinner-silk gown that clung to her form and did little to conceal her bulk. Jax found it somewhat startling. What looked bad on one variety of humanoid, he reflected, was often considered immensely flattering on another. Not knowing anything about the species, he could only assume that, given the clingy nature of her attire, Vindalians found size attractive.

In addition to the gown, she wore a string of lightly polished green stones around her neck. No astrogeologist, Jax didn't recognize them. It was the only jewelry on her person. Given the Baron's status, he concluded that she was either being deliberately modest or else had not had adequate time to prepare herself to greet visitors. His gaze drifted back to Dejah, sitting alone on the couch. She wore no jewelry and the most basic and functional of attire, but to Jax she outshone the noble's mate by several orders of magnitude.

"Dejah has engaged this gentleman," Umber was saying, "in the hope of finding who killed Ves." Yet again he failed to mention the presence of I-Five. This time, thankfully, the droid kept his indignation to himself. Instead, he was studying the new arrival intently.

"Dear Ves." Kirma Umber blinked rapidly, which Jax assumed to be a sign of anguish among her kind. "Who would murder a harmless artist?"

I-Five had kept silent about as long as he was constitutionally able. "A serious critic."

Kirma glanced at him, the droid's sarcasm apparently—and fortunately—lost on her. "Are you having any luck in your investigation . . . ?"

"Jax Pavan. We've only just begun. We're trying to build a picture of Ves's last moments by interviewing those who were closest to him." He nodded in Dejah's direction. "Since you're the artist's primary collectors, we came here first."

"My husband is the one who is enamored of the light sculptures. Though I can certainly appreciate the skill that went into their construction."

"You're not upset at the artist's death?" I-Five asked.

"What a thing to say!" Kirma Umber's extensive lashes flared. "Ves Volette was a fascinating, devoted, and kind sentient. If he had been a lowly fashioner of cheap tourist trinkets, I would have been equally as fond of him. Of course," she added tersely, "being a machine, I don't expect you to comprehend such feelings."

"Of course not," I-Five said drily. He went silent again, for which Jax was profoundly grateful.

Kirma turned to Jax. "Aren't you duplicating the work of the police?"

"Supplementing." Jax smiled. "My friends and I

can work outside official channels. You never know what you may find there."

"You can see how upset we both are," the Baron said. "If there's anything I can do to facilitate your investigation, I insist that you make use of myself and my good offices."

"That's very kind of you." Jax glanced at Dejah. "I told you this wouldn't take very long."

"You've only just arrived." Umber stepped closer. From his body wafted a faint odor of pomegrail, though Jax was not sensitive enough to tell if it was natural or the result of a flattering additive. "Won't you stay for second-morn meal?"

"Thanks," I-Five responded, "but we're not hungry."

Even the Baron had to smile nominally at that. "There's nothing I can offer you?" he persisted, looking from Dejah back to Jax.

The Jedi hesitated. "Actually, there might be. I need a compressed energy crystal. Adegan or Luxum would be best, but I'd take whatever you'd be willing to part with."

Umber acted as if he hadn't heard correctly. "You want to buy one of my Volettes?"

Jax shook his head. "Not a sculpture. Just a CEC."

The Baron was horrified and made no effort to hide it. "The CEC is at the heart of each sculpture. No," he corrected himself quickly, "the CEC *is* the heart of each sculpture."

Though a bit taken aback by the force of the Vindalian's reaction, having already ventured the request, Jax persisted. "Pardon my ignorance—I'm not an artist, and I'm not exactly familiar with the genre—but couldn't you substitute something for a piece of Adegan? Another energy source? Marilite, maybe, or pressure-treated halurium grains?"

Umber was clearly restraining himself with an effort. "Since you are honest enough to readily confess your ignorance, I take no offense. You do not understand. Once the CEC is removed from a Volette light sculpture, it collapses. It cannot be restored, certainly not by replacing the energy source. One can have an image repainted, reholoed, retooled, or a carving of some solid material reproduced. While not the original, an excellent copy may be so obtained. But once a Volette light sculpture is deactivated, it becomes as dead as the unfortunate artist himself."

"What would happen if you tried it?" I-Five asked.

Kirma looked at the droid. "You would get an amorphous blob of light. That's all. Maybe with color, according to the design. But the shape, the dance, the aesthetic, would be lost forever." She eyed her mate. "Isn't that the truth of it?"

"Truth it is," Umber confirmed. "I would no more destroy a piece of Volette art than I would surrender a limb. Especially since there will be no more. What exists now is all that there will ever be." Turning away from his visitors, he let his gaze roam over his collection. Even without resorting to the Force, Jax could feel the powerful emotions emanating from him. "Even if I needed the credits, young man, I would not—*could* not—comply." He turned back to Jax, and his gaze was hard. "I do not have the *right*. Maintenance of the Volette sculptures is more than a joy, now. It is an obligation."

Dejah was nodding her head in agreement as she

spoke to Jax. "I told you what kind of collector the Baron is. What kind of friend he's been to Ves and me."

"Yes, you did." Jax sighed. If he was ever going to acquire a CEC to power a lightsaber, it clearly wouldn't be from here. He would have to find another source. Unless, he reminded himself, Den had better luck.

After his wife excused herself, the Baron escorted them toward the exit. "Just as a matter of personal curiosity, what does a private investigator want with a compressed energy crystal? I realize that such a scarce article has a multitude of uses, but I can't see how it would prove useful to someone in your profession. Leastwise, not sufficiently to justify the cost." He paused, adding, "Of course, you don't have to explain yourself. It's none of my business what you want with a CEC."

"He's a budding inventor," I-Five explained. "He wants to make a functional probe that'll enable him to trace the neural paths to all the abnormal synaptic connections in his own brain."

As they reached the doorway Jax shot the droid a look. "Speaking of abnormal synaptic connections, maybe it's time someone took an aligner to the back of your skull."

"You see?" I-Five gestured by way of reinforcement. "Verbal confirmation of what I just said."

Umber forced himself to repress a smile. "In addition to being remarkably, even dangerously, outspoken, your droid effects a most distinctive sense of humor."

"No, he doesn't." Jax stepped aside to let Dejah

exit. "He's just rude. As to your question, Baron—I am looking for a CEC to use in my work. I'm sure you understand that someone in my position can't go into intimate details."

Umber's eyebrows rose in response. "*Intimate,* is it? Well, then, I won't pry any further." As Jax looked on, he put his arms around Dejah. Jax thought the clinch lasted a good deal longer than civility required, but the lag was understandable. Those who had the opportunity to embrace red Zeltrons, especially of the opposite gender, were reluctant to let them go.

Stepping back, the Baron finally released her, though he still hung on to her extended hands. "If you need anything, Dejah, anything at all, Kirma and I are at your beck and call."

She smiled. "Thank you, Baron. For everything. Ves would thank you, too, if he were here."

"He is." Turning, Umber nodded back into the domicile. "Vindalia willing, he always will be."

They were in the lift that was taking them back to the aircar hangar when Jax voiced the conclusion he had reached. "I don't think this Baron Umber had anything to do with Ves's death."

Dejah nodded knowingly. "I told you. He was our best friend on Coruscant. Whenever there was a problem of any kind, Ves trusted him to take care of it."

"You divine a lot from a brief conversation in someone's home," I-Five commented to Jax.

Jax eyed the droid. "You disagree with my assessment? If so, give me reasons. Other than the fact that anyone could see you took a personal dislike to the noble."

"I did no such thing." The droid didn't seem irritated. "I reacted to him and treated him exactly as I would have any other potential lead we might investigate."

"Loutishly."

"Directly," I-Five countered. "I am not confrontational. Merely straightforward. That's how one obtains desired information most rapidly."

"Maybe when communication is machine-to-machine," Jax said. "As a protocol droid, you should know that interviewing organics requires patience, understanding, and something else that seems to have been wiped from your memory."

"Which would be—?"

"Tact. If I'd let you run your vocabulator, we would have been thrown out of that dwelling in the first three minutes."

I-Five executed a shrug. "Small loss, since your client had already half convinced you there was nothing to be gained from speaking with the Vindalian anyway."

An exasperated Jax fell silent, prompting the droid to prove he was still a protocol model by adding, "I'm sorry he wouldn't sell you a CEC."

Jax shrugged. "Art lovers. A species unto themselves."

Dejah put a hand on his arm. The simple gesture immediately calmed him, redirected his thoughts, heightened his emotions, and took away much of the frustration of having wasted half a day learning essentially nothing. Those were only a few of the things the Zeltron touch could do.

"At any rate, I don't disagree with your assessment," the droid said, "because I assume that you utilized the Force to subtly probe the Baron while you were conversing with him."

Jax nodded as the three of them stepped out of the turbolift. At this time of day the hangar was not an especially busy place, and they took their time to enjoy the expensive décor of their surroundings as they waited for their transportation to unlock, activate, and arrive.

"I did," Jax assured the droid. "I was monitoring him the whole time we were there. I got nothing that would indicate he's in any way involved with Volette's murder."

"Neither did I. Galvanic response, eye contact, epidermal flush—none of it provoked anything like a suspicious reaction."

"Good. That settles it."

"Did you check the female?"

Jax raised an eyebrow. On his right, Dejah stared at the droid in disbelief. "Surely you don't think Kirma Umber had anything to do with Ves's death? That's absurd!"

I-Five replied calmly, "Why?"

Taken aback, Dejah had to think a moment. "Well, for one thing, she wasn't even that interested in Ves's work. The Baron was the real aficionado. I mean, she certainly admired it—how could anyone not? She shared the Baron's respect for it, if not his passion."

"That doesn't persuade me that my observation constitutes an absurdity." The droid turned to Jax.

"Surely everyone who had contact with the dead artist is a reasonable suspect."

"Even me?" Dejah challenged him.

"Even you, although you've been ruled out due to physical inability."

"Physical inability? You ambulatory circuit board, I'll show you—"

"All right, you two." Jax spoke sternly to the droid. "Dejah's not a suspect, I-Five. If she had anything to do with her partner's death, I would have sensed it."

The droid made a sniffing sound. "That, at least, I can appreciate." He looked at the still-angry Zeltron. "You see? I always respond to rational conclusions." To Jax he continued: "My question remains—what about the Baroness?"

Jax shrugged. "I suppose I should have probed her, just to fulfill the formalities. Still, I think Dejah is right. The Baroness was a friend to them even if she didn't entirely share her husband's boundless enthusiasm for Volette's work."

"And please keep in mind," Dejah said with asperity, "that I have empathic abilities of my own—which rang no alarms."

"In any event," Jax said, "I suspect Pol Haus and his people will perform their own thorough checks on the both of them."

I-Five still wasn't satisfied. "I doubt that the prefect's forensics team will include an investigator versed in the ways of the Force."

Further conversation was interrupted by the arrival of Dejah's convertible. As they slipped into the traffic stream, Jax chewed his lower lip. He waited for her to slide in beside a transport that was as ugly as it was functional. Within less than a minute they were accelerating on automatic. Then the Zeltron looked at him. "What now?"

"I suppose you have a list of the rest of Ves's buyers and of any nonprofessional social contacts?"

She nodded. "Whoever killed him left the studio intact. I haven't made a detailed check of it yet." Her gaze turned forward, to take in the massive flow of traffic between the towering buildings. "If nothing's been disturbed, then all that information will still be there. After I drop you and I-Five off, I'll collect it."

"Good. We'll make a list and start following up."

"What will we be looking for?" she asked.

"Any close acquaintance who's gone missing, or simply moved away. Anyone who tried to buy one or more of Ves's works just before he died. And especially anyone who might have reason to hold a grudge against him. Political, professional, you never know in situations like this. A sale that was withdrawn. A negotiation for a particular piece that fell through. Something as seemingly insignificant as a perceived insult delivered at a meeting." He glanced over at her. "We'll be relying on you to recall any such incidents."

"I'll do my best," she promised.

The aircar accelerated as the Zeltron pulled it out of line and headed downward in the direction of Poloda Place.

twelve

Aurra Sing entered the chamber of her new employer. The two Red Guards escorting her stopped at the entrance. The door hissed shut behind her, and she was alone with Darth Vader.

She stood, taking in her surroundings but not letting herself be absorbed by them. The room was dimly lit by human standards, but the low-level lighting posed no obstacle to her vision. She could clearly see the dimensions of the small chamber, could see there was no furniture save for a single formfit chair and desk. One of the walls was inset with graphic readout screens, serial port plugs, and other devices she didn't immediately recognize.

Vader stood at the room's far end, the stentorian sound of his breathing, regular and even, filling the air. The insectile orbs that covered his eyes—if indeed he had eyes—were turned toward her, but with Vader, one could never tell what he was looking at. His vision seemed to encompass every direction. And what he did not see through his eyes, Sing knew, he sensed through the Force.

She wondered how he slept—or, indeed, if he slept. One of the many rumors about the being hidden in the biosuit held that he had been hideously burned by either acid or fire, and as a result of the damage done to his lungs and throat he required the constant monitoring and assistance of the portable respiratory apparatus, which prevented him from lying down for little more than brief periods at a time. So, according to speculation, he was forced to rest while sitting or standing erect.

Most of the rumors of his origin, disparate though they were, agreed on one thing—that Vader was more machine than man. She wondered what motivated him, what drove him forward through the days. Even a Sith Lord, which Vader was rumored to be, needed incentive to carry out the assignments that Palpatine had chosen for him or that he had selected for himself, to push him to complete tasks that another might find overwhelming.

She thought she knew.

Hate drove him.

Hate motivated Vader to get through each day and night. Hate was the fuel that fired his existence. Having given himself over to the dark side, he had done so unreservedly and completely. Sing was sure that nothing remained within him of humanity, of compassion, of sympathy for his fellow humanoids or any other sentient species. Her own connection with the Force was strong enough to tell her that Vader did not distinguish or discriminate among any of them. Those brought into his presence could be certain of one thing: all would be treated equally without mercy.

For hate to succeed as a form of motivation, it requires focus. One needs a subject, or subjects. Sing suspected that this was not a problem for Vader. There was always someone new to despise, some previously unrecognized individual to draw his attention and his enmity. And if a fallow period manifested itself, he could always rely on the Emperor to supply him with fresh subjects to investigate and deal with. Palpatine also hated indiscriminately, she had heard it said, but he could control it better, could more exquisitely manipulate the full power of the dark side. No doubt Vader aspired to exercise such mastery one day as well.

But for now the hate that filled him and overflowed from him was an uncontrollable firestorm, a raging river, a reactor on permanent overload. Fury shot through him with every beat of what was left of his heart. It drove him the way some unseen goal or deep desire or unfulfilled need drove other, lesser, men. Sing could feel it, like the radiant heat that escaped from a closed blast furnace. He couldn't completely damp it; the best he could do was direct it. In that regard, she knew, purpose was useful.

Which was where Jax Pavan figured. And her as well.

There were, undoubtedly, great maneuverings afoot that demanded the majority of the Dark Lord's attention. It could not be easy, Sing speculated. Such vast governmental changes did not happen in one single swoop or by a day's worth of orders. There was still much to be done: important politicians and nobility to convince, persuade, bribe, or assassinate; great commercial concerns to bring into the fold; and species both humanoid and nonhumanoid to be bound by treaty or bombed into oblivion. However much he might have enjoyed personally tracking down and ridding himself of that turbulent Jedi, Jax Pavan, when the fates of entire worlds were at stake, attention must be focused on the business of the Empire. He had to resign himself, at least for now, to dealing with Pavan through a second party. A professional.

Aurra Sing.

She was unarmed, of course. Her weapons had been confiscated at the Palace entrance. While Darth Vader was master of all he surveyed, she did not deem him foolish enough to rely altogether on the Force to ensure his safety. It was all well and good to let the dark side flow through one. To be truly effective, however, it needed not only to be manipulated by skill but also be guided by intelligence. Force or no Force, Vader was by no means foolish enough to permit something as simple, utilitarian, and lethal as a primitive bomb or blaster into his presence.

"Sing." A single monosyllable of acknowledgment.

"Lord Vader." She didn't bow, save for a slight inclination of the head. If Vader was bothered by that, he gave no sign of it.

"Your presence precedes you."

"Only to someone who knows the Force." Without being prompted, or given permission, she came several steps closer. "Quite a residence—this antechamber doesn't do it justice." She glanced at the wall's electronics, then back at him.

He waved a black-clad hand. "My . . . lifestyle . . . requires the constant attention and utilization of certain technical accoutrements that are alien to most."

Nodding, she examined the sharp angles that had

been molded into the ceiling, the jagged cartouches on the walls. "In design you favor the abstract, I see."

"I am most comfortable when bounded by inorganic patterns and mathematical precision."

"Yes," she agreed, lowering her gaze to regard him directly. "Your passions are, so it is said, quantifiable and clinical." Her tone turned curious. "Or are they mere divertissements?"

His tone did not change, but nonetheless seemed colder. "Do you presume to try to comprehend my motivations? They are beyond you. They are beyond anyone."

"I presume nothing," she told him. "I like to have the best understanding I can of whoever employs me. In my line of work it's important to know all you can about your target. It's also useful to know all you can about who pays you."

"Credits." The massive dark figure before her let out a derisive hiss. "What a weak thing to motivate and bind people together."

She shrugged. "Works for me. What would you have it replaced by?"

His voice rose, as did a clenched fist. "Unity! Organization!"

She said wryly, "I'll take the credits, thanks."

He made a gesture of dismissal. "Even among those from whom one might expect better, the braying of fools deafens."

Sing tensed. She had no weapons, but that did not mean she was unarmed. "Are you calling me a fool— *Lord* Vader?"

He laughed.

Few people had heard the Dark Lord of the Sith

laugh. When amused, his reaction as promulgated by the specialized respiratory equipment that enveloped him inclined more toward a hissing sound. But this was a real laugh, as genuine as it was humorless.

"You amuse me." He leaned slightly forward. "A rare occurrence, one that by itself justifies a portion of what the Imperial government is paying you."

Letting her left foot drift slightly backward and lowering her upper body, she glared at him. This monstrosity in black fabric and metal was causing her to lose her temper. On the rare occasions when that happened, it usually resulted in someone dying.

"I'm nobody's court jester. You engaged me to capture someone or, failing that, to kill him. I'm not averse to slaying two for the price of one."

Vader's amusement was now boundless. Black-gloved hands spread wide. "But if you kill me, Aurra Sing, then who will remain to authorize payment of the credits you so ardently desire?"

Turning her head to one side, she spat deliberately onto the polished floor. "I've already filled out the necessary forms."

"Wonderful!" he said, laughing again. "You are more than I hoped you would be. I foresee the development of a lasting and mutually beneficial professional relationship between us."

Flattery washed off the bounty hunter like mercury off steel. "I only continue to work for someone whom I respect—and who respects me."

"So it's respect you want, is it?" He took a step forward and she tensed, both hands clenching slowly. "I thought it was only a sum of credits. Money is easily

given, Sing. It is nothing more than chaff. Respect—
respect cannot be given. It must be earned."

She came straight at him.

It took only a few steps. A little of the Force perfectly in tune with bands of lithe muscle. In a second
one out-thrust fist would be in his face and she would
see what that composite armor was made of. She
knew of no one who had ever seen what lay beneath
that mask. She intended to be the first.

Her fist never made contact. Raising his right hand
and bringing it around in a swift arc, Vader blocked
the blow and sent the body behind it flying across the
room. As she flew, a startled but still wholly self-
aware Sing tucked and rolled. She hit the opposite
wall hard, bounced off, landed on her feet, and immediately came at him again.

"The reflexes of an animal," Vader murmured. His
lightsaber hung at his waist. He ignored it, his fingers
going nowhere near the weapon. "That's what the
Empire needs: a few more well-trained, domesticated
animals."

"Domesticated? I'll show you who's domesticated!" She leapt high, kicking out, and in midthrust
somehow bent sideways to kick harder with her other
leg.

In a movement preternaturally fast, but which somehow looked almost languid, Vader ducked, reached
up, and with one gloved hand lightly tapped her in
the middle of her back. A serious thrust catching her
in that position could have broken her spine. The
Dark Lord's touch was more of a caress. He was letting her know what he could have done.

Landing in a crouch, a feral expression on her face,

she raced at him again, low this time. Her speed was startling: a droid would have been hard-pressed to match her acceleration. She dropped low to the floor and swung her right leg around in a powerful circle sweep. Her intent was to take his legs out from under him.

She might as well have been trying to cut down a bronzewood tree. At the last instant the Dark Lord thrust both hands downward toward the spinning bounty hunter. A profound surge in the Force rippled through the room. Guards posted at a distance in the hallway nearby were nearly knocked off their feet by it. But the strength of the emanation had not been directed at them.

Casually, as if inspecting a new exhibit that had been donated to the Imperial Museum, Vader walked around the now motionless figure on the floor. Aurra Sing lay on her back, unable to move. It was as if a giant weight pressed her down. Seething in impotent rage, she watched the Dark Lord pass through her field of vision and beyond.

She felt, rather than saw, him make a negligent gesture, and she could move again. Sing reached up with one hand to clutch at her throat. Momentarily stilled, the fury that had boiled up within her began to return. She rose to her feet.

Without even looking in her direction, Vader waved diffidently at his visitor. "Enough, assassin. You repeat the fatal error of one who knows but a tiny bit of the dark side."

Holding herself back with an effort, she stood panting and glaring at him. "And what might that be?"

"You don't know how to control it. You let it control you. This is the difference between mentor and student. You make good use of what access you do have to the Force, but I fear you will never master it."

She still held her hands up in a defensive posture. "If you're going to kill me, stop talking and do it."

"Kill you?" For the first time, Vader sounded surprised. "Why would I want to kill you? Imperfect as you are, you are still more useful than the vast number of incompetents I deal with on a daily basis. You show courage, skill, determination. Those are not qualities to be wasted, even in one so foolishly headstrong. Why would I kill that which can be helpful to me?"

He adjusted something on the front of his chest, and his voice grew slightly less harsh. "Now then: what progress in your search for the Jedi Jax Pavan?"

Sing's breathing slowed. Unclenching, her hands dropped to her sides. Relaxing thus left her defenseless, but against Vader it did not seem to matter whether one prepared for battle or not. The outcome was foretold, and she did not need access to the Force to see that.

"I have been making inquiries. Although my reputation is widespread, I'm not personally known on Imperial Center to many of those of whose services I'd normally be making use. It takes time to satisfy underlings that one is who one says one is." She smiled. "I've had to break an assortment of bones and cartilage."

"All in the service of the Empire," Vader observed. "Do what you must. Methodology does not concern me. I am only interested in results."

She nodded. "That's as I was told."

"Is there any access you require that is being denied you? A single word from me and—"

She dared to interrupt him. "I know. I'm getting closer. It won't be long. I can feel it."

"Through the Force? I didn't realize you were that close."

"Not the Force," she told him. "Instinct. Something different from the Force. Call it feedback from a lifetime of doing this."

"I know that you live long. May you continue to do so."

Now she did bow slightly. "To serve you, Lord Vader."

The helmeted head dipped a bit in return, then drew back. "The dog can learn after all, it would seem. Encouraging. Go now, dog, and return with the bone I sent you to find."

For a second time she bowed. Then she grinned mirthlessly, turned, and stalked out of the room.

It had not been a conventional meeting, but it had been a useful one. Leaving, she felt she had shown something of herself to the Dark Lord. And any encounter with Darth Vader that did not result in the death or maiming of the visitor could be accounted a successful one.

thirteen

The Ploughtekal Market was probably not the biggest on Imperial Center, but then, it was hard to say for certain, since no one had ever measured its full extent. Furthermore, its physical boundaries and the density of merchants to whom it was home were constantly shifting. Those who did their business there, and often lived there as well, were reluctant to extend much cooperation to the authorities. If they could be censused, they could be taxed.

It was said of Ploughtekal that you could find anything in the galaxy within its hive-like depths. Legal, illegal, unimaginable: it was all there for those who knew how to work the innumerable streets and multiple levels. A large number of shops were not even listed on the electronic registries. You had to find them the old-fashioned way: by walking and asking directions.

Word moved almost as fast by mouth on the streets and avenues of Ploughtekal as it did via holocast. Intel would reach the sector police of an establishment engaged in especially antisocial dealings, and by the time the cools had arrived at the indicated location, the entire business would have pulled up stakes and vanished—only to reappear somewhere else, kilometers away and levels up or down, under a completely different name and appearance. It was a game with hundreds, thousands of continually moving pieces, like a stadium full of dejarik masters all playing on one another's games simultaneously.

It was, in other words, a place that Den Dhur considered nothing less than designer hell.

The street was narrow and crowded with merchant booths hawking everything from strips of roasted hawk-bat to risqué holos, and made even more crowded by the heterogeneous assortment of sentients appraising these wares. The cacophony of shouts, squawks, hisses, moans, stridulations, and other means of communication made Den fearful of getting an earbleed. Add to that the heady, humid reek of open-air cooking, from Gungan bouillabaisse to Wookiee luau, spices, death sticks, stimsticks, other mind-altering vectors, and, as always, the staggeringly multiphasic stench of unwashed bodies, and the result was a full-out synesthetic assault. It made his time on Drongar seem pale by comparison.

As he walked Level H-26, Den studied the readout on the compact Multi-Tasking Assistant, or MTA, that he carried. It contained a list of all the components Jax required in order to put together a rudimentary lightsaber. They were the absolute minimum items necessary to construct the elegant and deadly instrument that identified a Jedi. A second list accommodated those components that would make the final construct not just functional, but also worthy of its owner.

The cheap pack that jounced against his back was

half full. Certain parts were innocuous enough—focusing lenses and an emitter; a superconductor and a power cell—and therefore comparatively easy to obtain. Despite Ploughtekal's resources, other components were proving either more difficult or prohibitively expensive. Slowly, methodically, the latter constraint was yielding to the reporter's contacts or negotiating ability. Even so, Den realized glumly, without the CEC the rest of the components were pretty much useless.

"Hey, watch it, floob!"

The massive male Herglic who had nearly stepped on Den hastened to shift to one side. With a contrite *hauum*, he gestured his apology. He could easily have crushed the irritated Sullustan with one step, but Herglic tended, as a species, to be embarrassed by their size, which was why Den had felt secure in being rude. Had the near collision been with the pair of supple Cantrosians following immediately behind the Herglic, he would have been less blunt. A quick swipe of one of their paws could have left him with a bad case of Cantrosian-scratch fever.

He sighed and looked at his MTA list again, electronically checking off several more items. *Personally,* he thought, *I think we've done pretty good to have gotten all that we have.* Especially considering the limitations on time and funds. Between his efforts and the stuff Rhinann had assembled during his earlier quest, Jax should have enough now to at least get started. Den had to admit that, intolerable as the Elomin's company could often prove, the tusk-crowned humanoid knew his business.

Moving from shop to shop, from contact to contact, he somehow managed to come up with part after part at prices they could afford. But the lightsaber's key component—the CEC—continued to elude him.

"I'm not done yet," he muttered. There were still a few places deep within the market's center that he intended to try.

Though it seemed impossible, the crowds actually grew denser as he worked his way ever deeper into the seething, frenetic complex. Typical of any such market, Den knew, but in one the size of Ploughtekal the constant crush could grow wearying, if not actually dangerous, especially for someone whose kind ranked at the lower end of the humanoid size scale. On the other hand, his comparatively diminutive height allowed him to squeeze into places that the representatives of bulkier species could not access. Unfortunately, none of these booths had anything even faintly resembling a CEC for sale. At last he was ready to admit defeat.

With what we've managed to acquire and with what he's already got, Jax can assemble a lightsaber, he thought as he made his way toward the eastern borders of the great market. *It just won't work.* The Sullustan's step was plodding as he neared a marketplace exit. He was worn out from being pushed around or ignored by larger, clumsier beings. *Oh well—if he makes it heavy enough, he can always throw it at people.*

Just as he was about to exit, however, a flash of something caught his eye. He turned and beheld a kiosk that sold, among many other illegal things, replicas of sector police badges. Den stopped and looked at them thoughtfully. He'd seen phony ID before, and he had to admit the quality of these was quite good. The rank, picture, and shield number seemed to float, crisp and clear, a few millimeters above the badge itself.

The kiosk's owner, an old and rheumy Toydarian, noticed his interest. Rummaging around beneath the counter, he brought forth another badge, the picture ID of which was a Sullustan. With a grin he held it up. "Eh? Eh? Perfect likeness, is it not? Only four credits—a bargain!"

It wasn't a perfect likeness, as Den could plainly see. The person in the holo had thinner ears and lips; also, his skin was somewhat lighter in tone. But he also knew that such subtle differences didn't matter to anyone except another Sullustan. To most sentients, representatives from any species other than their own were all but impossible to tell apart.

Abruptly, he reached for his pocketbook. He had an idea . . .

The teeming surface of Imperial Center was dotted with innumerable buildings that had been designed primarily to impress. For example, what made the Orvum Stadium unique was not its capability to seat hundreds of thousands of patrons, but the fact that every single seat could be adjusted to accommodate the individual needs of hundreds of different species. Clustered together a short distance away, the Protorian Polygon consisted of five towering spires linked by a completely transparent glassine bubble that contained three gourmet restaurants and a tourist pedway.

Its shape sustained by powerful tractor and pressor fields, the Aquala Tower rose only a modest distance into the sky—but it was composed entirely of water. Nonaquatic visitors could don underwater breathing gear at the top or bottom and swim through multiple levels of real sea life, while citizens from water-breathing worlds could relax and enjoy the scenery without being burdened by specialized hydrorespiratory equipment.

The greatest companies in the galaxy constantly competed to create corporate headquarters that were the most spectacular, the most innovative, and the most recognizable on Imperial Center. Mobolo Machines' office complex consisted of half a dozen sky-towers in constant slow motion. Demonstrating the proficiency of its product line, Kiskar Repulsorlifts' headquarters floated exactly five meters off the ground. Anyone could walk underneath the enormous structure and marvel at the power and technology that kept it not only aloft but also in the same exact position, day after day.

Captain Typho stepped out of an airtaxi on the fringe of a structural complex that was not as tall as certain cloudcutters, not as elaborate as most commercial centers, and not as eclectic as the majority of Coruscant's great entertainment venues. Notwithstanding a deliberate architectural modesty, the buildings that stretched out before him were in their way some of the most impressive on the planet, for they constituted the bureaucratic hives of the Imperial government.

For the headquarters of his civil service divisions, the Emperor had chosen to adapt and modify an existing business complex. Ostensibly this was done to save time and money. The actual purpose was to divert attention from the many interior modifications installed, some of which would have appalled the few long-established citizens' rights groups still extant under the New Order.

From the outside the group of office structures retained their original innocuous, unprepossessing appearance. Within, they had been customized out of all recognition. In addition to a highly secure and specialized prison designed to temporarily hold dangerous and politically sensitive detainees, there was a complete medcenter intended to provide the best available care to the Imperial staff. Living quarters boasted varying degrees of opulence; the most modern and efficient communications facilities kept the new government in touch with its vast, far-flung member worlds, colonies, and allies. As with the Imperial Palace itself, there were redundant life-support systems capable of sustaining a habitable environment indefinitely. If necessary, the extensive compound could function without any contact with the outside world, which meant that, should the rest of Imperial Center fall into chaos and collapse, the Imperial offices would continue to function.

As he entered, Typho was impressed but not awed. The purpose that drove him, that had brought him here all the way from Naboo, was bigger than any building, more powerful than any threat, and exalted his spirits higher than the crown of any cloudcutter.

Once inside, he slipped into a steady stream of visitors. While the flow was more or less orderly, representatives from a majority of the civilized worlds occasionally jostled and pushed for position. No one came to this place for leisure; everyone was engaged in business of one form or another that required their personal, as opposed to holographic, presence. Typho understood this quite well. His own concern certainly warranted it. Revenge was not a matter best conducted from a distance.

Though the complex was enormous, it was designed to allow visitors and employees to carry out their assignments or complete their work within a day. It had to be that efficient. It wouldn't do to have outworld suppliants camping out in corridors in the hope of resolving their problems sometime the following days or weeks.

Typho was among the least likely to suffer such a theoretical delay. As an officer and bureaucrat himself back on Naboo, he understood the workings of government complexes. While this one was incomparably bigger than any counterpart on his homeworld, the guidelines by which it operated were similar. Despite the occasional setback or dead end, he had little serious difficulty filling out the required flimsiwork and navigating the facility.

His persistence eventually found him a modest room occupied by a dozen beings seated at workstations. Half of them were human; the rest comprised various species. The middle-aged bureaucrat he eventually found himself before checked his vital data and acknowledged their validity with a squeal of approval.

Typho had encountered Jenet in such positions before. Short and stocky, with rodent-like facial features, prominent teeth, and white hair and facial fur, they were not, from a humanoid perspective, the most attractive of bipeds. But they were hard workers and particularly famed for their near-infallible memories. While the Emperor was well known for his humanocentric policies, he was smart enough to hire the right species for the job. And who better, Typho reflected as he took a seat across from the smallish creature, to serve in a sensitive bureaucratic position where recall of detail was essential?

The Jenet's low voice was interrupted by a good deal of ancillary huffing and puffing, but his command of Basic was all in all quite admirable.

"So. You are called Typho, a captain of Royal Household security from Naboo."

"Yes."

"I am Losh. I have seen pictures of your home-world. Unsightly, water-ridden place."

Typho nodded. "Perhaps so, but for sheer global repulsiveness little can compare to Garban."

At this insult to the planet that gave rise to his species, the Jenet's whiskers twitched. He was much pleased, and not a little surprised.

"You are familiar with Jenet society?"

"With the basics," Typho conceded modestly. "As a security officer I have to know galactic protocol. It wouldn't do to greet someone from the Tau Sakar system, much less Garban itself, with a flowery compliment."

"Indeed it would not." The bureaucrat was impressed; visitors who knew and understood that the Jenet traditionally greeted one another with insults were few and far between.

"It's clear you are who you say you are. Certainly your vitae check out clean." Caressing a whisker on the left side of his bright pink face, the official studied the information floating in the air before him. "According to the records, this is not your first visit to Imperial Center."

Again Typho nodded. "I have had the pleasure before, yes."

"I hardly need tell you there is much to see and do here." His sigh emerged as a series of short, soft squeaks. "Though as a midlevel functionary, I am fortunate if my family and I can spend more than a week or two each year availing ourselves of such pleasures. What is your purpose here, Captain Typho?"

Affable and welcoming though the interviewer was being, Typho didn't relax his guard for a minute. The Jenet was merely doing his job in the most efficacious manner possible: Put your guest at ease, set his mind at rest, and then probe for the information you really want.

"I'm no tourist," Typho told him straightforwardly.

Whiskers jerked. "I guessed as much. Coming to this place does not fit the profile of a sightseer. So, again: what is it you want?"

"Information."

"What else?" With a casual wave Losh indicated their surroundings. "The Emperor did not cause this complex to be compiled to provide entertainment. This section deals with government travel. You are a government official, albeit of a minor planetary system. Let me guess: you seek particulars regarding the travel of someone from Naboo. Someone who has used government funds to visit Imperial Center on nongovernmental business."

"No," Typho told him.

"Ah. Then you are tracking someone who has violated Naboo security and has either fled here, or come seeking to avoid arraignment."

"Not that, either." While the bureaucrat's second guess was much closer to the mark, the captain was still able to respond honestly.

The Jenet's curiosity was piqued. Since this represented a break from the daily monotony, he engaged more than usual. "Something out of the ordinary, then. Captain, much as I enjoy conversing with you— even though the sight of your ugly face makes me bilious—I still have a daily administrative quota to meet. How can I help you? Be concise."

"You can use those filthy scavenger's eyes of yours," Typho replied politely, "to research the names of visitors to a certain world on a couple of specific dates."

"Travel details." Whiskers bobbed. "Simple enough." Pink fingers hovered in the air, poised in front of the luminescent, insubstantial control images above the desk. "Go on."

Typho tried not show his nervousness as he provided the parameters. "On the date in question Senator Padmé Amidala of Naboo suffered fatal injuries at a mining site on Mustafar. At the time she was under the protection of a Jedi named Anakin Skywalker." This was where his inquiry could get tricky—and dangerous. "I need to know if the Jedi in question survived and, if so, his possible whereabouts."

The Jenet's whiskers stiffened sharply as he dropped his hands away from the floating aura of instrumentation. "The Jedi are all dead. The Emperor has cleared that particular infestation from the galaxy. It is a violation of Imperial law to seek any data on them. As a security officer, you of all people should know that, Captain."

Typho had anticipated this reaction. "The unexpected and apparently violent death of Senator Amidala, who was much beloved by her people, was a tragedy from which many on Naboo have not yet recovered. As the officer in charge of her personal security, I have a special interest in finalizing the events concerning her passing. Even though you are obviously an official who's failed his way upward into a position far too complicated for his feeble mind, I'm sure you can understand and sympathize with that."

"As an official who has to deal daily with intrusive idiots like yourself, I suppose that I can. Sympathizing, however, is not a component of my job description."

"I'll take information over sympathy any day," Typho assured him.

As the official hesitated, Typho tensed and did his best not to show it, knowing that the Jenet could terminate the visit at any moment and send his visitor packing. If that happened, Typho would have to start all over again elsewhere, in a different section with a different bureaucrat. And instant cross-referencing would reveal to a second interviewer that the captain had already been granted a previous session, which meant that he and his request would likely be dismissed out of hand, if he was lucky. If he wasn't—inwardly, Typho shuddered, although his concern was still about failing Padmé, rather than saving his own hide.

After a long moment, Losh's fingers began moving again through the instrumentation display floating before him. "I'm not sure why I'm helping you. I'm not required to do so. Researching the travels of Jedi falls far outside my purview."

"You're doing it because you're a lonely, frustrated, obnoxious excuse for an administrator," Typho told him.

The Jenet's pink head bobbed, the white hair streaming down his back shifting slightly with the movement. "Or perhaps I'm inspired to take a break from routine by the meaningless ravings of an obviously psychotic offworlder."

Typho repressed a smile. "Could be."

Typically, it took longer to input the request than to receive the desired information. "Somewhat surprisingly, there is data in the files relevant to that which you seek. So that the galactic populace may know what end justly befalls common criminals, the detailed fate of each Jedi is noted. Have a look for yourself." With the sweep of a finger, the Jenet caused a duplicate of the readout he was scanning to appear before the anxious Typho.

His gaze traveled at high speed down the list. Opposite each Jedi's name were the details of that individual's passing. Occasionally the words UNVERIFIED, UNKNOWN, or, even more rarely, POSSIBLY STILL EXTANT appeared. To be certain of his conclusions, he made himself read through the entire list, though not all the pertinent details, until he reached the name he sought.

Interestingly, among those listed as extant and POS-
SIBLY ON IMPERIAL CENTER was a name he had encountered recently: Jax Pavan. That was the Jedi the
bounty hunter Aurra Sing had been looking for.

Well, that was Jax Pavan's problem. The captain's
concerns lay elsewhere.

He read the entry for SKYWALKER, ANAKIN. His
heart pulsed as he noted that the Jedi in question had
indeed perished on the volcanic world of Mustafar.
Though he scanned carefully through every subsequent name, there was no mention of Padmé. Despite
his disappointment, he knew that was to be expected.
The list recorded the passing of Jedi, not "ordinary"
galactic citizens. Such details of Padmé's death were
widely available in the general media, especially on
Naboo.

He read through the listing again. There was no
mention of what Skywalker had been doing on
Mustafar at the time of his death, though Typho already knew that. He was supposed to have been
guarding Padmé. More surprisingly, there was no description of his manner of passing: merely that he had
met his end on that fiery, inhospitable world.

Typho thought furiously. Skywalker had not been
just any Jedi. He had been one of the best, personally
driven to protect his ward and exceptionally skilled in
the use of the Force. Try as he might, Typho could not
imagine who else on Mustafar at the time could have
killed Padmé in the strange fashion consistent with
the official autopsy.

Suppose Skywalker had indeed killed Padmé, but
had somehow subsequently made his escape? But
then why would the official report show him as dead?

Regardless of whether or not the Jedi had slain Padmé, the Emperor wanted all Jedi dead. No one in officialdom would protect him. If anything, knowing that he had killed Padmé would have made him a perfect example of a traitor for the Empire to hold up.

Assume the opposite, then. Take the official record at face value. Anakin Skywalker was dead. Though his manner of passing was not described, Mustafar, after all, was a place where fiery death awaited at every step. If the Jedi had perished as a consequence of falling into boiling lava or being buried by an eruption, why wouldn't the record show that? The omission implied that he had died by other means.

By other hands? Typho wondered.

He had seen for himself Skywalker's skills and mastery of the Force. If natural means were not responsible—and if they were, there was no reason the captain could think of why that should not be reported in the official record—then it suggested a person or persons might be to blame. That made sense. Whoever wanted Padmé dead and had slain her by such ingenious means would understandably have to kill her bodyguard first. Was it possible an individual existed with the power to overcome a Jedi as powerful as Skywalker?

The Emperor himself could have done so, Typho knew. But Padmé's death had occurred before Palpatine had declared himself, and in any event, Typho couldn't conceive of any scenario in which her death would have been politically advantageous to Palpatine's ascension. Who else, then? Another Jedi, perhaps— but why would one Jedi want another dead, not to mention a renowned, respected, and well-loved Senator from Naboo? Who possessed that kind of mastery of the Force, and that kind of raw hatred?

That was when it hit him. That was when it all came together in his mind.

A Sith.

Only one of the Dark Lords commanded enough skill with the Force to overcome a Jedi as strong as Anakin Skywalker. Only one of that malevolent brood could casually dispatch someone as good and pure as Padmé. As to who might want her dead— well, with her outspokenness on behalf of the Republic, the Senator had made plenty of enemies, both within the old Senate and without. Many who favored the transition to the Empire would have been delighted at her passing, including the Sith.

He needed to be sure, of course. At the moment he was only speculating. But the more he thought about it, the more he compared possibilities and alternatives, the more it made sense.

Now he needed a name. An individual. But he could hardly expect the mundane official seated across from him to have access to the movements of the Sith.

"Are you all right?" Losh asked. "Not that I care what happens to a miserable supplicant such as yourself."

"I'm fine. Just making sure I have the information I need, you useless lump of worm-munch."

The Jenet's whiskers inclined forward. "Even though you are here on official business, don't forget to indulge in the delights of the world-city." A beady red eye winked. "The lower levels in particular offer certain pleasures not to be found on any other planet.

Of course, being mated and with family I wouldn't know anything about that."

"Of course not." Typho rose from the chair. "Thank you for your time and assistance. I hope you drown tomorrow."

"And may yours be the bloated corpse that rises from beneath to lift me up." With a wave of his hand the bureaucratic rodent wiped the floating, glowing information from the air between them. The consultation was at an end.

No one bothered Typho as he wandered the halls. He passed through security scans without being challenged, having left his blaster and the lightsaber he'd taken from Sing in a secure locker before entering the complex. All those individuals in the swirl of beings around him were caught up in their own concerns. Since the Imperial complex was not a place in which to waste precious time, everyone who passed the captain from Naboo assumed he was engaged in important work of his own. Security did not question him. They were looking for those likely to cause a disturbance or enter sections that were off-limits. Security droids stepped or rolled or floated around him, ignoring his presence as he ignored theirs.

How could he find out if a Sith Lord had been on Mustafar at the time of Padmé's death? If one had been present, it would explain a great deal. He paused long enough to enter an eating establishment. Like any machine, a body functioned better when properly fueled. So he ate and drank, but the food could have been made of tree dust for all the impression it made on his taste buds.

Where and how to begin? To another such a quest

might well seem hopeless, but not to Typho. He was experienced and knowledgeable as well as determined. And, having already gained entrance to the Imperial complex, it would be easier to do so next time.

What he needed to do struck him during the last few bites of his meal. A Sith capable of killing a Jedi as strong as Anakin Skywalker would undoubtedly be one the Emperor would keep close to himself—to keep an eye on as much as to make use of him. It might well be possible to learn if any Sith were based at the Imperial complex. Typho had heard it said that the Sith Order had for centuries been pared down to a total of one Master and one apprentice, but he doubted the truth of that—it seemed a perilous way to keep the Order extant. It was far more likely that there were many of them. Far from depressing him, the idea was heartening: it meant that Padmé's killer might be close at hand, lurking in a corridor or doing the Emperor's bidding somewhere in the complex around him. The notion stimulated his thoughts and strengthened his resolve.

Tomorrow, he told himself. After a night's rest he would return in search of information far more dangerous than that which he had sought today. It would not be easy. After all, no one in their right mind deliberately sought to make the acquaintance of a Sith. But Captain Typho was not in his right mind.

He was in love.

PART II

RITES OF PASSAGE

fourteen

There was a reason why the Qarek'k was literally and not just colloquially called a dive in the Neimoidian tongue. To enter, one stepped through a portal off the street and then dropped a full story down to a waiting pedway. Powerful repulsors positioned on either side of the drop slowed visitors one by one, holding them suspended until security equipment mounted overhead and on both sides could run a thorough check on each and every visitant. Those who passed were allowed to drift gently to the ground and enter the establishment. Those who failed, argued, or otherwise tried to make trouble were sent back up to the street.

Weapons were permitted. In this region of under-level Coruscant, it was the unarmed pedestrian who was considered unconventional. The no-nonsense owners of the Qarek'k had no problem whatsoever with customers packing multiple instruments of destruction. Patrons were welcome if they entered weighted down with everything up to and including a tactical nuke. *Use* a weapon in the establishment, however, and one would find oneself set upon by what was considered the toughest security team in the sector, comprising grizzled veterans of the Clone Wars who had seen and dealt with everything—several times.

Into this sordid den of thieves, killers, and other miscreants dived an especially toothsome-looking female humanoid of indeterminate age, flame-red hair, and snow-white skin. Aurra Sing could easily have emphasized her entrance by executing a couple of forward flips or twists as she let herself be grabbed and slowed by the entryway's field. However, she saw no reason to exert herself to entertain the Qarek'k's dissolute clientele. So she just jumped from the street and waited patiently for the security system to examine her and lower her to the floor.

The identification that had been provided for her acknowledged her as a private agent on Imperial business. It was not questioned. Not even the lightsaber, which for anyone not working for Vader would have been cause to summon a platoon of stormtroopers and Inquisitors, raised so much as an eyebrow. Vader's authority was indeed all-pervasive.

She paused as the bouncer, a Sakiyan, looked her up and down, performing one last manual matching check between her person and her hand-carried ident. The folded hundred-credit note on the underside of the card was adroitly slid up the bald humanoid's sleeve, and he gestured curtly for her to proceed.

Although her outward expression did not change, Sing smiled to herself as she strode deeper into the labyrinthine warren of rooms. Even with Imperial clearance, it was never a bad idea to get on the good side of the head bouncer.

She allowed herself to be subsumed by the noise

from half a dozen different live bands. A storm of lights—some fixed, some ambulatory—bathed the adjoining rooms in every possible color and combination thereof, including the infrared and the ultraviolet. Depending on one's species, subjecting oneself to too much of one hue or the other could result in a serious burn or minor cancer. The owners assumed no responsibility for such developments. Anyone old enough, bold enough, and sold enough on the delights of the Qarek'k to chance entry did so at their own risk.

She finally found an empty stool in a chamber called the Crimson Redrum. Arms extended wide, the Amanin pubtender gazed up at her. "Something to drink, hard-case?" The hypersonic bubble encasing the bar made conversation possible despite the two competing bands.

Sing was quietly amused. "What makes you think I'm a hard case, flat-head? Don't I look soft and cuddly to you?"

The Amani's small red eyes, adapted to seeing in weak light, focused on her. "There is nothing of either about you, humanoid. I have seen your kind in here many times before."

"You're perceptive," she told him. It was a male, she saw by his coloring.

"I'm just a pubtender," he replied. "I don't want any trouble."

"Don't curl yourself into a ball just yet. I'm looking for information, not trouble. I'll have a Merenzane Gold, on the rocks."

The pubtender hesitated. "Expensive."

Sing flashed the expense chit that had been provided her. The Amani frowned. "You pay with a chit. Cash is better."

"But you'll make an exception in my case."

He took the card without further protest. "What kind of rocks would you like?" He gestured behind him at the curved floor-to-ceiling storage bins. "We have everything from pure silicates to rare nonferrous metals."

"Frozen water will suffice."

She listened to the two bands that filled the Redrum with wall-to-wall noise. Each comprising multiple species, they seemed to be competing with each other to see who could play not the best music, but the loudest. The Amani was back in less than a minute. She took a sip of the liquid that gurgled in the tall glass and smiled lazily.

"Good. Now—you spoke of cash." Reaching down to the pouch riding at her waist, she unsealed the top length and let him have a good look before she resealed the pouch. What was visible within caused the Amani's small eyes to grow almost as large as her own.

"You should not bring so many Imperial credits into a place like this," he admonished her. "A mere humanoid such as yourself could get seriously hurt."

"Don't worry about me," she replied. "Now—for liquid refreshment, I pay credit. For food, I pay credit. For information—I pay cash."

The Amani was too short to lean over the bar. Instead, he pushed himself up on his long, dragging arms until his face was level with her own. "What is it you wish to know? What data do you seek?"

"I'm looking for someone. His name is Jax Pavan,

though he may be known around here by another name." She held up a holobase. It immediately expanded to provide a three-dimensional, rotating portrait of the man in question. "He's a Jedi, though not much of one."

The Amani's thick lips curled downward into a rubbery frown. "The Jedi are all slain. Slain by minions of the Empire." He stared at her a little harder. "Are you a minion of the Empire?"

"I work for myself. Actually, I'm employed directly by Lord Vader."

The bartender hesitated, stared, then broke out laughing. "A hard case with a sense of humor. That's rare. Well, it's no matter of mine who you work for."

"Glad you appreciate the absurdity of it." She pocketed the holobase, and the image disappeared. "Maybe he's not a Jedi. Maybe I was given wrong information. Personally, I don't care if he's the Grand Master or a local scrap recycler. I just need to find him."

"I wish I could help you, hard-case. I have an excellent memory."

"I know. That's why your kind are often employed as trackers." She smiled enticingly. "I appeal to your mercenary nature."

"I can't give you information I don't have. I'd slime myself if it would jog the memory you seek, but there's just nothing there." Raising a huge three-fingered hand, he pointed toward the next room, the Green Dystopia. If anything, the music reverberating from within it was even louder than in the Crimson Redrum. "You might try talking to my colleague Calathi, in there."

The things one does for money, freedom, and a Dark Lord of the Sith, she told herself as she slid off the stool.

Starting toward the next room, she found her way blocked by three patrons. Her first impression was that they had been engaged for some time in a contest to see who could become the most drunk while continuing to remain upright and marginally functional. Her second impression was that it was a three-way tie.

Not as far as the inebriated trio was concerned, however. Obviously hammered enough to cheerfully contemplate miscegenation, they surrounded her. The Zabrak was the most aggressive. A lupine Shistavanen hung back at one angle, while a large, stocky Utai blocked the other direction.

Sing sipped her drink and calmly continued toward the green room. The Zabrak shifted to intercept her. He was tall, muscular, and "soused to his horns," as the saying had it. He smiled down at her, revealing impressive canines. "Haven't seen you in here before, little snowflake."

"Haven't been in here before. If you'll excuse me . . ."

Reaching out, he put a powerful hand on her left shoulder. She glanced at it, turned slightly, and he let it slide off. "I wouldn't do that again."

"Why?" The grin grew wider. "Don't you like my touch?"

"Not particularly. I also don't like your appearance, your attitude, your breath, and particularly your body odor. You stink." She eyed the Zabrak's intoxicated companions. "As a matter of fact, you all stink. But at least there's variety to your stench."

The Shistavanen and Utai exchanged amused glances. "You're a real hard case," the Utai said.

"Funny, that's what the pubtender said. Maybe I need to change my hairstyle."

The Utai scowled. "Maybe you should be more polite," he suggested.

"That's right," the Zabrak agreed. "Be a shame to see a pretty snowflake like you get hurt when all we want is some nice." He reached out and grabbed her shoulder again.

Aurra Sing felt abruptly, unutterably weary. She had no time for this. But, she reminded herself, keeping a low profile was paramount when on the hunt. She would give them one more chance. "I told you not to do that," she told the Zabrak. "Move it or lose it."

The Zabrak leaned in close, his breath an alcoholic miasma. "Give us a kiss."

No one saw what happened next. They knew it happened because they could see the results, but it had taken place so fast that when questioned later all anyone could recall was two blurs: one of flesh and one of light.

One moment the Zabrak had been leaning in toward Sing. The next he was staggering backward, staring at his left arm, which had been cut through at the elbow with surgical precision by a single sweep of her lightsaber. His hand spasmodically clutched her shoulder for a moment before falling to the floor.

The Zabrak staggered backward until he collapsed on a divan, staring in shock at the cauterized stump of his upper arm. The other two were momentarily paralyzed as well, but the immobility of shock did not last long.

"*Get her!*" shouted the Utai as he and the heavy Wolfman lunged forward. Vibroblades flashed, aiming to mutilate and maim.

Moments later the Shistavanen's head was staring at the variegated ceiling, having been separated from his body. The Utai still stood upright, looking bewildered. Then a hair-thin line of red, straight as a laser, materialized down the center of his body, from head to crotch. An instant later the body's two halves fell neatly in opposite directions.

The Amanin pubtender spoke into a comlink: "Cleanup in Section Seven-B."

There was not a lot of blood, the lightsaber having cauterized the massive wounds even as they had been inflicted. Having spilled not a drop of her drink in the course of the melee, Aurra Sing calmly deactivated her weapon and turned to regard the wide-eyed Zabrak.

"I'd have a large drink, if I were you," she suggested. "The shock will wear off soon, and you'll want to be self-anesthetized by then." She paused, then added, "But have it somewhere else."

The Zabrak, clutching the stump of his left arm, stumbled backward and let the crowd—which had scarcely paused in their frenzied dancing to observe the altercation—swallow him up.

Clipping her lightsaber to her belt, Sing turned, walked back to the bar, and placed several credit slips on the counter in front of the Amani.

"I don't have time to answer questions. Not from

your security, nor from sector police. This should cover any awkwardness."

A three-fingered hand made the money vanish as deftly as any magician. "What awkwardness?"

She smiled thinly, turned, and headed for the room called the Green Dystopia.

fifteen

The quarters they had taken on the forty-fourth level, Quadrant Q-1, had the virtue of anonymity, if little else. The mixed bag of species that inhabited the surrounding resiplexes provided excellent cover. The cul-de-sac was also sufficiently out of the way to allow Dejah to come and go without notice. Once her Nucleon dropped below the fortieth level, the media mynocks who drew income from harassing the bereaved survivors of celebrity casualties tended to lose interest.

While waiting for her arrival, Jax was assembling the components that Rhinann and Den had managed to acquire. On the surface it seemed a pointless endeavor; the result might look like a lightsaber, but its lack of a CEC rendered it little more than a prop. Nevertheless, he was determined to persevere. When and if they managed to acquire an energy crystal, everything else would be complete and in readiness.

Nearby, Den was relaxing with a priviewer. It was a visor and earphones melded into a single unit that wrapped around his head like a too-large high-tech crown that had slipped down over his eyes. Occasionally he would let out a hoot of appreciation or a chuckle of laughter as whatever he was viewing tick-led his fancy. Settled on the other side of the central work center, Laranth was cleaning one of her two blasters. The Gray Paladins did not carry their weapons for show; nevertheless, they took pride in having clean and functional ordnance.

In the far corner of the room, Rhinann was dozing, arms folded across his reedy chest. All the walking, talking, and endless negotiations he had engaged in on behalf of Jax had tired him out. He deserved a rest, he had told them, and he was of no mind to aid either the Jedi or the Paladin in their menial pursuits. Verbal as opposed to manual dexterity was his strength. He would save his energy and his efforts for more dignified pursuits, thank you very much.

I-Five stood nearby. He was outwardly immobile, but Jax knew that the droid's mind was humming away as it perused multiple matters simultaneously. It was something few organics were capable of, because most organic brains couldn't self-partition.

Jax wondered what topics occupied the droid. By this time he knew better than to ask; he had no desire to grant the metal man any more opportunities to flaunt his maximized self-awareness. The truth of the matter was he was still getting used to the idea him-self. The concept of a droid being fully conscious was something he had accepted only reluctantly. It still made him uncomfortable at times to muse upon the ramifications of a truly sentient machine. Before he'd met I-Five, his feelings about a droid's place in or-ganic society had been the same as everyone else's: droids were tools, convenient ambulatory mecha-nisms to be used or discarded as necessity dictated.

He would not have thought twice about ordering one to jump into a vat of acid or carving it up for parts if doing so served his purpose on a mission. Droids were expendable and an infinitely renewable resource: if one became defective or was otherwise compromised in any way, it was simply recycled for parts and a new one ordered, at the Temple's expense. There was never a shortage; to be the head of a production company such as Trang Robotics or Cybot Galactica was like having a license to print credits.

While it was true that some sentients developed feelings of attachment, even affection, for their droids—Master Obi-Wan, he recalled, had been adamant about his astromech accompanying him on missions during the Clone Wars—for the most part people viewed the automatas the same way they might view a more sophisticated version of a bread crisper. Jax certainly hadn't had occasion to wonder about any inner lives they might have been hiding.

That attitude had changed when he'd met I-Five. He'd been forced to change his opinion not just about the droid, but also about I-Five's "partner," Lorn Pavan—the father he had never known.

The droid had told him much about his father's life, but had been maddeningly vague about the specifics of his death. All Jax had been able to glean was that his father's fate had been ordained by someone highly echeloned in the Republic—someone who might even have had access to Palpatine himself, back when he had been Supreme Chancellor. I-Five would be no more specific than that, and Jax couldn't tell if the droid knew nothing more or wouldn't say anything more, or both. He suspected the last possibility,

however. Whatever his father had done must have re-
verberated considerably through the halls of power
back in the waning years of the Republic for the droid
to be so closemouthed about it more than two
decades later. He had hinted darkly that Lorn and
himself, along with a Jedi Padawan named Darsha
Assant, had been pursued by an all-but-unstoppable
assassin whose sole purpose had been to retrieve a
holocube that Lorn had attempted to fence on the
black market. Both the Padawan and his father had
died, and I-Five had escaped only by luck.

Jax paused in his work, thinking. He'd attempted
to learn more about his father's mysterious end on his
own, but he was at best a journeyman slicer, and digging for data that old required far more skill than he
possessed. Come to think of it, though, someone with
the requisite skill was no farther than the other side of
the room.

As if telepathically alerted, Rhinann bestirred himself long enough to check his chrono. "Your lady
friend is late."

Pushing the magnifier up on his forehead, Jax
replied, "She's not my lady friend. And I'm sure she
has a good reason for being late. At any rate, it's not
our business."

"She's a Zeltron. They're not known for depend-
ability." The Elomin closed his eyes again.

The exchange had been loud enough to draw Den's
interest. The Sullustan lifted the priviewer up over his
head and set it aside. "It should be at least partly our
business, Jax," he said. Pulling from his pocket a
finger-sized unitary, he unfolded its screen with a flick

of his wrist. "You want to know why? Take a look at our credit balance."

"I doubt that organic vision is capable of resolving so tiny a figure," I-Five said.

Jax gave him a look of displeasure, then turned back to the Sullustan. "How bad is it, Den?"

"Well, it's not a crisis. We have enough in the account to eat tomorrow. The day after that . . ."

"I see no problem, then. For me," the droid said.

"We'll have to move, too," Den added.

"I see." Pulling off the magnifier, Jax set it on the work center. "What will we be able to afford?"

The Sullustan studied the readout on the unitary. "I think there's a public park over in Sector Nineteen."

"I didn't realize it was that bad."

"It's not," Den assured him as he collapsed the screen and pocketed the unitary. "It's worse."

"Why didn't someone tell me before?"

"Someone tried," Den told him. "Several times. You kept telling me or Rhinann that the Force would provide. Well, now would be a good time to crank it up."

"We could sell the *Far Ranger,*" Laranth suggested.

Both Den and Rhinann glared at her. "No way," the Sullustan said. "That ship's our only chance to get off this rock. Which I'm still hoping will happen once you two idealists decide to get practical. Because if you don't, we may wind up living in it."

"If I may be allowed to venture a suggestion . . . ?" I-Five said.

"Since when have you ever asked permission?" Laranth put aside the blaster she had been working on and started on its mate.

"Dejah Duare," the droid continued, "is the sole beneficiary of a well-known, well-respected, and, most importantly, well-recompensed deceased artist." His photoreceptors focused on Jax. "I see no reason why if, prior to her departure, she still wishes us to continue our efforts to locate Volette's killer, that we should not be paid for them."

"Hear, hear," Laranth murmured while checking the emitter of her second blaster.

"A capital suggestion, in both senses of the word," added Rhinann.

"Works for me," Den said.

Jax was horrified. "I can't do that. As a Jedi I'm sworn to help those in need and to assist those who request my aid. I can't *charge* for it. Especially not someone in a disturbed emotional state. It's not ethical." He spread his arms. "In fact, it's one step short of bounty hunting. I'd feel like a mercenary again. I swore I'd never again sink that low."

Den had to kick out with both legs to get off the couch, which had been designed to accommodate much taller species. Approaching Jax, he waved a stubby finger at the reluctant Jedi.

"You do the work, and let the rest of us worry about the metaphysical fallout." Evidently Jax's conflict was plain to see, because Den added, not unkindly, "It's not that we're asking you to go against any deeply felt personal beliefs, Jax—"

"Yes it is," I-Five said without hesitation.

Den glared at his mechanical friend. "It's only that," he continued to Jax, "no matter how noble your intentions or how worthy what we're currently doing, there are mundane and uninspiring matters that simply can't be ignored. Like the rent."

"And food," Laranth added.

"Minimal appearances must be maintained," put in Rhinann.

"All right, all right!" Jax took a deep breath and checked his chrono. "When she gets here I'll . . . talk to her." He let his gaze rove around the room. "If this only involved me, I'd continue to say no. But we're all in this together, so in this one instance I'll allow myself to be outvoted."

"Never underestimate the humanoid affinity for rationalization," I-Five said.

The reporter turned to the others. "We should each find something else to do when Dejah arrives." He spoke to all of them, but he was looking at Laranth.

The Twi'lek hesitated, glanced at her unfinished work on the bench, then at Jax. The Jedi was puzzled by that look, which seemed compounded of equal parts amusement and annoyance. She said nothing, however; she merely gathered up the disassembled pieces of her blaster.

The main domicile entryway chose that moment to announce the arrival of a visitor. Its integrated evaluator declared the caller to be unaccompanied, unarmed, and, insofar as could be determined from outward appearances, not a representative of the police or any other branch of unwelcome officialdom.

"We'll let ourselves out through the secondary exit," Den informed Jax as he headed for the far side of the communal room. Rhinann followed close behind, together with I-Five. Laranth was the last to leave. She lingered a moment.

"Secure an agreement and fix a suitable retainer," she told Jax. "Take your time. But not too much time."

He frowned uncertainly. "I don't follow your meaning."

Laranth gave him another bland look, which still seemed somehow annoyed. "What I mean is, we don't have time to waste."

"We have plenty of time. The Whiplash hasn't even scheduled Dejah's departure yet. They still have to secure passage and—"

"My mistake." She turned, fast enough to send her lekku whirling, and strode out, head high.

What in the worlds has gotten into her? the Jedi wondered. He had little time to ponder it, however, because a twitch of the Force's strands reminded him that Dejah was at the door.

When he let her in, she didn't look around; by now she was familiar with the surroundings. "I'm sorry to ask you to meet us here, but it's my experience that dwelling in borderline squalor is good for security. I'd rather be safe than comfortable."

She waved off his apology. "Where's everyone else? Even your impertinent droid is gone, and he's usually no more than a meter from your side."

"Would you rather wait for them to return?"

"No, that's not necessary." She smiled, which made him feel slightly uncomfortable. "I'm sure you can fill me in on whatever I need to know."

Jax felt momentarily at a loss, then drew himself up. This was ridiculous. Master Piell would have considered being alone with a Zeltron of the opposite gender nothing more than a test. After all, he had the Force to counteract her pheromones.

It didn't seem to be helping all that much, however.

"I need to go over some predeparture details with you," he explained. "Things you need to do before you wrap up your final affairs, ways to go about them so as not to arouse suspicion, how to terminate any close relationships—that sort of thing."

"Travel information. Good."

He hesitated again. "Uh, you might want to take notes."

"Not necessary. I have a good memory." She sat, hugging her knees to her chest and giving him her undivided attention.

As he began to recite some of the procedures that would be necessary for her to ensure a safe and anonymous departure from Coruscant, he couldn't help but be aware of the bodystocking that covered her like a second, lucent skin. He used the Force to deflect the pheromones he could feel pulsing from her, but the visual alone was enough to keep him stumbling over his tongue like an anxious Padawan. Dejah pretended to notice nothing unusual in his behavior, of course. She simply sat, curled up in a supple tangle of arms and legs, and listened attentively. With her empathic talents, however, there was no question but that she was acutely aware of his inner turmoil. As he strode back and forth in front of her, taking care to keep a certain nominal distance, he was positive that he could feel her inner glow of satisfaction, hot as an undamped reactor core.

Eventually he ran out of things to say to her—except, of course, for the one thing he'd been dreading saying since she walked in the door. Despite having reached an agreement with his companions, now that the time had come to propound it, his Jedi training continued to resist.

She stared at him. "Was there something else, Jax?"

"No—yes." Girding himself in every respect, he sat down beside her. "Dejah, I don't want to do this. I've been trying to think of the best way to ask it of you, the least offensive way to make this request."

Her eyelids fluttered, and her crimson skin was positively aflame. "I'm Zeltron, Jax. Whatever request you want to make, I'm sure I've heard it before."

"Good. That makes it easier—" He broke off in shock at what the Force showed him behind those eyes. She'd chosen to reveal her thoughts, of that he was sure; no one with her psychic sensibilities could be read so easily.

He stood hastily. "That's, uh, that's not what I mean—at *all*."

Her expression turned uncertain. "I don't understand. Then what kind of request are you having trouble making?"

"What I'm trying to say, Dejah, is that we're about out of funds, and if we're going to continue to help you, I'm going to have to ask for—a retainer."

There—he'd managed to get it out, though the request still sounded obscene to him. He looked away. *I should have let Den do this,* he told himself unhappily. *Or Rhinann. Or even I-Five.* Asking for money wouldn't have bothered any of them in the least.

He felt ashamed to look at her, reluctant to use the

Force to sense her feelings. How would she react? Would she be hurt? Insulted? Angry?

He forced himself to turn and face her—and saw that her right hand was unsealing her jeweled carry-bag. "How much do you need? Do you want cash, or a credit transfer?"

Relief left him momentarily weak in the knees. She was watching him with a coy smile that seemed to say, *There now—that was easy enough, wasn't it?*

Less than an hour after he'd brought her up to date and she'd left, his colleagues rejoined him.

"How'd it go?" Den inquired anxiously. "Did she balk at the request?"

"Yes," Rhinann wanted to know. "Do we eat well tonight?"

I-Five made a snorting sound with his vocabulator. "It's always about food with you organics."

Jax, affecting an air of complete and utter confidence, said, "I am happy to say that, thanks to the gracious and understanding Dejah Duare, we now have an open line of credit through the planetary banking system under two new assumed identities, either of which any of you can now freely access."

Rhinann's tusks quivered in gustatory anticipation. "I thank you, Jax. There is nothing worse than being a gourmet in a world of indiscriminate eaters."

"Except having to listen to one," Den said. "But seriously, Jax—good work."

"Yes," I-Five agreed. "It would have been enough to have secured a promise of token payment. But an unlimited line of credit—your efforts exceed my expectations. I may go so far as to indulge in a logic board tune-up."

Basking in their praise, Jax noticed that compliments were lacking from one of the group. Having once again taken her seat at the work center, Laranth had resumed her equipment upgrading without a word.

He shrugged. He thought briefly about probing her feelings with the Force, but decided to respect her privacy. If the Paladin had a problem with him, his past experience with her guaranteed that she wouldn't be reticent to let people know when she was ready.

Still, it did somewhat dampen the celebratory mood . . .

sixteen

"I'm looking for the Cragmoloid Boulad. I was told you might know where I could find him."

The Green Nikto sitting in the ticket kiosk of the sleazy holobooth looked Typho deliberately up and down.

"Who told ye thet?"

"Does it matter?" Courteous and diplomatic most of the time, Typho could be tough when the occasion demanded. Here in the bowels of Coruscant, occasion did more than demand: it positively screamed. "Can you help me or not?"

"Depends." The Nikto groomed his facial scales with his long claws. "C'n ye pay?"

"I didn't take you for a philanthropist." Typho unsealed a pocket and brought out a fistful of credit chits. Avarice replaced some of the disinterest in the Nikto's large obsidian eyes. He licked his narrow lips.

"How d' I know ye're net thee police?"

"Get serious. Do you really think a dreg like you is worth the sector's time?"

The Nikto cackled, halting only when his laughter degenerated into a hacking cough. Typho made sure to stay well out of respiratory range while waiting for the attack to finish.

A clawed right hand swept the credits from the captain's grasp. "Twenty-third level," the Nikto said. "Quadrant D-three, Sector Two-Twelve. Ye didn't hear eet from me."

"Hear what?" Typho turned and walked away.

Nighttime downlevel on Coruscant wasn't all that different from daytime. In the abyssal ferrocrete depths the sunlight hardly ever penetrated to any perceptible degree; the light came from fluorescents, electroluminescence, and other sources. Even so, the combination rarely amounted to more than a perpetual twilight. Down here life surged and pulsed to rhythms unsettling to the average citizen. It was best, Typho had found, to move at a brisk clip, to project a don't-mess-with-me attitude. Uncertainty, more than anything else, drew the attention of predators and scavengers.

The entrance to the address Typho had been given was on the bottom row of what appeared to be a rundown resiplex. Even though he couldn't see them, he knew his body was being scanned by a plethora of security devices. If he could see them, he reflected, they wouldn't be very secure.

"You're armed," a voice accused from a hidden speaker.

"Of course I'm armed. What kind of idiot would come to a place like this without being armed?" He hoped the scan had only registered his blaster. The lightsaber was secured in the inside lining of his jacket, along with a small confounder that was supposed to render it invisible to detection.

"The exact extent of your idiocy is yet to be determined." There was a click, and double doors parted. They were much higher and wider, Typho noted as he entered, than was necessary to accommodate the passage of the largest humanoids on Coruscant.

The female Cragmoloid who met him displayed no weapons. Given her impressive size and bulk, none were needed. "Check your lethal devices, please."

"Certainly." Typho had no compunction about handing over his blaster and vibroknife. Not in light of the fact that the female asking for them stood more than three meters tall, massed over two hundred kilos, and could kill him with a blow of one massive fist. It was strange, however, to be frisked by a trunk as well as by hands. Despite their immense size, they traveled over his person with surprising delicacy.

Satisfied that she had relieved the visitor of every instrument of destruction, regardless of size, she stepped back. "Follow me."

The chamber where she left him was occupied by one other. It spoke to Boulad's confidence that he would meet alone with a complete stranger. Of course, help was likely only a trumpet away, and while it was one thing to talk oneself into the fixer's presence, it would be rather more difficult to get out in the event that things did not proceed as intended. The fact that the average adult Cragmoloid had the strength of half a dozen large humanoids was threat enough.

Boulad's kind were known for their directness. Typho's host did not disappoint in that regard.

"The fact that you found your way here means that you seek something you cannot find anyplace else."

Typho could feel the deep, sonorous voice vibrate the floor beneath him, heard it echo off the cavernous walls. The entire block of resicubes, he realized, had to be a façade, a hollowed-out shell that formed the Cragmoloids' lair. This chamber was dimly lit, sparsely furnished, and big enough to house a sky lorry. It also smelled faintly like hay.

He responded to Boulad's statement. "Your perception flatters you."

This produced a deep grunt that might have indicated satisfaction, recognition, or perhaps indigestion. Unfamiliar as he was with Cragii punctuation, Typho chose to accept it as encouraging. He gestured behind him.

"Your mate? A niece, perhaps? Attractive as well as competent."

The Cragmoloid's tiny eyes opened wider. Typho had chosen his opening well. He knew that the pachydermoids would rather discuss clan or relationships than just about anything else, so they spent the next twenty minutes talking family, with the captain letting his host carry most of the conversation. By the time Boulad had finished waxing rhapsodic about his current wife, Typho had been accepted as an honest broker, if not quite a member of the family.

"For one of the feeble trunkless, you are a pleasant exception," Boulad told him. "Still, it is time that you stated your business."

"Just so," Typho agreed. "I seek the disposition of any Sith on a certain world at a specific time."

Even for the representative of a species that valued honesty and directness above all, Boulad was taken aback. His trunk elevated in surprise. "Why not ask me something easy to obtain, like the Emperor's personal taste in beverages, or the home of the current mistress of the Senate vice president?"

Typho proceeded to fill in his host on the necessary details. When Boulad had recorded them all on an appliance designed to accommodate his massive digits, he grunted anew.

"All this is a simple matter to research, except for all of it."

"You understand," Typho said, "why I couldn't walk into Imperial Records and ask for a hard copy."

Boulad's trunk waved affirmation. "By now there would be little of you left to question. The Emperor does not like anyone prying into such interdicted material, even for something as simple and innocent as travel itineraries. How resourceful of you to find it all by yourself, without any assistance from anyone. Especially anyone like me."

The captain smiled. "I amaze myself sometimes."

"And now to the matter of money, which cannot be avoided. For such a dangerous service, at risk of inviting potentially lethal attention, I must charge five thouand credits. If you cannot pay such an amount, then you may utilize the exit, for our business here is done. I respect your manner, but I will not take such a risk for anything less. And if you know the people of Ankus, you know that we do not bargain in such things. Our word is our bond."

Typho was not a man of unlimited means, by any stretch of the imagination, but he had determined from the beginning of his quest that money could and would be no object. "Very well," he said, pulling out his coinpurse. "I assume cash is acceptable?"

"Mandatory." Boulad leaned forward, towering over his guest. "My people have already secured the information you want. At least, as much as was available."

Typho blinked in surprise as he paid his host. "That was fast."

"I was curious to know the why and wherefore of what you sought. If you were able to pay for it, so much the better. If not, it was worth researching to see if it might prove valuable to someone else."

A flicker of fear shot through the captain. If the Sith or any of their minions learned that someone was delving into their travel records . . . without thinking, he said as much to Boulad.

His host was no Jenet, for whom Typho's uncertainty would have been a compliment. "You wound me, visitor! I am an honest broker, as are all in my family." He gestured to his left from where another, somewhat smaller Cragmoloid was joining them. "Including my third son Arlumek, whom I believe has brought the information you requested—and have now paid for, in full."

While the elder Cragmoloid counted and pocketed his payment, Arlumek placed a small emitter in front of the expectant Typho. Heavy hands manipulated instrumentation, and words appeared in the air between them. They obviously meant nothing to the younger Cragmoloid, who turned away in disinterest.

To Typho, however, they meant a great deal. The strictly prohibited records that the slicer's family had somehow managed to access indicated that one Darth Sidious had journeyed to Mustafar, was there at the same time as Padmé and Anakin Skywalker, and had returned shortly thereafter.

His mind whirling, Typho excused himself. Now that their mutual business had been concluded, however, Boulad was reluctant to see the human go.

"Stay!" he entreated his visitor. "I would hear more of your excellent family."

"Sorry." Typho headed toward the door. "I have pressing business to attend to."

"A pity," the jovial Cragmoloid called after him. "If you ever have something similar to trade, you know where to find me."

Typho spent the rest of the night wandering the underlevels, his thoughts churning. Twice he was approached by footpads, but a glance at his face was enough to convince them that easier pickings lay elsewhere than on the corpus of the half-crazed human.

Padmé, Padmé, he whispered to himself. *Retribution is at hand. Retribution and justice. I know now who killed you.*

Like any puzzle, it was simple to solve once you had all the pieces. Who could have penetrated her security on Mustafar? Who could have slain the Senator's resourceful, determined bodyguard and suffered dearly in the fight that would surely have followed any attempt to harm her? Anakin Skywalker would not have gone down easily. Yes, the answer was clear now.

Darth Vader had killed them both.

Therefore, Vader must die.

He wasn't worried about getting close enough to the Dark Lord to finish him, even though he knew that one as adept in the Force as Vader surely would detect any threat. Typho knew from his own work as a specialist in security that, given sufficient knowledge, determination, and ability, coupled with a disregard for his own life, an assassin could get to any public figure. A soldier such as himself had both of those assets. Early in his quest he had realized that to avenge Padmé, it was reasonable to assume he would have to sacrifice his own life, and he was fully prepared to do so.

The problem lay in getting physically close enough to Vader to strike. What would draw Vader away from the security that undoubtedly surrounded him? What might induce the Dark Lord to forgo his usual caution and meet alone with an unfamiliar intermediary? As aide to the Emperor, Vader needed nothing. That didn't mean he was devoid of desire, of course. But what could such an incarnation of evil want?

Abruptly, he remembered what the bounty hunter Aurra Sing had said during their confrontation in the ruins of the Jedi Temple: "On behalf of Lord Vader I was hoping to find evidence here of a Jedi named Jax Pavan."

Vader was looking for a surviving Jedi named Pavan. And Typho recalled seeing the name *Jax Pavan* listed on the Imperial administration complex readout as being possibly still alive.

So the Dark Lord wanted this particular surviving Jedi badly enough to send a bounty hunter as celebrated as the relentless Aurra Sing after him. She had been searching for him locally, in the ruins of the Jedi Temple. Which meant that, unless the bounty hunter was way off the mark—not likely, given her reputation—Jax Pavan was somewhere on Coruscant. Not only on Coruscant, but somewhere nearby.

That was it. That was the solution. Jax Pavan would serve as the bait to bring Darth Vader within killing range. How precisely Typho was going to carry out the assassination was something he still had to plan, but he had no doubt a means could be managed. Having spent his entire professional life learning how to keep people from being killed had taught him how best they could be slain.

No question about it: Darth Vader was going to die. Padmé Amidala would be avenged and so would Anakin Skywalker. But before he could begin to put the final plan in motion, there was one more thing he had to do.

He had to find Jax Pavan.

seventeen

It seemed to Jax that no matter how hard they worked, they couldn't get a break.

It wasn't as if no one on the streets had heard of Ves Volette. Ever since the devastation that had been wrought on his homeworld, every prominent Caamasi on Imperial Center had been fodder for media interviews, commentary, and a good deal of *tsk-tsk* gossip. The violent death of one as famous as Volette made his name even more widespread.

But this was Imperial Center, the world-city, home to billions upon billions and workplace to billions more. Here, the murder of an artist, no matter how well known, was minor news at best. If not for the Caamasi connection, it would have required a dedicated search by those with a particular interest in such matters to determine that it had even occurred.

Jax and his friends had performed such a search, and come up devoid of clues. Ideas they had in plenty; the trouble was, none of them were panning out. The Jedi's only consolation was that the sector police were no nearer solving the crime than he was. Of course, had Prefect Pol Haus made it a priority and devoted all his resources to its resolution, his department doubtless would have made better progress. But the prefect's bailiwick included dozens of levels, thousands of buildings, and more species than Jax could name. The murders alone, considered apart from all other violent crimes, were backlogged by years.

At least, Jax thought, *there are five of us to focus on a single crime.* That was encouraging. Just not very much. Deprived of the resources of a modern police department, all they had to go on were the answers to the several questions they had deployed among contacts who, with luck, were in the know. Thus far these had proved erroneous, futile, or leads to dead ends. Jax dreaded every communication with the disheartened Dejah Duare, because each time he was forced to report the same lack of progress. They were getting nowhere, and his feeling of guilt only increased every time he deposited the Zeltron's money into their communal account.

They were bound to eventually learn something worthwhile, he told himself, if only through the virtue of sheer persistence.

For the most part, his colleagues went about their assignments with minimum complaints, but without an overabundance of enthusiasm. He was in particular concerned about Laranth, who seemed to be growing more and more withdrawn. The Twi'lek had always been moody, but even Rhinann, who wasn't exactly a draft of fresh oxy at his best, had had occasion to remark on her state. She had, over the last few days, taken to tucking her lekku stump behind its mate, instead of letting it hang freely as she used to. That meant something, Jax was sure. He just didn't know what. Also, he noticed that when she spoke to him it was always in brief, curt syllables, never stating or asking more than was absolutely necessary.

Den carried out his tasks with crisp efficiency, but without noticeable enthusiasm. And instead of assisting his companions, I-Five had taken to spending periods of time uplinked to a HoloNet grid—at considerable expense. When Jax had asked his purpose, the droid had replied, "You're not getting many results with your tactics, so I thought I'd try some things on my own, at a more reasonable dataspeed rate. Frankly, watching you organics laboriously process information is like watching supercooled hydrogen flow."

"Anything worthwhile to report?"

"Not yet."

There came at last a day when it seemed that their luck might change. A bored Rhinann received a communication from a local police outpost, which he duly relayed to Jax.

"Excellent," the Jedi said. "Something from Haus's people, at last." He searched the Elomin's dour face. "What is it? Have they finally picked up a viable suspect? Did someone actually confess? Or is it a good lead they feel free to share with us?"

"None of those." Rhinann handed Jax a copy. "Read it if you wish. I'll spare you the details. The gist is that one of us needs to go to sector police subpost one eighty-six to bail out a certain Sullustan named Den Dhur. Unless—and this is the course of action I personally recommend—you would rather he remain in custody."

Laranth was at the work center repairing a comm unit. She didn't speak or look up. Even Den's longtime companion I-Five did not break whatever silent cybernetic conversation he was involved in to voice his opinion.

Jax put the hard copy aside. No point in reading it; the meticulous former bureaucrat would, as he said, already have read and analyzed every aspect of the official document, if only to alleviate his boredom. "What charge are they holding him on?"

"Impersonating a police officer. But not to worry— I'm sure a word or two from your close personal friend the prefect will see him back on the street within minutes."

"I suppose we can't do anything via comm channels?"

"No. If it's to be done at all, his release must be realized in person. I nominate you."

Jax gave him a look of annoyance, an effort that was wasted since the Elomin had already turned away. The Jedi turned to I-Five. "You want to come with me? There might be details I'll need to quick-check." But the droid, lost in the maze of cybernetic data processing, did not respond. Jax shrugged. "Guess I'll go by myself."

As he started for the door, Laranth looked at him. "Come back to us," she said to him. Encouraged by her tone, he paused and looked back.

"Are you saying you'd miss me if I didn't?"

"No," she replied, utterly deadpan. "I'm saying that we don't have sufficient funds to bail out two of you, and I don't want to have to decide which of you goes free."

* * *

Ennui had its uses, Jax decided as he and Den exited the heavily armored, windowless front of the police subpost. It was a state of being that crossed species lines. It was as good a reason as any why the cools had walked (or, in one case, slimed) through the necessary interviews and the hectares of flimsiwork that had eventually allowed the Jedi to extricate the Sullustan from custody. The bail that had been required to accomplish Den's release was as good as forfeited, he knew, since Den had no intention of reporting for trial on the date set.

"What were you thinking?" he asked as they made their way down the Level 14 street, heading for the nearest public transport.

"I was looking for a way to get some information out of a certain Vernol—a real mopakhead named Shulf'aa. He's a merchant over in—"

"We've spoken with dozens of merchants, all to no avail."

"Ah, but not in the capacity of an investigating police officer."

Jax looked at him. "Tell me you learned something."

"Shulf'aa's an art dealer."

Some of Jax's enthusiasm faded. "Let me guess: he owns some of Ves Volette's sculptures."

"Two pieces, to be precise," Den elaborated. "They're still in one of his several galleries, because the artist's price has gone way, way up since his death. And each time it goes up, Shulf'aa raises his asking price. It's a fairly straightforward piece of commercial brinkmanship. He keeps hoping that one day a buyer will pay at the top of the asking bid.

"But that's not what I found especially interesting."

"He told you something he didn't tell the police?"

"He told me something, in my transitory guise as a police representative, that he hasn't had a chance to tell Haus and his goons, because they hadn't asked him yet. It seems that the two Volette light sculptures Shulf'aa acquired didn't come to him through normal, that is to say legal, channels."

"They were stolen?"

Den was enjoying his moment of triumph. "Less than a year ago."

Jax said slowly, "Dejah never said anything about that."

"Why should she?" the Sullustan pointed out. "We didn't ask her.

"Anyway, so I pressed Shulf'aa, threatened to take him in for attempting to vend stolen goods, and he offered me a bribe to keep quiet about the whole matter. I told him that I would—but that he could keep his money, in return for the name of the individual who provided him with the goods."

"Which is?"

"Spa Fon. A Nuknog fence and extortionist."

Jax thought about it. Even shorter than Sullustans, the typical Nuknog would barely come up to the Jedi's waist. As a species they defined the concept of *looking out for number one;* Nuknogs stuck their necks out for no one. Since their necks were longer than their legs, this was probably a good idea. They were cunning, greedy, and totally amoral, as well as being deft manipulators with sharp eyesight and keen hearing. Such a being would make a superior thief—

provided he didn't have to run too fast. Jax could certainly envision one stalking and ultimately burglarizing an artistic member of a trusting species such as the Caamasi.

"It gets better," Den continued. "Fon's local."

Jax grinned at the Sullustan. "I take back everything I've said about you, Den."

"What have you been saying about me? Never mind, I'm sure it can't be any worse than what I-Five says about me."

"I even take back everything he says about you. Thanks to your imaginative stunt, we've got more than a clue—we have a suspect. What's the address?"

Den rolled off a street name and number. Jax overlaid the information on a mental picture of the immediate region of Coruscant. He was not surprised to find that the address was nearby. Most thieves dwell in close proximity to their victims. It simplifies transportation.

"Let's go have a little chat with this Spa Fon."

eighteen

The address the batrachian art broker had reluctantly revealed to Den was, surprisingly, located on the 42nd Level, in a neighborhood that could at least lay claim to potential gentrification. Which was to say that one was marginally less likely to be mugged and robbed there on a dark night than on many of the innumerable levels below. Nevertheless, Jax and Den did not relax as they exited the transport and made their way on foot to the complex where, according to the information Den had been given, the Nuknog made his business as well as his home.

This portion of Level 42 was infused with photonics, so that wired or radiant lighting was not required. Shopfronts flaunted their goods without the usual security bars or alarm beams, and the guards out front actually wore uniforms instead of just harsh expressions and weapons. It wasn't the Manarai Hills, not by the length of a comet's tail, but it was considerably more upmarket than either of them had anticipated. *Business must be good,* Jax mused.

The address given to Den was almost comically nondescript—so much so that it was impossible to tell whether they were looking at the front of a residence or a business. There were no windows, no other doors, not even any visible vid pickups: just a floor-to-roof rectangle of dull gray carbonite composite with a number floating half a centimeter to one side of the center.

Jax knocked loudly. The response time was long enough to make him think that no one had heard. But as he raised his fist to pound again, a portal appeared in the center of the gray wall, revealing a Lonjair standing there. Barely half a meter tall, skinny and indigo in hue, it regarded them out of four bright turquoise eyes beneath a single tuft of pale blue hair that rose from the crest of its skull.

Jax had never seen a Lonjair before. There weren't a lot of them in this part of the galaxy. Normally shy and species-centered, they tended to keep to themselves in three closely packed systems far out on the South Arm. Like every other civilized species, they had representation on Imperial Center, but to see one in private service was unusual. Perhaps Spa Fon, being of modest stature, preferred servants even less physically imposing than himself. Certainly the Lonjair's high, squeaky voice was not exactly daunting.

"Yeh geets aftrah beedness wi' Spah Fhoon?"

Den stepped forward. "We do."

The Lonjair looked the Sullustan up and down. "Yeh dawn't lahks d'sarht."

Jax said, "Does the redoubtable Spa Fon judge business acumen by appearance?"

In quick, smooth succession, one after the other, four eyes blinked at the Jedi. "I aftrah beh nahdin' nahmes."

Jax supplied two, making them up on the fly and

hoping his companion would remember his. Den's previous profession had taught him to retain minutiae, so the Jedi wasn't too worried.

The Lonjair instructed them to wait, and disappeared into a hallway. He wasn't gone long; when he returned, he ushered them in with a gesture.

As they entered, Den whispered to Jax, "Don't you find it peculiar that Spa Fon didn't have his servant ask us our business, or have you disarm?"

"Everyone has a different modus. Sometimes it's defined by tradition and not logic. If nothing else, it indicates that Fon isn't afraid of us."

Den nodded in the direction of their diminutive guide. "Why should he be, with a bodyguard like that?"

Spa Fon was waiting for them in a chamber that was, thankfully, high enough to allow Jax to stand erect. Whether the Nuknog had arranged it out of courtesy to customers and contacts bigger than himself or whether it simply reflected the existing architecture was open to question.

Spa Fon sat on a thick yellow cushion, his small blue servant taking up a stance beside him. Fon's hospitality might include a ceiling of reasonable height, but it evidently did not extend to furniture. His visitors were obliged to either stand or make use of similar cushions.

Den dropped gratefully onto one of the pillows. It took Jax a moment to fold his longer legs beneath him. The position brought back a quick flash of memory: he felt as if he were back in beginning levitation class, trying to absorb the teachings of Master Yerem.

The sharp jab of longing for such simpler times surprised him with its intensity.

Impatient, as were most of his kind, Spa Fon scowled at them. "Erppah tells me you're here on business. I don't recognize either of you. Give me a reference or I'll have you thrown out." At this, the Lonjair tilted back his head and assumed an air of unmistakable haughtiness.

"Relax." Den made a soothing gesture. "We're here on the recommendation of Shulf'aa the Vernol."

"Ah! That sly slink." The Nuknog let out a sniff of approval. "What's old wart-face up to?"

"Oh, the usual," Jax responded casually. "Business is good. In fact, we were told that when we met up with you, we were to solicit additional stock on his behalf."

The high-ridged head bobbed appreciatively. "Such stash as Shulf'aa requires is not easy to come by. Exclusive goods are as well guarded as they are regarded by his customers. But tell him I will see what I can do. Now then"—he shifted his lumpy backside on the luxurious cushion—"what brings you to me, specifically?"

Den looked at Jax, who nodded encouragingly. The Sullustan turned back to their host. "You provided Shulf'aa with two Ves Volette originals. He'd like more."

The Nuknog rolled his eyes in opposite directions. "I bet he would, the old bug eater. Does he think Volettes are like shafts of wandering sunlight, to be gathered freely with a photon net? Since the artist was killed . . ."

It was the opening Jax had been waiting for. Casually, offhandedly, he said, "Yes, that was a gifted bit of work on your part. I'm curious as to how you managed it."

"*Managed* it?" The Nuknog's tone took an abrupt turn toward the unpleasant. Beside him, the Lonjair stiffened. "I *managed* no such thing. Why would you accuse me of such an act?"

"Well, it's intuitively obvious," Den said. "You stole from the artist two of his works, which you then flogged to Shulf'aa at considerable profit. So you tried it again. But this time Volette had prepared for a similar break-in. Or perhaps your timing was bad and you encountered him by accident. In the ensuing struggle, you killed him. Not that we care."

Spa Fon glanced at the Lonjair, who blinked in response. When the Nuknog turned back to his guests, it was clear from the narrowing of his eyes that he now saw them in a new and not nearly as favorable light. "I think that you do care, very much. I think maybe in fact that you're police, here to try to get me to confess to a crime I didn't commit because you can't solve it any other way."

"We're not police," Jax began honestly. "We're—"

"And," the Nuknog interrupted, "I think it's time for you to leave." Raising a reddish, bony arm, their host gestured.

The curtain covering the back wall parted, and a shape emerged. As it stepped into the room behind Spa Fon, Jax recognized the species—Cathar. Feline in appearance, covered in thick gold to yellow-brown fur, and clad in a leather vest and kilt, it stood much taller than him and probably massed three times his weight. Beneath the fur, Jax could see, was mostly muscle.

"Well," Den said briskly, edging backward toward the exit, "Obviously you have other appointments, so we'll just be—"

Den froze as the Cathar took a step forward. On his head, between the pointed ears, he wore a diadem of silvery metal fronted by a single mangana aqua cabochon. That meant something in Cathar culture, Jax knew. He just couldn't remember what.

He took a deep breath. "There's no need for this, Spa Fon. We're all friends here."

The Nuknog glared at him. "Friends do not accuse friends of murder."

"I'm sure it was an accident. It was his sculptures you wanted, not his life." Smiling broadly, the Jedi spread his arms wide. "Hey, there's no shame in admitting to an accident."

"I'm glad you feel that way," replied Fon. "So you'll experience no hard feelings over the accident that is about to befall you both now."

The Cathar approached Jax, ignoring Den. "I am Sele," he growled. "I will pull out your tibia and use it to pick my teeth." Snarling, the leader of the Nuknog's bodyguard exposed sharp, white canines.

"Is this any way to treat customers?" As Jax took a step backward, his right hand slid inconspicuously to his waist. "You can't make deals in a hostile atmosphere. Why don't we all take a breath and—"

Letting out a roar that shook the room, Sele reached for Jax with one huge paw. Though the Cathar was faster than one might expect for a creature of such bulk, Jax was considerably more nimble.

Dodging to his left, he drew and activated the Velmorian flamesword in a single motion.

The Cathar paused a moment at this unexpected move; he was, however, completely confident in his ability to subdue any hostile interlopers. Given his size and strength, it was an assurance not misplaced.

But he had, in all probability, never faced a Jedi before.

Sele drew a poniard as long and heavy as the Jedi's leg. Ducking beneath a swing powerful enough to decapitate a reek, Jax leaned forward in a long thrust that sent the tip of the flamesword through the Cathar's fur and a centimeter deep into his thigh. Howling, the bodyguard stepped back and swatted at the smoke rising from his singed fur. When he looked up again, his expression was by itself enough to paralyze a typical opponent.

Now I remember the significance of the headband, Jax thought. *It signifies him as the mightiest warrior of his clan. It figures.*

Rushing forward, Sele brought the weighty blade of the poniard down in a swipe that would have cut the Jedi in half from crown to crotch—had it landed, which it did not. Dodging right this time, Jax feinted with the flamesword. His adversary sidestepped left; Jax whirled, leapt with the Force's aid, and brought the Velmorian weapon down. Flinching, Sele managed to block the blow, but the overflow from the sword seared a black streak across his right shoulder. For the second time the Cathar let out a howl of pain.

Though he had lightly wounded his opponent twice, the Jedi knew that Sele had to land only one of his substantial blows to win the fight. He continued his strategy, using the Force to keep him just out of his foe's reach while letting the laws of physics work in his favor. At his mass and size, there was simply no way the Cathar could move as quickly or as nimbly as Jax, even without the Force's aid.

At last, smoldering like a house afire from more than a dozen slashing wounds inflicted by Jax's flamesword, Sele had no choice but to acquiesce to his opponent. The hulking creature bent one leg and bowed his head. He laid the poniard on the floor between them. "By the rules of the Blood Hunt," he said in a throaty growl, "I surrender to you all that I own and all that I am."

"Accepted." Breathing hard, Jax turned to face the still-seated and now obviously stunned figure of Spa Fon. The Lonjair was nowhere to be seen. "Bad business," Jax said. "Something like this could ruin your reputation if word got out." The fence didn't reply; he just sat and stared. "Don't you agree, Den?" Jax continued. "Den?"

Turning away from the seemingly paralyzed Nuknog, Jax searched the room with his gaze and the Force. Where was Den?

"Interesting thing, reputations. They're so often undeserved."

Stepping from behind the same dividing curtain that had earlier revealed the now chastised bodyguard, the Sullustan rejoined his companion. Squirming beneath his right arm but failing to break free was the Lonjair. With a flourish, Den dumped him in front of the Jedi.

"My friend, meet the real Spa Fon."

Jax looked from their supposed host down to the slightly built Lonjair. "*You're* Spa Fon?"

"Don't hurt me!" the Lonjair whimpered. Black spots of panic had broken out all over his body. His four eyes were rolling in so many directions at once that looking at them made Jax dizzy.

"I'm just a simple dealer in wanted goods," the bona fide Spa Fon whined. "I take but I don't harm. Don't hit me, please!" Jax noticed that the thick patois the Lonjair had affected earlier had been replaced by perfectly understandable Basic. Off to the side, Sele growled something unflattering under his breath. The unabashed display of cowardice on the part of his former employer forced the Cathar to look away lest he share in the Lonjair's shame.

Den gestured toward Jax. "My friend spoke the truth: we're not police. We're independent contractors, doing a job. Except we don't hide behind a disguised droid." He looked contemptuously back at the bogus Nuknog. "Now, for the last time—how and why did you murder the artist Ves Volette?"

Four desperate eyes goggled up at the Sullustan and the Jedi. "I didn't, I didn't! Not I, nor any of my people! Sure, I wanted more of his light sculptures. They're quick and easy money. But I swear, I steal but I don't kill!"

Jax leaned forward and reached out. The Force that he perceived as linear extensions of himself, as threads of purposeful intangibility, touched the pitiful creature lying before him. It took only a moment. "He's telling the truth."

* * *

"What now?" Den asked as they headed back toward the terminal.

"Back to our place," Jax said. "I have Rhinann engaged in some research on an unrelated matter that I want to check on."

Den shrugged. "Whatever." He checked his chrono. "Just as well—it's almost happy hour."

nineteen

Rhinann sat before his access console, pondering his next action.

It had seemed a simple enough appeal from Jax: find out everything still extant about his father, Lorn Pavan, a small-time information broker, dealer in stolen goods, and, before that, clerical assistant employed by the Jedi Temple. All of this two decades and more in the past. A straightforward request for anyone save one of the Elomin, who were accustomed to seeing labyrinthine complexities and subterfuge beneath the surface of anything that seemed initially innocent. The fact that Jax had also enjoined him not to speak of this task to I-Five only added to Rhinann's suspicion. He had made it seem casual enough, like an afterthought—"Oh, and by the way . . ."—but his studied insouciance only made Rhinann the more wary of a hidden agenda. For an Elomin, the concern was never about being too paranoid—it was about being paranoid enough.

"Open channel," he murmured to the console. The holoproj responded by showing him the gateway to the HoloNet. Rhinann interlaced his fingers and pushed his palms out, limbering up his digits and cracking his knuckles. Then he bent over the instrumentation projection.

Five hours later he pushed back his formfit chair and stretched, feeling the muscles of his rhachis reluctantly unkink. He was too deep in thought to be aware of the trilling sound made by the passage of his breath over his vibrating tusks.

There was much to think about.

What he'd managed to put together was fascinating. Jax's father had been a minor-level accountant and file clerk for the Jedi until his two-year-old son had been found to have higher-than-normal midichlorian levels. The elder Pavan had been approached by representatives of the Council, who'd urged that young Jax be taken into the Temple as a Padawan.

It was, Rhinann knew, considered quite an honor to have one's child offered an opportunity to become a Jedi Knight. Even though it meant giving up that child forever to the cloistered corridors of the Order, few parents turned down the Jedi, because it also meant a secure, honorable, and purposeful life for their offspring, which was something all parents wanted.

Lorn and his wife, Siena, had resisted, however. Though not rich, they were by no means destitute, and the thought of giving up their only child, even though it might be deemed in his best interests, horrified them.

Reports as to what happened next were conflicting. Lorn had either quit his job or been let go, and the child Jax had been either taken by or given freely to the Order—although a grievance, filed by the parents, was on the public record accusing the Jedi of what amounted to kidnapping. Rhinann got the impression that there had been collusion in high places to bury the story, even before Lorn's name was linked to the missing Neimoidian holocron. In any event, nothing had come of the grievance. Siena Pavan had left her husband not long after, and Lorn had begun a long downward spiral, literally as well as figuratively, that had eventually deposited him on the mean streets of Coruscant's underworld. Here he had met the protocol droid I-Five, and the two had begun their singular partnership.

All this was public record—or had been before the data purge of anything having to do with the Jedi. Even so, it had been relatively easy to suss out. The next stage of Lorn's saga, however, had been systematically and thoroughly purged. The shunting, decryption, and maneuvering around countless pyrowalls had taken much time and patience. Rhinann had painstakingly applied enhancement and reconstruction of the various data bins, some of which had been removed from the vaults, leaving only quantum residual traces. At some points he'd had to rely on nodal seeker algorithms to reconstruct and best-guess the graph probabilities of the data conduits. It hadn't been easy; obviously the story he was trying so scrupulously to piece together had been thoroughly scrubbed, by orders from someone very much on high. He'd had to move cautiously indeed to avoid the myriad alarms, trip wires, and deadfalls that lay in wait around every virtual corner, and when he'd finally disengaged from the hunt, the story was still by and large piecemeal.

The essence of it was simple enough—Lorn Pavan and his droid partner had come into possession of a data holocron containing intel concerning the Neimoidian trade embargo of the planet Naboo that had occurred twenty-three years previous. Rhinann wasn't able to ascertain the exact nature of the intel, but it was obviously severely compromising to at least one highly placed government official, if not more. In response to this, a death mark was issued on Pavan and, by extension, I-Five.

So far, his extensive and exhaustive reconstruction of past events had yielded little that hadn't already been vouchsafed by I-Five. What Jax was most curious to know was the identity of the mysterious assassin, as well as his employer. These data were buried the deepest, and took the most effort to exhume.

"I found nothing but rumor, essentially," he told Jax later. "The Imperial Security Bureau categorically condemns all such speculation as innuendo and calumny, and the slightest suspicion of illegal interest is enough to warrant an investigation by the Inquisitorius. My slicing past their pyrowalls did not activate any alarms, which is how I intend to keep it. What I have discovered is everything I can get without putting us all at great risk. Don't ask me to investigate further; I won't chance a cerebral meltdown for you or anyone.

"I will tell you this once, and then I intend to forget it. Make of it what you will, but know that you didn't learn it from me. It is, at best, hearsay.

"A fragment of a sector police communiqué, dated, as closely as I can determine, approximately eighteen years ago, from the time of the Naboo trade embargo, mentions the death of a Hutt nightclub owner and local racketeer, along with several of his minions, at the hands of a Zabrak assassin. The killer's targets were apparently a human male, most likely of Corellian or Alderaanian origin, and a protocol droid."

"I-Five and my father," Jax murmured.

"Almost certainly," Rhinann agreed. "They escaped, and were pursued by the Zabrak."

"That correlates with what I-Five told me. The thing he refuses to specify is the assassin's identity."

"If my suspicions are correct," the Elomin said, "he had a good reason for not doing so." He paused.

"Tell me," Jax said. He felt the hairs on his arms and the back of his neck rising in anticipation.

Rhinann said, "The weapon used by the Zabrak was a double-bladed lightsaber. A *red* lightsaber."

Jax stared at him. "A *Sith*?"

The Elomin regarded him impassively. "You tell me."

"But—" Jax felt his mind whirling. According to Temple lore, a Sith Lord's lightsaber was always red, constructed by following an ancient, secret formula. It had been thus ever since Darth Bane had instituted the Rule of Two, more than a thousand years ago. In addition, the Jedi had traditionally eschewed the use of double-bladed lightsabers. The style and color of the Zabrak's weapon, therefore, all but guaranteed his identity to be that of a Sith.

His father had been killed by a Sith. And I-Five had known this.

twenty

When they returned to Poloda Place, Den immediately noticed that I-Five was still jacked into the HoloNet. Plugged in, jacked in, turned on, wired up: however an organic chose to describe the condition, it was the mechmind state of oneness with other artificial intelligences. Den knew that, while in that state, the droid could exchange information instantly, without having to first translate it to Basic and then back again. He could receive replies at the same speed, instead of waiting for the cybernetic equivalent of hours for an organic to finish a couple of sentences.

It did no good, the droid had told him more than once, to try to explain such things to organics. Even those with whom he had surrounded himself, who were smarter and more empathic than most, could at best only nod courteously and declare their understanding—when in reality it was plain they understood nothing, and that their comprehension was irredeemably restricted by the limitations imposed on their thought processes by the very nature of their protein-based synaptic connections. He gave them credit for trying, though—especially Den, who, like most of his kind, was sharp of mind as well as tongue.

Jax immediately met with Rhinann, and the two of them disappeared into an antechamber to talk. A few moments later Jax reentered the room, his expression grim. He crossed to the wall where the droid was jacked into the interface. "I-Five," he said tightly, "we need to talk."

Something in his tone made Den take notice. It also got through to I-Five. The droid removed his digit from the interface socket and turned to face Jax.

The Jedi glanced at Laranth and Den. "Can we have the room, please?"

Laranth nodded and left. On the way out she grabbed Den by the shoulder. "Come on," she said. Den thought briefly about resisting, but only briefly; the Twi'lek was much stronger than he was.

"No fair," he protested feebly. "If this is about the case, shouldn't we be there, too?"

"It's not about the case," Laranth said.

"How can you know?"

"You're a reporter," she said. "How can you not?"

I-Five said mildly, "How may I help you, Jax?"

Jax repressed an urge to grab and shake the droid, knowing that it would do no good. "The man who killed my father was a Sith. Why didn't you tell me?"

"What good would it have done?"

"What *harm* would it have done? As a Jedi in particular, I had a right to know."

"And now that you know," the droid said with maddening complacency, "what do you plan to do?"

"Well, I—" Jax paused, realizing that he'd formed no real course of action. "I'll find out if this Sith still lives," he said, somewhat lamely, "and—"

"And no doubt get yourself arrested and tortured by the Inquisitorius," I-Five finished. "It's a New Order out there, remember? *If* the assassin is still alive—a low probability, given the attrition rate in his kind of work—he is not the hunted. You are."

"He was acting under orders," Jax said. "Orders from very high up. Orders that may possibly have come from Palpatine himself."

"And?" When Jax didn't reply, the droid continued, "Do you dream of taking the fight to the Emperor? Weren't you the one who told me not too long ago that the very concept teeters on madness?

"You're doing everything one life-form can do, Jax. A great deal more than most do. Would you throw it all away to avenge someone you never even knew?

"I knew Lorn Pavan better than anyone, I daresay. I can call up memories of him that seem as real as you. And I'm certain he would tell you to let the past care for the dead."

"So you didn't tell me his killer was a Sith because you knew that I'd feel honor-bound, both as his son and as a Jedi, to bring closure to all this?" Jax shook his head in disbelief. "How? You didn't even know me at the time."

"I knew your father," I-Five said. "And I came to know the Jedi over the years. And I *saw* the Zabrak. Nothing could stop him. Lorn wouldn't have wanted you cut down like he was."

Jax's head was spinning. If there was the faintest possibility that a Sith did still exist, it was his duty as a Jedi to hunt him down. Added to that was the urge to avenge the father he never knew. But he had to admit that I-Five was making a lot of sense. As a Jedi, his first duty was to help the people, not pursue personal vendettas. Also, the galaxy had changed: to be identified as a Jedi Knight now wasn't the automatic ticket to awe and respect that it once had been.

But he couldn't simply let it go . . .

I-Five said quietly, "I was wrong not to tell you everything, Jax. It's not my right to choose your path. But now that you know, should you decide to investigate this further, I can at least help level the playing field." So saying, he opened the hatch to a small, hidden aperture in his chest plate, in what would be the upper left quadrant of a human's torso. He reached into the chest compartment and withdrew a small vial. After a moment, Jax recognized the clear tube, about the size and length of his index finger, as the vaporizer delivery ampoule for a non-invasive epidermic injector commonly referred to as a skinpopper.

"This is, as far as I can determine, the sole remaining sample of bota extract in the galaxy," the droid said. "Bota was a broad-based ergogenic plant native to Drongar."

"I've heard of it," Jax said. "It was the reason the Separatists and the Republic fought there . . . until it mutated and became worthless."

"Yes. It is—was—what's commonly known as an adaptogen: a panacea that has various, mostly salutary effects on differing species. To Neimoidians it's a narcotic, to Hutts a psychedelic, to humans an antibiotic, and so on.

"During her tour of duty as a healer, Jedi Barriss Offee accidentally discovered that a dose of the distillate greatly enhanced her connection to the Force. She described it as being linked to all beings, all places, throughout all times." The droid hesitated, then added, "Jedi Offee wasn't one to overly indulge in hyperbole, so I assume that her assessment was a straightforward one, metaphysical as it may sound."

"I believe you," Jax replied. "How did you come into possession of it?"

"When I finally finished reconstructing my synaptic grid links, I remembered that I'd made a promise to Lorn once. He asked me to watch over you, if you'll recall."

"Hard to forget, with you reminding me at every opportunity."

"Jedi Offee offered me the privileged status of being an envoy to the Temple by carrying the distillate with me back to Coruscant. When Den and I arrived, however—"

"There were no Jedi to deliver it to—until you found me." Jax looked at the ampoule, held it up to the light, admiring its translucence. It reminded him, for some reason, of the pyronium nugget. "But why didn't you give it to me when we first met?"

Again, I-Five hesitated uncharacteristically. "Because," he said at last, "you're one of the last few surviving Jedi. I had to make sure—"

"That I was worthy. That I wouldn't use the bota in the service of the dark side."

"Forgive me. I had to be certain. According to Jedi Offee, the enhanced connection with the Force is potentially so powerful that, were it to fall into the wrong hands, the results could be cataclysmic. She felt that it opened a channel to what she referred to as the Cosmic Force. I assume you know what she was referring to."

Jax nodded, lost in thought. Most philosophers and students of the Force, including many members of the erstwhile Council, believed that the Force was above intellectual concepts of good and evil, and that the terms *light side* and *dark side* constituted nothing more than a merism. Nevertheless, many also felt a case could be made for viewing the Force, as it was generally understood and utilized, as a subset of a grander and all-pervasive unifying principle.

It was this "living Force" that was the aspect most Jedi—and most Sith as well—were familiar with. If one's connection with it was strong enough, one could accomplish what seemed to most folk to be miracles: telekinesis, healing abilities, supernal strength, speed and stamina, even a certain amount of precognition.

But, according to the Old Teachings, this was only one aspect of a greater whole, much as one planar surface represented only a fraction of a hypergem's multidimensional wonders, known variously as the unifying, cosmic, or greater Force. One connected with the greater Force only through a lifetime of meditation and sacrifice, but the reward of doing so was, it was said, a unification with all of space and time, an ability to manipulate matter and energy on the most elemental levels . . . even, it was said by some, the ability to throw off the shackles of the flesh in favor of an immortal body of energy.

If bota extract lived up to Barriss Offee's description, it would seem to offer a shortcut to the enlightenment of the greater Force. If it could indeed potentiate the effects of his body's midi-chlorians to such an unprecedented degree, and if it could make such power available to *any* Force-sensitive—well, then *cataclysmic* was definitely an understatement.

If Vader were to somehow learn of it . . . Jax couldn't finish the thought. But then another thought, even more frightening, occurred to him:

What if he already knows?

What if Vader knew, somehow, that Jax was intended to be the recipient of the extract? He might not know the exact time or vector of its delivery, might not suspect that it had been carried to Imperial Center by a mere protocol droid. But if he had any foreknowledge at all, either through the Force or simply through mundane intel, of the miracle distillate's properties, that was surely reason enough for his unflagging pursuit of Jax.

He said as much to I-Five. The droid agreed, adding, "Perhaps it would be best to hide it—ideally by someone else in a place unknown to you, so that a truth-scan wouldn't reveal its whereabouts."

Jax looked again at the clear amber liquid in the ampoule. "You had to pick a time like this to tell me about it."

"And a better time would have been . . . ?"

Jax had no anwer for that.

twenty-one

The meeting room wasn't large. It was hidden behind a false wall in the kitchen of a charity that fed the homeless and hungry representatives of several species. It was surprisingly crowded, however. Jax found himself standing against the rear wall as the cell's leader spoke from the makeshift forum at the front of the room. That the partisans had passion and were driven by determination could not be denied. Passion and determination were, however, poor substitutes for Star Destroyers and divisions of stormtroopers.

The speaker was a Gossam, elaborately dressed in the style favored by his people. His tone was sharp and his words, eloquent. His passion was easy to understand. Among the nonhuman species, Gossams had been especially singled out by the Emperor for continued persecution.

"Hear me well, disgruntled masses. First the stormtroopers will come for the peaceful nonhumans such as the Gossams and the Caamasi. Then they will come for the defiant nonhumans. Then the humans who object, and, finally, they will turn upon and devour themselves in an orgy of mindless destruction and self-loathing, until the galaxy turns back to barbarism and all semblance of kindness, decency, and civilization is lost!"

It went on in that vein for some time, individual members of the audience frequently murmuring their agreement. There was no applause; the speaker's words were too solemn for applause. Jax listened with half a mind, the other half being occupied with studying those in attendance. In addition to the humans there was a representative smattering of sentients from all across the galaxy, as he had known there would be. The Whiplash drew support even from some of those species seemingly favored by the government.

As a member of the subversive organization, he attended the clandestine meetings whenever he could, to reacquaint himself with familiar faces and to meet new ones as well.

A tall and elderly human female took the podium from the exhausted Gossam and started talking about organizations similar to the Whiplash that were forming on other worlds. Jax sat up. This was news to him, as it no doubt would have been to the general media. Was the government aware of these stirrings? If so, it would behoove the Imperial authorities to keep such knowledge quiet. A cluster of malcontents on one world was easily monitored. Individual groups of dissenters were each separately a simple matter to contain.

The woman was talking not merely of groups with similar ideas and aims, however, but of the first threads of cooperation among them. Of the Whiplash not simply talking to like-minded factions on other worlds, but of linking up with them. Of not just speaking out, but taking action.

What she was describing went deeper and broader than resistance. She was promoting organized rebellion. Not for now, not even for tomorrow; the advocates of resistance were too scattered and too few to risk anything like direct confrontation with the government. But the first notions, the preliminary inklings, were there, scattered throughout her speech. Some in the audience were moved to tears, others to cries to take up arms immediately. The speaker calmed the latter even as she dissuaded them. It was not yet time. Preparations had to be made. Measures needed to be taken. The groundwork had to be laid.

A now riveted Jax listened intently to every word. Clearly the Whiplash was becoming more than just an avenue for getting dissidents safely offworld. There was purpose growing behind it, and individuals who were dedicated and empowered.

Just individuals? he wondered. Or were certain planetary governments, disenchanted with the direction Palpatine was taking, having second or third thoughts about aligning themselves with the newly proclaimed Empire?

After the human finished speaking, the meeting broke up. Some attendees departed quietly and in haste. Others remained, gathering in small groups to further discuss the ideas that had been presented. The speakers had removed themselves quickly, departing one at a time and in different directions so that if any happened to be followed and picked up for questioning, their arraignment would not imperil their fellows.

Jax was leaving, too, when a sturdily built older human crossed his path and raised a hand.

"Your pardon, citizen." The man's gaze dropped to the deactivated weapon partly concealed at the Jedi's waist. "I couldn't help but notice the unusual weapon you're carrying. If I'm not mistaken, it's a Velmorian flamesword. An unconventional weapon, but one that can still be quite effective."

"You have a good eye for tradition, friend." Jax resumed walking. The man fell in alongside him.

"Weapons are something of a passion of mine," he stated. "There are few outside Velmor who could handle such a weapon with any skill." He eyed the increasingly uncomfortable younger man intently. "You are not Velmorian."

"No, I'm not." Jax lengthened his stride.

The persistent stranger kept pace. "Please don't misconstrue my curiosity." He indicated the meeting room behind them. "We are all here for the same reason. We share the same purpose: a discontent with the way things are. We are all renegades."

Jax slowed slightly. Probing with the Force revealed nothing hostile within the stranger. A tremendous intensity, yes, but nothing to suggest that he might be an enemy. Still, it was best to be cautious. He stopped and looked at his questioner. Though he was dressed in nondescript civilian garb, there was the unmistakable air of the military about him. He looked like he knew how to handle himself in a fight, and the antiquated eye patch did nothing to dispel that impression.

"Was there something you wanted from me, citizen, or did you just want to compliment me on my taste in personal armament?"

"No," the man responded apologetically. "I meant no intrusion. The flamesword caught my eye, was all. That, and an admitted curiosity to know what sort of person could effectively wield such a device. Other than a Velmorian trained in its use from childhood, one would think only a Jedi might have such skill."

Jax tensed, but though he probed deeply with the Force, there was still nothing threatening about this pushy interrogator. Certainly nothing to suggest he might be a government agent or a representative of the sector police.

"You have me all wrong, friend. I'm just a hobby-ist who picked this blade up at a market sell-through. I don't really know how to use it, but I like the way it rides at my waist, and the sight of it is enough to scare off those who might try to cheat me."

"I see." The man seemed disappointed, but willing to accept the younger human's explanation at face value. "At what would they try to cheat you, that you would feel the need of such a weapon to wave at them?"

Jax thought quickly. They were approaching the exit to the street, and this conversation was ap-proaching its end. "I'm a gambler, so I often have large sums of credits on me." He extended a hand. "It was nice to meet a fellow dissident, but I really have to be on my way."

"And I as well," confessed the stranger. "Might I know your name, young gambler?"

After a moment's concern, Jax decided, *Why not?* He was never going to see this fellow again. In another moment, the underlevels of Imperial Center would swallow them both.

"Jax Pavan. And you are—?"

The man appeared to hesitate, but not enough to unsettle Jax. As before, there was no sense of hostility or threat within him. As they shook hands in farewell, he said, "I am Captain Typho, late of Her Majesty's Naboo Royal Security Forces."

twenty-two

The droid was fast, Den had to give it that. Fast and sneaky. It popped up suddenly from behind a pile of rubble, firing four quick shots at Laranth. For all its speed, however, the Paladin was quicker. She whirled, her blasters clearing leather even as she crouched and turned, firing five shots in response. Each of the first four blocked an incoming charged-particle beam. The fifth shot nailed the droid right between the photoreceptors.

"And the crowd goes wild," Den said. He was relaxing in a dilapidated formfit divan, with his feet up on an old console cabinet, watching the Twi'lek going through her ritual with polite interest. "If we're ever attacked by a training droid, I have no worries about the outcome."

Laranth ignored him. She dialed the intensity scale on her twin DLs back into the lethal zone before returning them to their holsters. Then she reactivated the training droid and sent it back to its charging niche.

Den yawned. "Think Jax is back from the get-together yet?"

"When he is, we'll know," she replied. "Or rather, I'll know."

"Cub, I wish I'd had that all-purpose intuition mojo like the Force back when I was a reporter. Would've come in awfully handy some—"

Laranth made a quick, lateral slicing movement with her left hand, its intensity rendering the fierce accompanying "*Shhh!*" superfluous. Den shut up. He watched the Twi'lek. She stood straight, in an attitude of listening. The passion with which she sought to connect with the Force was so obvious he half expected the fleshy tentacles her species wore in lieu of hair to rise like organic antennae, aiding her in her quest.

She stood for a long moment as if carved from jade, then abruptly looked at him and said, "Tell Jax I had to investigate something." Without waiting for a response, she stepped back into the resiplex, emerging a moment later clad in a hooded cloak.

"You sure you want to go out there alone?" Den knew the question was foolish; if ever a creature existed who was designed for the mean streets of Coruscant, if ever urban natural selection had produced a predator better at stalking the city-planet's duracrete jungles than Laranth Tarak, the Sullustan didn't want to be in the same universe with it. Still . . .

"Wait for Jax," he urged her. "Whatever they're talking about at the Whiplash meeting can't be nearly as important as whatever you're up to looks to be."

Laranth shook her head. "It could be nothing. I'll be back this evening, most likely," she said. Then, before he could say anything more, she walked away into the night.

* * *

Aurra Sing's nostrils flared, almost as if she could actually smell her quarry. In a sense she could, if one could attribute something of that sense to the Force. *Here,* she said silently to herself, *and close.* Making her way steadily but unobtrusively through the crowds, she smiled her feral smile. She wasn't 100 percent certain that it was Jax Pavan she was about to encounter, but it was someone steeped in the Force. Of that she had no doubt.

The trail brought her to an ongoing funfair in one of the deeper sublevels. Here there were tri-dee arcades, virtual rides, exhibitions from the farthest reaches of the galaxy—or at least what claimed to be such—and other attractions. Sing let herself be swept along in the polymorphic crowds, keeping her awareness extended.

Where are you, young Jedi? Where are you hiding in this hive of filthy, useless souls? I am coming for you. The Dark Lord wants you. This is easy for me. Don't think you have a chance of defeating me; I have killed Jedi far more skilled than you.

A lover of chaos and confusion, Sing delighted in the funfair's surroundings, where deafening noises and eye-smiting illumination, along with the multifarious commingling of species, all came together to produce a bedlam that she found pleasurable. Many of the attractions were genuinely clever. There was the Corrobor, where one didn't just have the opportunity to race flying starships or participate as a crew member—one could also *become* the starship. In a neuralstim booth, one felt as if one was temporarily transformed into a thing of metal and composite,

circuits and lights, weapons and engines. In the
Droidome, similar virtual realities gave any sentient
the temporary appearance and persona of a droid,
from security to construction, from translator to en-
gineer. Real droids found this particular entertainment mildly obscene, not to mention unrealistic. The
worst that a customer could experience did not extend to such real-world droid tribulations as casual
disposal or dismemberment.

There were high-tech massively multiplayer multi-
species combat games, food and drink to sample from
one end of the galaxy to another, live shows that one
species would find unremittingly dry and another utterly hilarious, as well as body-switching simulations
that permitted one to experience another species'
physicality, or gender, or sensoria. Size-distorters gave
one the perspective of a giant or a germ. Transport
sims for many known planets let one walk, float, or
fly around the surface of a multitude of worlds.

Sing ignored them all. With her white epidermis,
skintight jumpsuit, lithe figure, and shock of red hair
geysering from her otherwise bald skull, she drew
many intent looks from other patrons, some from
wildly different species. To each she responded in one
of two ways: by ignoring them or by giving them a
look as hard and intense and burning as the open core
of a nuclear reactor.

*Where are you, young Jedi? Where are you, Jax
Pavan?*

She ignored the tempting diversions through which
she strode. Ignored food, and liquor, and proffered
stimulations of other kinds. Ignored come-ons and
thoughtless invective, swiping hands and assurances

of instant wealth loudly promised. Nothing could divert her from her task.

Close now, she told herself. She could practically taste her quarry, could visualize the shock that would freeze his expression as she tickled his navel with the tip of her lightsaber. Not that she needed anything to encourage her stalking, but her claustrophobic surroundings, underground and filled with shoving, jostling representatives of numerous species, reminded her of nothing so much as the zenium mines on Oovo 4.

Very close, now . . . An occasional celebrant caught a glimpse of her face, the look in her eyes, and made haste to get as far out of the way of the fast-moving white humanoid as possible. And then, abruptly, she found herself before the entrance to one of the fair's main amusements: a Holo House.

Whoever the Force-sensitive she'd been tracking was—and she was virtually positive it was her quarry; the Force told her that its association with the entity Jax Pavan was very strong indeed—he was somewhere inside the building. She could simply storm in by the simple expedient of removing the head of the humanoid checking entrants. But that would draw unwanted attention, and, this proximate to her prey, that was the last thing Sing wanted. Despite her rising level of excitement, she forced herself to lower her heart rate and respiration. *Look normal,* she told herself. Relaxed, calm . . . just a single working woman out for an evening's entertainment. Which wasn't that far off the mark. She paid the entry fee, was assured the building was not crowded, and entered.

The attraction was like a house of mirrors, only without the mirrors. In their place, illuminated laser lines crisscrossed multiple levels. At the intersection of any two, a holoimage of one or another visitant from anywhere else in the place might appear. Being a holoproj, the image wasn't mirror-reversed; there was no way to distinguish it from reality. Reach out and your hand would pass through the image, be it one of yourself or someone else. You could step through it and onto another pathway or level—unless, of course, it was not an image but an actual being. The result was confusion, bemusement, mistaken identity, and—ideally—widespread hilarity. Any vestige of the last emotion, however, was absent from the bounty hunter as she moved purposefully through the maze.

Laughter and conversation from other, distant visitors echoed through the passageways. Sing had her lightsaber out, but had not yet activated it. No need to alarm the paying customers—or to alert her target. Clenched in her gloved right fist, much of the gleaming metal was hidden from view. If necessary, she could bring it to full activation in less than a second.

She passed a handsome young couple amusing themselves by kissing their respective images, and felt her lip curl. Foolish, wasted lives, there for a few brief seconds and then gone in an instant, vanishing without ever having impacted the fabric of civilization. Not like her, Sing told herself. She had an effect. She made a difference. Perhaps not one that those who encountered her took pleasure from, but certainly one that they and those around them would long remember—assuming they survived.

Finding someone in the place was next to impossible without the Force's aid. The multiplicity of levels, routes, and images offered too many choices for most people. Aurra Sing, however, would have been able to track her quarry through the lambent maze even had she been blind and deaf. The Force was her guide. A touch of the dark side was all that was needed to lead her through the multiple images, levels, and corridors, until . . .

There! Right in front of her, no more than five meters away, stood the target, clad in a cloak and cowl and looking in the opposite direction. Sing's fingers tightened around the haft of her lightsaber. Moving silently, she drew near. As she did so, several replicated images of herself appeared to her left, right, and overhead. Each was equally determined, each equally grim.

It was too easy. Sing hesitated. She could feel the Force emanating from her target, but could sense no suspicion, no wariness. Why didn't he sense her approach? Insufficient training, perhaps. Not properly attuned. Vader had told her that Pavan was hardly a master of the discipline. No matter; the Force was clearly present here. If this was in fact her quarry, she would bring him back alive to the Dark Lord; if not, then he was just another rogue Jedi or a Force-sensitive, and either way she would be allowed the pleasure of the kill. But she would not strike without first seeing the face of her victim. For the bounty hunter this was not a matter of ethics; it was all about personal satisfaction.

Clutching the lightsaber in her right hand, her thumb's pressure just short of activating it, she reached out with the Force across the few meters separating them and gently "touched" the individual standing before her. Light as Sing's mental goad was, the figure whirled at the sensation. The hood of the overcape fell back, and Sing's gaze met the other's.

Sing had just time enough to register that it was a female Twi'lek who stood before her. Then, before she realized it, her lightsaber was activated and parrying blasts from the twin DL-44s in the other's hands.

Sing threw herself sideways. Half a dozen replications of herself duplicated the move with unnatural precision. Lightsaber whirling, she not only deflected incoming fire but struck back as well, knocking the bolts back toward her foe.

Using the Force, the Twi'lek leapt upward to the next level of the structure. The multiple images of herself that accompanied the jump offered no protection from a killer whose eyes could be deceived but to whom the Force spoke clearly.

Sing was right behind her. Spinning, whirling, jumping, she deflected every shot fired in her direction. A glimpse of one of her doppelgängers showed her lightsaber moving so fast, she appeared to be engulfed in a sphere of green fire.

But the Twi'lek's aim was better than it had any right to be; it was on the same skill level as that of someone taught in the Temple. A bolt from one of the blasters slipped past Sing's whirling lightsaber and singed her left shoulder. The bounty hunter gritted her teeth and slashed an opening in one of the plasti-form walls. Several surprised customers, seeing the fearsome form and a number of attendant images of her appear through the wall, fled screaming.

This wasn't going well. The combination of the

kaleidoscopic images and the panic-stricken civilians caused her grasp on the Force to briefly lessen. It was only for the fraction of a second, but that was enough time to allow the real Twi'lek to land a punch on her jaw that caused the world to momentarily dim.

Enough of this, Sing decided. She had a mission to perform, and, although her opponent wasn't the Jedi she'd been sent after, the Twi'lek was still somehow connected to her prey. She would have to be taken alive and questioned.

Easier said than done, however. Eluding a complex swing of her lightsaber, the Twi'lek managed for just an instant to get under Sing's guard. She fired. Sing felt the heat of the bolt and barely succeeded, aided by the Force, in arching backward enough for it to miss her face. Her high left cheek instantly acquired a four-by-one-centimeter sunburn. The dangerously close miss was enough to compel her to do something she had not done in some time.

She pulled her own blaster.

Handling the lightsaber with her right hand, she snapped off several bolts with the blaster gripped in her left. One burst caught the Twi'lek unprepared, blowing a hole in the floor beneath her feet. When the dust cleared, the Twi'lek was nowhere to be seen.

Reluctantly, Sing decided that it was time to break off the confrontation. In the distance she could hear the warning squeal of approaching police skimmers. Although her Imperial ident would extricate her from any confrontation with minor officials, she did not want anything that might be perceived as a failure getting back to Lord Vader.

While she didn't doubt her ability to take the

Twi'lek alive, she had now realized that her antagonist was most likely a member of the Gray Paladins. The blasters were the clue. That meant she was a Jedi, and not likely to be very forthcoming about a fellow Jedi's whereabouts, even under torture. Add to that the very likely possibility that, if Sing was circumspect enough, she might be able to follow the Paladin back to Pavan without arousing suspicion, and she was left with only one sensible choice.

Gathering herself, Aurra Sing thrust her lightsaber over her head and leapt straight upward, smashing through two floors. She landed on the roof, then leapt again, and again, using the Force to augment the power of her muscles, until she was beyond the fair's boundaries.

Then she stopped and waited. She could sense the Twi'lek's Force connection, could tell if it was coming toward her instead of going away. For several minutes the blip on her mental radar stayed mostly in the same area—no doubt because the Paladin was searching the Holo House for her. But then it began to move slowly away from her.

A grim Sing began to follow. This time she would be more circumspect; would bide her time until the situation was less crowded, with more chance of success.

The hunt was rapidly coming to a close.

twenty-three

Jax got the comm call from Laranth just as he, I-Five, and Den were leaving to rendezvous with Dejah Duare. The Twi'lek was typically laconic:

"Someone wants you dead."

"How?"

"Badly."

"No, I meant how do you know this?" *And whoever it is,* Jax added silently, *tell 'em to get in line.*

"Because I just finished dancing with the assassin who's looking for you. I could feel her more than a klick away, which is why I went to investigate. Not the best idea I've had lately."

Jax nodded. "I take it that she's still ambulatory."

"And lethal. You're being hunted by the best, Jax, if that's any consolation. Where are you now?"

"Sari Street, near Caspak Boulevard."

"Wait for me there," Laranth said.

As he listened to the Twi'lek elaborate on her adventure, Den realized once again that he was not a happy life-form.

"Aurra Sing?" he asked. "*The* Aurra Sing?"

A grim-faced Laranth nodded slowly. "Unless you

know of another who matches the description." Her voice was as dry as a year on Tatooine.

"Flattering, in a sense," I-Five said. "I read up on her while I was uplinked to the police grid. She's infamous, and she doesn't come cheaply."

Jax nodded. He knew that there was no need to wonder who would set a bounty hunter with Sing's reputation on him. Only one person could have afforded the credits to hire her.

Nice to know I warrant the best, he thought wryly.

Den grabbed his ears in a Sullustan gesture of exasperation. "I think," he said, "that it's long past time for us to grab the next freighter to clear its cradle and leave, Jax. I mean, Sweet Sookie's aunt!" He shook his head. "If Sing's after you she won't rest until most, if not all, of us are dead—and don't ask me to place odds. We have to get off this overpopulated pit of perversion. Not that I have anything in particular against perversion, mind you. It's just that I take umbrage when part of the perversity is trying to kill me."

"We gave our word to Dejah Duare."

"*You* gave our word, Jax. Sure, her credit is generous and useful, but we can't spend it if we're dead. We need to relocate to a new neighborhood. On a new planet. In a new galaxy."

"Quiet," Laranth admonished them both. "We have company." At the same time that she spoke, Jax heard the rising whine of repulsorlifts. A moment later the first of three police skimmers settled down in the street beside them. Other pedestrians gave the cools a wide berth, and any civilian vehicles that had been in the vicinity suddenly found other venues more attractive.

The police contingent was led by the sector prefect himself. Jax could see that he didn't look happy to see them, but then he doubted that Pol Haus ever looked happy to see anyone in his line of work.

"So we meet again." He paused, singling out Jax and I-Five. "Just what are you two up to now?"

"We're just out for an evening's entertainment," Jax said, and smiled.

"Right," the prefect responded. "And why does the kind of entertainment you favor always seem to involve breaking the law? I see the Zeltron's not with you," he continued, without waiting for a reply. "Interestingly, however, we just received a complaint from a local arcade, describing two female humanoids who did a considerable amount of destruction there in the last hour." He looked appraisingly at Laranth, who met his gaze squarely. "One of them, it seems, was a Twi'lek."

"I apologize for my species," she said. "We can be rambunctious at times."

"There's also," Haus continued, "a complaint on file from a well-respected art dealer named Shulf'aa, asserting that a certain Sullustan . . ."

Den did his best to shrink behind Jax's legs.

". . . claimed to be a police officer in an effort to extract information from said art dealer, under pain of shutting down his business."

"A misunderstanding," a small voice said from the vicinity of the Jedi's thighs. "Easily explained, I'm sure."

"No doubt," Haus murmured. "Not so easy is the allegation from another broker, a Lonjair who calls himself Spa Fon, that you two"—he looked at Jax and Den—"entered his business premises under false pretenses, whereupon you intentionally and with malice threatened his person while delivering a merciless beating to one of his helpless and entirely innocent former employees, who—"

"Hold on," Jax interrupted. "First of all, that Lonjair 'broker' is a professional thief. Second, the 'helpless and entirely innocent former employee' was a subspecies of Cathar who probably massed a quarter metric ton of pure meanness and who threw the first punch, and third—"

"Never mind." The prefect sighed as he waved off Jax's indignation. "I'm not really interested. But when your locator rings showed up near this latest disturbance, I figured it would be appropriate to check in, just for old times' sake." His tone grew stern. "I don't know exactly what's going on here, Pavan, beyond your amateur attempts to aid Fem Duare in her hope of identifying her partner's killer, but I do know that you're becoming an irritation. I have enough daily irritations in my position without having a semi-permanent one latch on to me. I say *semi*-permanent because it's not going to persist. It's not going to persist because if anything like this comes to my attention again, you"—he pointed to Jax—"and the rest of you as well, are going to find yourselves exploring the many and varied cultural delights of the sector jail. Do I make myself clear, at every end of the spectrum?"

"Perfectly," Jax assured him.

The prefect scowled again and, accompanied by his squad, moved off into the crowd.

Den stepped tentatively out from behind Jax. "Spa

Fon, Pol Haus, and now the infamous Aurra Sing. Whose list will we make next, Jax? Darth Vader's?" The Sullustan snapped his fingers in mock realization. "Oh, wait, I forgot—we're already there."

Silently, Jax regarded his friends. He was proud of them all, proud of how they had come together as a team. Proud of how they had handled every danger and problem that had been thrown at them since they'd been with him. Did he have the right to ask them to endure more, to chance possibly greater risks? What would Master Piell have done?

Laranth would stay dirtside no matter what, he knew—the resistance movement was all she had to give her life meaning. But did he have the right to ask Den and I-Five, as well as Rhinann, to put their lives on the line every day for him?

He took a deep breath. "All right. I'll have one more meeting with our client, and on the basis of that we'll decide how to proceed. Maybe it is time to seek our fortunes elsewhere."

"Good call." Den was visibly relieved. Behind him, however, Laranth's continued silence bothered Jax slightly. But then, he reminded himself, she had been moodier than usual lately. He didn't need the Force to tell him that.

Mindful of his friends' concern as well as his own interests, Jax was determined to be as firm and straightforward as possible in the course of what well might be his final meeting with Dejah. It was a determination he set his mind to before he left for the meeting the following afternoon, that he maintained in the course of the journey to her residence, and that he continued to hold right up until the time he was admitted to the domicile she had shared with the late Ves Volette.

At which point, determination vanished like a solar sail in a sun flare.

Zeltrons were noted for the flamboyance of their attire, but what Dejah was wearing when she greeted him seemed to be shocking even for her kind. A shimmering silver drapery, as much cloud as cloth, it clung to her body while remaining in constant and revealing motion. It was if she had slipped into a pearlescent mist that coated the shore of a moonlit beach. It flowed in all directions, maintaining the shape of her body while giving fleeting, suggestive glimpses of it. A necklace and bracelet of matching Alderaanian sequat shells completed the ensemble. Definitely not a knockoff she'd picked up at the local discount house. It had probably cost more than most folk made in a year. Or ten.

"Come in, please, Jax. Follow me."

He did so, forcing himself into a detailed examination of the walls and ceiling until they had arrived at the conversation chamber. It was a sunken circular seating area with a riverstone-surrounded fountain in the center that could spout water, fire, or any of a dozen other entertaining visual enhancements, according to the whim of the dwelling's occupants. At the moment, it was spraying a deep orange liquid. Off at the far end of the chamber were three now nearly priceless Volettes, each dancing and contorting to its own individual encoding. They supplied all the illumination the chamber needed.

The shifting light made it difficult for him to think.

The cloud of intoxicating pheromones she was emitting—not to mention the intoxication factor of the cloud-like subtance she was wearing—did nothing to improve his focus, either. Using the techniques in which he had been trained, he regained his equilibrium. But even with the use of the Force, it wasn't easy.

She didn't make it any easier by sitting down right next to him.

"So," she began, "what did you want to talk to me about, Jax? You said it was important."

"It is. Dejah—could you possibly damp your, ah, emissions?"

She sat back from him—but only slightly. "You could have put it a little more subtly," she said with a slight, petulant moue. "Why? Do you find my personal emanations unpleasant?"

"No. Quite the contrary. That's the problem. I'm having a hard time focusing in such a . . . potent atmosphere."

"Oh, well then, if it's unsettling you." She did nothing visually, but suddenly the room seemed to clear and he was able to think reasonably straight again without invoking the barrier of the Force. Her smile left no doubt that being distracting bothered her not in the least.

"Thanks," he told her. It would have helped his concentration even more if she could have done something about what she was wearing, too, but asking her to eliminate that would in all likelihood only make things worse. "I'm here because of the job."

Her expression went from moue to full-fledged pout, which, although intended to convey a sense of disappointment, only ended up rendering her even more alluring. "What's wrong, Jax? Isn't the retainer I'm paying you and your friends sufficient? If it's inadequate, I suppose I could—"

"It's not the money," he assured her quickly. "It's just that other factors have come into play. For one thing, the sector prefect is growing increasingly irritated at our probing, to the point of threatening us indirectly but unmistakably with incarceration if we persist in our inquiries."

Her eyes flashed. Set against her pale red skin, the effect was positively destabilizing. "Tell me his name. I'll pay him a visit. I guarantee you that afterward he won't threaten you again."

Afterward he'll probably run naked down the Imperial parade thoroughfare if you ask him, an increasingly unsettled Jax thought. "Better to stay away from the police. That's what we're trying to do. But there are other complications. For example, there's a woman—"

"That truncated Twi'lek?" she interrupted him.

"No, not Laranth." *Why would she think of Laranth?* he wondered. "Someone else. Someone very dangerous. I'm concerned for the well-being of my friends."

"I could pay her a visit, too."

Her suggestion helped Jax remember why he was here. "This is one being I don't think even your persuasive abilities would affect. I'm afraid, Dejah, that we're going to have to terminate the agreement between us. My friends and I will still do our best to get you safely off Coruscant. But under these new circumstances, for us to continue the search for your partner's killer simply poses too much of a danger. To you as well as us."

Dejah buried her face in her hands and started sobbing. A fresh flush of pheromones burst forth from her, different from those that had enveloped him earlier but no less affecting. Despite the resistance he immediately put up, her empathic projections, combined with the desperate bouquet she was emitting, threatened to undermine his renewed resolve. He started to reach for her, to hold her and reassure her. Then, realizing what a mistake that would be, he remained where he was and let her weep.

It broke his heart.

After a couple of moments she looked up, wiped at her eyes with the backs of her hands, and folded them in her lap. Even that simple gesture was fraught with sufficient implication to unnerve him, but he still didn't move.

"Isn't there *anything* I can do to make you change your mind, Jax? If not more money, then what?" The promise that shone in her eyes and hung expectantly in the air between them was almost powerful enough to shift a small planetary body in its orbit.

He felt himself wavering. *Stall, blast it!* "It's just that," he began, playing for time to get a new grip on his emotions, "we don't seem to be making any progress. Or at least, not the right kind of progress. We've learned a few things, but they've just sent us off on different tangents. What we need is a fresh start. A new angle. Is there *anything* you can tell us that you haven't told us before, that you haven't told the police?"

"Well," she said, "I have been doing a little questioning of my own. This is a pretty exclusive residential area, and people of all species here tend not to want anything to do with established authority. But they'll unburden themselves to me."

A Sullustan rockrender would unburden itself to you, Jax thought. "So what have you found out?"

"Probably nothing. But . . . there's an old Drall who lives several domiciles down from here. You know the Drall—they're so absorbed in their libraries that they hardly ever socialize. Because of that I don't know if the police ever interviewed this elder. But the Drall are also noted for their jewelry work, and she used to sometimes have a chat with Ves about how art crosses species lines.

"She dropped by just a couple of days ago to finally offer her condolences. Said she would have done so sooner but that she was occupied with some important bit of cataloging. I invited her in and brewed up some dianogan tea she had brought." Dejah smiled coquettishly. "Well, you know what *that* stuff can do. We had a good time." The Zeltron leaned toward Jax, and this time her pheromonic discharge was rigorously muted. "In the course of our conversation she let slip that she had seen a large Vindalian in the neighborhood a few nights before Ves's death."

Jax frowned. It might be sheer coincidence that a Vindalian was seen in the vicinity when Volette had been slain. After all, it wasn't as if the Baron and his mate were the only two Vindalians on Coruscant, or even residing in the better regions of the Imperial Sector.

But what if it wasn't a coincidence? What if there was some kind of a tie there?

As he pondered it, there came the muted chime that indicated a presence at the entry. Grateful for the interruption, Jax sent tendrils of the Force to investigate.

What he encountered was cause at first for surprise, than unease. The entity requesting an audience was none other than Sele, Spa Fon's Cathar bodyguard—or former bodyguard, before Jax had shamed him by defeat. He and Den had left the huge felinoid creature back at Spa Fon's, where, he'd assumed, the warrior had expiated his shame through the ritual of *Gi-an-ku'rii*. Instead, here he was. How had he found Jax? Was he seeking a rematch?

Jax sighed and loosened the flamesword in its sheath. "Wait here," he told Dejah. Then he stepped outside to confront the giant once again, realizing with grim irony that in some ways a death match against a being twice his size was preferable to being alone with Dejah and her pheromones.

Before he could say anything, however, the Cathar gave a low, submissive growl. "If it may please my conquerer," he said with bowed head, "I have overheard certain scraps of gossip and hearsay on the streets that might have bearing on your quest." He paused, waiting for permission to continue.

"Go on."

"An acquaintance of mine, a Geroon, has a droid that he sometimes hires out as domestic help to members of offworld gentility. This droid told him that he saw a skimmer wearing the seal of Umber House parked near the conapt of the artist Ves Volette on the night of his death." The imposing creature lowered his eyes. "I pray that this information may be of some small use to you."

"It is indeed," Jax said. "In fact, it buys you manumission. I return to you your autonomy. Go in peace."

Sele raised his eyes in surprise and gratitude, and lost no time in making himself scarce.

Jax returned to Dejah's sitting room, where the Zeltron eyed him inquisitively.

"Who was that?"

"I think," Jax said, "it may have been the answer we've been looking for."

twenty-four

It had taken time, but his instincts and his searching—all his hard work—had finally paid off. Where better to look for a renegade Jedi, after all, than at a gathering of renegades? Yet when the several meetings he had attended had resulted in nothing, not even a lead, Typho had been about to give up and focus on his other lines of inquiry. And then, at the last gathering he had decided to attend—success.

Perseverance was ever the key to victory.

Of course, the young man could be another Jax Pavan with the same name, and not the Jedi whom Aurra Sing had been charged with finding for Darth Vader. But given that Typho had found him at a Whiplash meeting, he found the possibility dubious, to say the least. As he trailed the young man from a distance, the captain utilized all the skills he had mastered in the security forces to conceal his presence from his quarry. Mentally, he fought to keep his attention on anything and everything else: the drifting aroma of cooking food, the passing of an attractive humanoid, an argument, an offer, a whisper overheard. If the fellow preceding him through the crowds was indeed a Jedi, Typho knew he had to exert every possible effort to keep from creating a disturbance in the Force that might alert Pavan to being followed.

At least his quarry didn't turn and look behind him as he made his way confidently through the biodiverse throng. Perhaps the glut of various emotional emanations from the crowd prevented him from singling out his tracker. Or perhaps, feeling safe in familiar surroundings, he simply wasn't paying attention. The reasons didn't especially interest the captain, as long as the latter's anonymity was maintained.

Eventually he saw Pavan enter a block of residences in a cul-de-sac. While automated residential security prevented Typho from following the object of his attention inside, still, he was confident he now knew the location of the man's domicile. It was enough for his purposes. A dozen individual dwellings might lie behind the single secure entrance, or a hundred. It didn't matter. It was enough that he had tracked the Jedi to this locality. Because, even if events proceeded as he planned and Vader was unable to snare his thoughts with the Force, Typho still wanted an ace in his field. He felt no compunction about giving up Pavan's location, if by doing so he kept the upper hand for a few moments longer. Luck favored the prepared—every soldier knew that.

And besides, he planned on sending the young Jedi a gift that, if things didn't go well, would at least see Pavan somewhat more prepared to face a Sith Lord. It was tempting to give in to the irony inherent in using it himself, but he knew he had to maximize his chances of success.

Vader wanted the renegade Jedi Jax Pavan—so

much so that he had sent the infamous bounty hunter Aurra Sing after him. Too bad, then, for Aurra Sing, because Typho had found him first. He smiled grimly. How could an unknown minor planetary official possibly gain an audience with the Emperor's wristhawk? By offering him something he desperately wanted.

Unbeknownst to him, Jax Pavan was Typho's ticket to a meeting with the Dark Lord. The last meeting Vader would ever take.

There were ways of arranging such things. Ways of making contact, even with the Emperor himself, if one knew how to work the proper bureaucratic channels. Typho's status helped, of course. It was not as if the peculiar roundabout communiqué was coming from some addled citizen off the street with an exaggerated sense of his own importance. As Typho tracked it, he saw that his message was making steady progress toward its designated recipient. He had little doubt what the reaction would be when it got there.

Vader would contact him directly. He wouldn't go through an intermediary for something that was evidently important enough to hire a bounty hunter of Sing's caliber. And Typho would respond of course, but not without taking proper precautions. It was said that the Dark Lord could read a sentient's true intentions at a great distance. That might be nothing but bilterscoot—but as a security professional, the captain would take no chances. Thus his preparations, in additon to ascertaining Pavan's whereabouts, included paying a visit to a certain apothecary with a less-than-salutary reputation. Between the two, he should be ready.

The place was located on a dark street in an especially poorly lit section of Underlevel 20. This was not because it was a particularly bad neighborhood—quite the contrary, actually. It was simply that the nonhumans who inhabited the area tended to be members of species who preferred dim light.

Even so, the Kubaz still wore the diffusion goggles favored by her people when dwelling on planets with brighter suns than that of their homeworld. The black bristles on her head twitched and her long snout flexed upward in the equivalent of an unctuous smile as she greeted the new customer with a flourish of hand gestures.

"*Krsft.* How I be's of service, sor?" Beneath the barely adequate overhead light, the chemist's green-black skin appeared almost devoid of color.

"I want to buy a taozin skin nodule."

Delicate fingers were already tracing relevant notations in the holoproj that hung in the air between them. "*Dzzt.* A rare curiosity. Expensive."

"Cost doesn't matter," Typho said. "Do you have one?"

"*Hmm-ezz.* Possibly." Drawing images and symbols in the air, the Kubaz checked her inventory.

"Got one inna stock." She calculated the cost. "It gonna be . . . *mfft-zza* . . . nine hunnert creds total."

Expensive indeed, Typho thought, then shrugged. There was no help for it; the taozin, also known as a Force dragon, was an extremely rare giant transparent invertebrate native to the jungle moon of Va'art. Some were also rumored to live in the abyssal caverns far beneath the lowest subsurface levels of Coruscant. What made the creature of interest to Typho was its invisiblity to Force-sensitives. According to legend, the spherical excrescences from the creature's skin produced a strange void in the sensorium granted to some by the Force. So it was said, at any rate. The captain hoped the legend was true; he would only have one chance to test its efficacy.

The Kubaz handed him a transparent envelope that contained a sphere about the size of his fist, colored the faint yellow shade of a rancor's tusk. The captain regarded it for a moment. Strange, indeed, to think of so small a talisman laying low the great Lord Vader. But that was the special thing about talismans, wasn't it? They always promised more than they appeared capable of delivering. That was, after all, how magic worked.

Typho turned and strode from the building, his talisman held tightly in his hand. He had one final chore: the package for Jax Pavan.

After that, he would be ready.

twenty-five

The silver-coated protocol droid could not look surprised, but its reaction to their presence was conveyed through its voice.

"Citizen Pavan." Peering past Jax, the mechanical noted those assembled behind him. "And your friends." The droid's gaze stopped on a more familiar figure. "Dejah Duare, you are, as always, most welcome in this household."

Den took a step forward. "How about the rest of us?"

The droid appeared momentarily confused. "You did not announce your coming. It's not in my file."

"The Baron and his mate are in?" Jax asked.

"They are in residence, yes." Glistening lenses regarded the Jedi. "May I assume that your appearance here concurrently with that of Prefect Haus is not a coincidence?"

"You could assume that," Den said, "since we arranged to meet him here."

"Please announce us," Jax said.

The droid hesitated, then turned and shuffled away through the plush carpeting. Jax and his companions waited outside the formal entry. The mechanical was not gone long.

"Please come in. The Baron is anxious, as ever, to hear what you have to say. And as always, I am sure he will be delighted that Dejah is with you."

"The Baron isn't the only curious one." Pol Haus stepped into view in the foyer. "I can't wait to learn your reasons for dragging me over here at this hour."

Once again they were impressed by the opulence of the Baron's surroundings. Umber greeted them convivially this time. His mate appeared shortly thereafter.

Pol Haus, who was there with a droid assistant, glowered at them. "Let's hear it," the Zabrak growled.

Jax nodded. Den and I-Five moved to opposite corners of the room. Their attitude was unperturbed, but their senses were alert. Everyone knew what Jax was going to say, even Dejah. They had discussed it beforehand, and all were agreed.

Now that the moment had come, Jax let the threads of the Force spread outward from him, to encompass everyone in the room. His effort to provide interior confirmation for what he was about to announce was disappointing. But then, he'd expected it to be.

"Very well," he replied in response to the prefect. "I know who murdered Ves Volette." He stole a quick glance at the Zeltron standing nearby. Having been prepared for the disclosure, she showed no reaction, either hormonally or telempathically. Satisfied, he returned his attention to their hosts and the police.

"A Vindalian skimmer bearing the crest of Umber

was seen near the artist's studio on the night he was killed." As a startled Baron opened his mouth, Jax raised a hand to forestall the objection he sensed was coming. "I know it wasn't you, Baron. I am as certain of that as I can be. You've—been checked out, and there's nothing to suggest you had any involvement in the murder. Quite the contrary."

"My investigations indicate the same, if anyone's interested," Haus added drily.

Umber settled himself. "I don't know whether to be offended or relieved by your words, Pavan."

"You are a true aficionado of Volette's art. There are ways of confirming these things. You love his work and you were clearly very fond of him."

"We both were," Umber declared.

Jax sensed the Force threads he had let flow drift back to him. Yes, there was definitely a sense of unease in the room, of rising disquiet. It only served to substantiate what he had come to suspect.

"Yes. But certainly you far more than your mate." Lifting his gaze, he looked past the noble. "Isn't that right, Baroness Umber?"

She looked straight at him. Unfamiliar as he was with her kind, he could not read her expressions properly. But there was no mistaking the anger that flowed through the Force.

"I would not deny it."

"Our droid"—and Jax indicated the watching I-Five—"succeeded in gaining access to your banking records." He glanced at Haus. The Zabrak said nothing, but he was watching Jax very closely.

"Really, Pavan! This is too much!" This time Umber was unable to keep his outrage under control.

Jax met his irate gaze without flinching. "Over the past three standard years you spent a considerable sum on the works of Ves Volette. So much, in fact, that your credit rating and ability to spend and borrow became impaired."

Umber could only sputter indignation. "I had it under control. At all times. Aside from the affront to my privacy, I fail to see how this has any bearing whatsoever on the identity of Volette's slayer." He turned toward Haus. "Prefect, surely this is a contravention of some investigative procedure."

Haus shook his horned head slowly. "Let's see where he's going with it."

"Someone else was worried about your finances as well, Baron," Jax continued. "Someone who apparently felt otherwise about how well you had them under control. Someone who was not quite as overcome by the Caamasi's creations as you were." Again Jax shifted his attention to the Baron's mate.

There was no question now about the uneasiness and anger that were flowing through the Force. He pressed on.

"You were the one Dejah's neighborhood acquaintance saw near Volette's studio that night, Kirma Umber. The witness said the individual she saw was larger than most Vindalians. I still don't know much about your species, but I know that the female is always larger than the male.

"You followed your mate because you feared he was about to purchase yet another of Volette's works, thereby further damaging your fiscal standing. After the Baron left, you confronted Volette and threatened him. Probably ordered him not to sell to the Baron any longer, or at least until you could get the family finances restabilized."

She was staring at him. "Many humans have vivid imaginations. I have to say that yours, Pavan, is far more florid than most." Her tone was calm, but what he sensed from her was quite different.

"Independent voice and artist that he was, Volette refused. You attacked him. Maybe not with the intent of killing him, but with enough force to stab him. Then you fled."

Baron Umber was staring at his mate. It was plain that he wanted to say something but could not find the words. Kirma looked at him, then back at Jax.

"You know something. I don't know how, but—yes. I followed my mate, and I confronted Ves. I did ask him to stop selling his work to us. But it had nothing to do with finances. When the Baron says that he has them under control, I know that to be true. He loves Volette's work, but he would never risk the family's financial stability in pursuit of anyone's art. Such a thing would be positively un-Vindalian."

"Then why?"

"You should know." Taking a step forward, the Vindalian female raised an arm and pointed. "It was because of *her*."

Unbidden, the attention of everyone in the room shifted immediately to the startled Zeltron. Dejah gaped at the Vindalian, looked at the Baron, turned back to the Jedi. "Jax, I—I don't know what she's talking about."

Umber spoke up without having to be prompted. "There was . . . an attraction between us, I admit." He turned to his mate. "But that was all. Nothing happened. Kirma, I had no control over my reactions when I was in Volette's dwelling and she was present." He gestured helplessly. "She's a *Zeltron*."

"Better you had stayed clear of her presence," his mate murmured.

"How could I do that?" he protested. "She was always there. When I was choosing a sculpture, she was there. When Ves and I were discussing payment, she was there. When negotiations were concluded or art was discussed, she was there. She was his partner."

Kirma Umber looked past her mate. Her emotions were now very different from those Jax had perceived earlier. "And she is a Zeltron. That explains, but does not excuse."

"*Nothing happened,*" Umber reiterated, with as much force as he could muster without shouting. His earnestness spread through the Force, and Jax believed him.

His mate met his gaze, held it, and finally turned to the Jedi. "I confronted Ves Volette. I left in a fury, but I left him *alive*." She turned back to Jax. "You must believe me! I didn't kill him."

A voice not yet heard from finally made itself known. It was calm, controlled, methodical. It was also from the last entity the Umbers and Haus were expecting to hear from.

"I did."

twenty-six

Typho's hands did not tremble as he entered the electronic address. There was silence after he finished, save for the faint susurrus of static. He imagined an aide speaking deferentially to the Emperor's second in command: *Lord Vader, the communication you requested be brought immediately to your notice is retained for your attention on channel six.* Or words to that effect. Typho wondered what sort of humor his attempt to contact Vader had left the Dark Lord in. His mind's eye saw Vader alone in a dark chamber, surrounded by humming, flashing technology, no doubt far more comfortable in such environs than in the presence of servile organics. His aides were in all likelihood unable to keep from engaging in the most obvious sort of fawning and scraping in the hope of incurring some small smidgen of their master's favor. Annoying as such types were, they were sometimes necessary; Vader couldn't do everything by himself, couldn't be everywhere at once, and seeing to the organization and consolidation of the Empire no doubt demanded every moment of his conscious hours.

Except for this one interruption. For something like this he would make time.

The holoproj flickered and took shape. Typho watched as the three-dimensional image of the Dark Lord swiveled around in a massive blue-black control chair and thoughtfully regarded him.

From Vader's point of view Typho was merely a human male, with his face masked. Though he felt nothing, he knew that the Dark Lord was reaching out with the Force, trying to divine the entity behind the disguise. He could imagine Vader's frustration as the latter found his attempt mysteriously blocked. He was betting everything on the taozin's skin node working now.

If Vader was being stymied in his attempts to read him, the Dark Lord gave no sign of it. "You know who I am," he said. "Who are you, who begs my attention?"

"My name is for my family," Typho replied. "I have something you want."

Vader nodded, the heavy helmet bobbing slightly. "So you claim. Whether you speak the truth remains to be seen."

"Then see, and believe."

The projection wavered slightly as a smaller image was superimposed within the first. It showed the end of some meeting that had just broken up, clearly recorded from a cloaked pickup. The assembly and its purpose would not concern the Dark Lord. What would catch his attention, Typho knew, was the figure of a young man coming toward the pickup's viewpoint. Automatically adjusting for distance, the device kept the human in focus and proper dimensions. There was no question of the identity. The image's voice—with that of the pickup's owner carefully and professionally deleted—provided what further confirmation was needed.

"Ah." Satisfied, Vader relaxed in his command chair. "The traitorous Jedi Jax Pavan."

"You want him. I can give him to you."

"And in return?" Vader sounded impatient. Whole worlds waited, no doubt, on his decisions.

"Nothing much. Five million Imperial credits."

"You are bold," Vader said, a note of amusement in his deep voice. "Resourceful as well, in your *attempt* to hide your mind from the Force. I find myself . . . intrigued.

"The credits will be transferred, according to whatever directives you provide. I will authorize payment to take place the instant the renegade Jedi is in my hands."

Vader didn't stoop to haggling, Typho noted with relief. Still, the game had to be played out to avoid arousing the Sith's suspicions. "How do I know I can trust you, Lord Vader?"

Vader seemed not in the least affronted. "You do not, and no guarantees I might make would reassure you. But money means nothing to me. I only want Pavan."

"Then you shall have him. Tonight, at first darkness. There is a condemned transport hangar in Sector Four-Gee-Two. Come alone to the sixth floor. A dozen stormtroopers or so might make me nervous and put a premature end to our transaction."

"I need no escort. I'll be there. And remember: I want him alive."

"No worries," Typho said. "I've gained his trust, and when his guard is down, I'll spike his drink with a double dose of dreamdust. By the time we three rendezvous tonight, he'll be so happily deranged you could tell him you were his long-lost Jedi Master and he'd believe it."

"A good plan." Without another word, Vader severed the link. The image imploded and vanished.

So, then—the meeting was set. Darth Vader, the conscienceless murderer whom he had come to Coruscant to confront, would be there in person at the designated location.

"It won't be long now, Padmé," he murmured.

"I did," the mild voice said. All eyes turned to the voice's source—the Umber family protocol droid. The Baron and Baroness stared in shock at the domestic mechanical, who looked calmly back.

"Yes, you did," Jax said. Through the Force he read surprise and curiosity from Haus. He looked at the stunned Vindalians. "I'm sorry, Baroness, to have accused you unfairly. It was the only way to induce your droid to confess."

"But how? *Why?*" Umber asked.

"Your droid has been in the service of the same family for a very long time," Jax said. "Much of the time we organics don't even notice droids. We've developed the ability to ignore their presence even in intimate situations." He smiled slightly. "I speak from experience. We know they're there, but we don't acknowledge them unless and until we need them. Yet that doesn't mean they're devoid of self-motivation." He glanced at I-Five. "Take I-Five, for example."

"But he's an exception," Den pointed out. "Your

social and interactive programming and related circuitry were illegally modified," he added to the droid.

I-Five looked down at his friend. "So naturally, you
would assume that I'm the only one who can be or
has been so modified?"

Across the room, Kirma Umber was moving slowly
away from her droid. Away from the machine that
had been in the service of the family Umber for longer
than she could remember.

"It's not possible," she said. "There was no reason . . ."

"I saw your distress." The silver protocol droid
spoke calmly. "I perceived it silently for years, while
the Baron paid his frequent visits to the artist Volette,
and his partner, the Zeltron Dejah Duare. I stood in
silence, not commenting, while you shouted aloud
your fears and worries in the privacy of your chamber.

"The last night you went to see Volette, I followed.
Security is, after all, part of my programming. I saw
no need to concern you with my presence. I observed
your argument with the artist. I registered your body
language, the raw emotion of your tone, the heightened conductivity of your galvanic skin response. I
determined then the way to best fulfill my programming and my obligation to the family Umber.

"I confronted the Caamasi and attempted to carry
out this programming with words. I was ignored, of
course.

"I decided at that moment that further action was
required on behalf of my owner. I therefore stabbed
Ves Volette in the anterior plex with this." The droid

held up its right fist and one of the digits shot up, transforming into a short, lethal-looking spike.

Kirma Umber gasped.

"Your data retrieval spike," Jax murmured. "You had more than enough strength to penetrate the protective cartilege."

"True. As there were no direct witnesses, once the Baron was cleared of involvement, I thought the matter, deplorable as it was, might fade away." His gaze was focused across the room, on Jax and I-Five. "I feel something that organics would term *curiosity*—a desire for heuristic extrapolation. How did you come to suspect me?"

I-Five answered. "While Jax and Den were questioning Spa Fon—" Haus coughed discreetly, to which Den offered a sickly smile. "—I was engaged in a cyberspatial data search." He looked at Jax. "If you will recall, I was still in the same mode when you returned. I was studying the details of the murder. In the course of my investigation I made good use of access to certain records of the sector police."

Den gawked at his companion, then looked at Haus. "And you thought what *I* did was illegal."

"When I was at the crime scene," Jax continued, "I noticed that many of the forensics droids were DN-Seven-Two-Fours, which I-Five's research indicated are quite similar to your design." He looked at the protocol droid, which stared calmly back. "They had a tendency to shuffle across the plush carpeting, leaving distinctive tracks—the same sort of tracks you leave in this carpet. That was what first aroused my suspicions. Further investigation by I-Five revealed that your model had a data spike perfectly suited for inflicting the wound that killed Volette." He didn't mention the biggest clue of all, which was, ironically, the lack of a clue. His inability to sense the guilty party, put together with his negative readings of the Umbers, pointed straight at their droid. Mechanicals were notoriously hard to read through the Force. He couldn't tell Haus this, of course.

The Baron started to speak. "If it was our droid, then a reprogramming should suffice to—"

The droid, astoundingly, cut his owner off. "Such an action would bring shame to the family. I am prepared to execute the appropriate resolution. It is only rational." The gleaming lenses dimmed visibly. A few flickers of light sparked from the base of the droid's skull. As the smell of ozone began to contaminate the room and the last of the sparks flared out, I-Five walked between the organics, stopping when he was within arm's reach of the motionless silver mechanical. As the others looked on, he extended his left hand. From the next to last digit a small probe telescoped, which I-Five inserted into a receptacle in the side of the other droid. A moment later it withdrew and retracted back into his finger. I-Five turned to the watching organics.

"Wiped. The neural net was fried. Not restorable by any specialist, no matter how talented." He tapped the side of the protocol droid. "Probably worth something as scrap."

Jax, who was watching Dejah, saw a single tear roll down her cheek.

"Well, that's just great," Pol Haus said. "What am I supposed to tell the upper crust, who've been clamoring for some closure regarding their favorite artist?

That a *droid* killed him? Oh yeah, that'll go down well."

"If I might make a suggestion," Dejah said, "surely there is no dearth of criminals on the streets who have gone free for want of evidence. I would think that this crime could be adjusted to fit one of them." She noticed the others looking at her in surprise, and shrugged. "As Prefect Haus has pointed out, there is no sense of justice to Ves's death as it stands. If some good can come out of it, maybe that will help."

Haus ruminated for a moment, then turned to his droid assistant. "Round up the usual species," he told it. "Maybe we can get something good out of this, after all."

Kirma Umber stared at the permanently frozen mechanical, then met her husband's gaze. The Baron smiled reassuringly at his mate. "We'll get another one. It was only a device, and it was getting old."

"Yes," she murmured. "It was only a device." A tear coursed down her cheek. "But loyal."

twenty-seven

The jet-black aircar had no driver; only its singular passenger. Typho watched from his concealment. Apparently Vader had acceded to his conditions. Well and good. The armored, automated vehicle arrived on exactly the indicated level and stopped at precisely the specified spot within the condemned transport hangar at one minute past the designated time for the meeting. A stickler for precision, Vader was.

Typho tensed. He knew he had but one shot at this. He had no illusions about his contemplated action. It had nothing to do with honor, with a fair fight. It was murder, pure and simple. He would have to strike from behind, swiftly and lethally, and from a distance with a blaster. It was murder, and murder for the most ignoble of motives—revenge.

He shrugged away the thought. He had come to terms months before with what he was doing and why. His soul might be irredeemably stained by his action tonight, but Padmé's would find peace. That was all that mattered.

"I came as you specified." Spreading his arms wide, Vader lifted his cloak. Darkness seemed to envelop the entire floor of the hangar. "Alone and unarmed."

It was time to trust in the small clump of mummified skin cells resting in his pocket. Time to avenge the woman he'd loved.

Time to strike.

Typho stepped quickly from his place of concealment on the floor above Vader. He'd chosen the spot with care. Directly before him was a hole six meters wide, and framed squarely within it was the Dark Lord's back.

Captain Typho raised his blaster and fired.

At first he thought the ionized gas cartridge in his blaster had backfired. It was as if a giant, invisible hand had snatched him up and hurled him with bone-breaking force against the far wall. Stunned, in shock, he watched Vader's form levitate through the hole in the floor. The black boots touched down next to Typho's broken body.

"How pathetic," the Dark Lord commented. He stood towering over his adversary. "Did you really think you had the faintest hope of assassinating me? It's been tried by far better than you."

Typho coughed, feeling his insides grinding together like broken glass. Blood stained his shirt. "You lied," he said, feeling the words lodge like stones in his throat.

"Did I? I told you I would come unarmed, and here I am," Vader told him. "You mistake the dark side for a weapon—something extraneous. It isn't—it is intrinsic. I could no more shed it than I could go about without my support suit."

He stepped closer. "I will give you one more chance," he rumbled, "to cease whatever game you're playing and provide me with Pavan's location."

"Or what?" Typho spat a mouthful of bright red blood. "You've already killed me."

"True. You will not last long in any event. But don't underestimate the power of the dark side. It can ease your passage. There is still a little time—unless you squander it." Vader stepped closer, bent to peer into Typho's face. "Why have you made this foolish attempt on my life?" The deep synthesized voice echoed through the empty hangar level. "Not that a specific reason is required or expected. But I should like to know. Those who speak their last should speak something of value."

He leaned closer at Typho's beckoning, to hear his final words. Typho was fading fast. He concentrated every fiber of his being on remaining conscious for one final act.

"This . . . is for Padmé," he rasped. And with a supreme effort, he spat a mouthful of blood directly into the surprised Dark Lord's mask.

Vader's reaction was not what he'd expected. After a frozen instant, ignoring the bloody spittle running down one plasteel cheek, he knelt and grabbed Typho by the hair, lifting the latter's head and eliciting a cry of renewed pain from him.

"What?" The flare in the Force that raced through the hangar was enough to shake the foundations of the building. The Dark Lord actually seemed to grow, to expand and become more terrible in his rage than Typho would have believed possible.

"Padmé," Typho mumbled. "Padmé Amidala. The woman I loved from afar, for years." He coughed again, felt more red shearing in his chest. "She . . . never knew. She was too busy, too deeply engaged in the . . . service of her people to notice me." Another bright scarlet flower bloomed from his mouth. "And I attended to my duty—I, Typho, captain of Naboo. But I . . . loved her. And now. . . now she's dead. Dead." Then, with an extraordinary rush of resolve, Typho managed to raise himself slightly, exerting himself through sheer force of will against Vader's anger.

"You killed her, Vader. You! I know it!"

Vader was silent and motionless again. When he spoke, his voice had the same deep inflection, the same synthesized thunder—and yet was somehow different.

"You know nothing." Vader straightened, letting Typho's head fall. "You're not worthy of uttering her name." Raising his arm, he flexed his fingers at the helpless Typho. The captain's mouth opened and his eyes bulged slightly as the flow of air to his lungs was constricted. Far down in his mind, a remote part of him commented dispassionately that this was no doubt how his beloved had met her end. Astonishingly, he found he still was able to choke out a final sentence.

"And you're responsible . . . for the death of the Jedi . . . Anakin Skywalker as well!"

The invisible, inexorable grip on Typho's throat momentarily relaxed as Vader drew back in slight surprise. That brief pause was followed by the horrible sound of a Sith Lord laughing. Three levels below, a pair of intoxicated humanoids heard just the echo of it and were immediately shocked into sobriety— the fearful clearheadedness that comes with realizing that untold terror lurks nearby.

When Vader extended his arm downward the second time, his control was more precise, more deliberate. "Yes," the Dark Lord said, his tone one of grim amusement. "Yes, I killed Anakin Skywalker. I watched him die. He was weak, was Skywalker. In the end he could not rule himself, could not control his contemptible human emotions. Most of all, he did not understand or appreciate the true strength of the dark side. And so—he died. The galaxy is better off without him."

The world was unraveling fast for Typho. The pain was going, finally, pouring out of him as fast as his blood. But he died with a smile on his face, for, although he did not understand the how or the why of it, he knew that dying with Padmé's name on his lips was a finer and deeper revenge upon Darth Vader than he possibly could have hoped for through confrontation. It was as if he could feel the man's heart and know that, somehow, he had ripped it open with her name alone.

He also knew that living was a far worse fate for Vader than death.

He was content.

Now he could go and find Padmé . . .

twenty-eight

The package came by courier just as Jax, I-Five, Laranth, and Den were leaving Poloda Place to rendezvous with Dejah and escort her to her ship. The Whiplash, aided by the Cephalon's prognosticative powers, had at last succeeded in securing a berth for her aboard the *Green Asteroid*, a trader in the Polesotechnic League. It would take her, over the next several months and by a roundabout route, to the pleasure planet of Zeltros. Dejah Duare was going home.

Rhinann had, as usual, elected to stay behind, citing "unfinished research."

Jax accepted the package, which was about thirty centimeters by two, from the delivery droid. There was no return address. He looked at his friends, who appeared just as baffled as he. He shrugged and started to open it.

Den backed hastily away. "Are you sure that's a good idea?"

"I don't sense anything negative or dangerous about it." Actually, that wasn't entirely true. The enigmatic parcel had definite vibes, though nothing about them indicated imminent danger. Instead, it seemed steeped in evil, marinated in blood. Whatever it was, death had not been far from it.

When he opened the package, he understood why.

It was a lightsaber.

A holocard projected a message inscribed in simple cursive: A JEDI SHOULD NOT HAVE TO RELY ON AN INFERIOR WEAPON. GOOD LUCK. It was signed, A FELLOW REVOLUTIONARY.

Jax examined the weapon. The hilt's design was elegantly simple, consisting of an ambidextrous grip of molded silver duralumin, with a locking activator similar to the one he'd lost in the Factory District. *Good,* he thought wryly, *because you never know when you'll have to overload another nuclear reactor.* He wondered what color the blade was. There was no way to know without activating it, which, given their location on a public street, seemed a trifle rash. He knew it was functional, however. He could feel the Force coiled within it.

Den, standing on tiptoe, was able to read the missive. "Well," he said. "That's serendipitous. Weren't you just trying to build one of these?"

I-Five took the card and looked at it. "A standard onetime holoproj chip," he said. "Nothing remarkable about either the writing style or the delivery mechanism." He cocked a photoreceptor at the Jedi. "I assume this comes as unexpected largesse?"

"You might say that. I can't imagine who could've—" Jax stopped abruptly, remembering the man he'd met yesterday at the Whiplash assembly. What had his name been—Typhon? About all Jax recalled of the man was that he'd sported an eye patch.

Could this have come from him? He'd shown interest in the Velmorian weapon, after all.

"I met a man yesterday," he said slowly, "who might be—" He stopped abruptly, struck momentarily silent by a sudden turmoil in the Force. Its origin was a psyche he'd encountered before, of that he was certain, even though he'd only experienced it indirectly. No Jedi—no one, in fact, with more than a smattering of midi-chlorians—could forget the impact of a will that strong.

Jax said, "Vader's nearby."

Den looked nervously around the crowded street, craning his neck in a futile attempt to see better. "Where?"

"*Nearby* is a relative term," Laranth said. "But I'd put the probability of his being in a ten-square-kilometer radius at pretty high." She gestured south. "In that direction."

"Okay," Den said. "So we'll be going *that* way, right?" He pointed north.

Jax and Laranth both stood quite still; then Jax said, "He's pretty upset. Not bothering to cloak his feelings at all."

"Intriguing," Laranth said.

"Not a word we want to be using right now," Den said. "Shouldn't we be pulling in our antennae, looking for a metaphorical rock to crawl under? Or maybe even a real rock? Instead of standing around here sticking out like a bunch of naked Jawas?"

"Don't worry," Jax said. "We're not pushing. And he's far too troubled to be aware of us." He hesitated, then added, "It does make me wonder what could disturb the Dark Lord to such a degree."

"Fine," Den said. "Wonder while we wander north."

With Volette's murderer finally identified—and conveniently self-immolated—Den was looking forward to events taking a more leisurely pace, for a time at least. One very large pressure had already been lifted from them for the foreseeable future: Dejah had insisted on continuing their stipend indefinitely.

"I insist," she'd told Jax, forestalling any protests he had been about to make. "You've set my mind easy insofar as Ves's murder is concerned. He has left me more credits than I know how to spend—and coming from a Zeltron, that's saying something. It would be my honor to subsidize you and the work you do."

Jax, typically, had done his best to talk her out of the deal, but Dejah, bless her, had been adamantine. And when faced with the persuasive power of her biochemical and telempathic arsenal, his resistance, he'd admitted, had been pretty pathetic. So she had gone back to her conapt to pack before meeting them at the local spaceport, and Jax had gone back to the others with a bemused look on his face.

Thus they had "creds and a shed," as the Ugnaughts put it, for the foreseeable future. And they had more than enough work to keep them occupied, between the UML and the investigations that Jax would no doubt keep getting them involved in. Den sighed. The chances of Vader locating Jax and bringing his booted heel down upon them all were still much higher than the Sullustan would have liked, which meant spacing as soon as possible was still the only sensible option. But he'd come reluctantly to realize that, for all their boasting of rationality, humans were most comfortable living in the nexu's den. *Actually,* he thought, *make that the nexu's mouth.* He'd come to terms with the lifestyle—mostly, at least—and it wasn't like they didn't have some firepower on their side. I-Five and Laranth were still spot-on deadly with their lasers and blasters, and Rhinann, he had to admit, could slice past any database, Imperial or otherwise, and leave not a single ion to trace, slicker than supercooled Tibanna condensate. Maybe he wasn't the most convivial of comrades, but Den could overlook that.

And then there was Jax. The Jedi was, he had to admit, growing into his role of a hero rather well. If he continued to survive Vader's intermittent attention, not to mention the thousand and one other dangers that loomed downlevel every day and night, he just might become a force—no pun intended—to reckon with. He had a good enough support group, although there did seem to be subtle changes in the overall group dynamic over the past couple of days between him and the others. Particularly as far as Laranth was concerned, though the Jedi was as blind as a space slug if he couldn't see how the Twi'lek felt about him. But there was a certain amount of tension between him and I-Five that was new as well. What was up with that, Den wondered. Hard to tell if anything was different as far as Rhinann was concerned; the dour Elomin kept interactions between himself and others at a minimum. And of late he'd become even more immersed in the HoloNet than usual.

Den shrugged. Well, after all, what family didn't have its bickerings and quarrels? It was important to remember that, because that was what they were—a family, albeit a pretty dysfunctional one at times. The important thing was that they all came together when needed to make a good team.

Jax watched their client approach the spaceport's entrance, noting with relief that she'd changed into traveling wear that was far less riot inciting than last night's attire. As she drew closer, he realized that she'd damped her pheromones and mental lures as well.

Good. Now let's get her onboard and offplanet before anything else can go wrong.

He felt slightly ashamed of his attitude—but only slightly. Though he had grown fond of Dejah, he was more than happy that she was moving on. Frankly put, she was trouble, even without the chemical and psychic come-ons.

Spaceport Nine was a large mass of surging, pushing, irritated, hurrying, frantic beings representing every species that was used to traveling between the stars. Which was to say that it was no different in design from any of the other many large spaceports on the capital world. What made navigating Nine a little more confusing, a little more difficult, and considerably more frustrating than working one's way through, say, Spaceport Eight or Ten, however, was the fact that Nine was undergoing a complete makeover under the supervision of the Imperial Spaceport Authority. Old structures were being demolished, new ones erected, traffic rerouted, and what was left still had to function, somehow, as a fully operational port.

In such circumstances, the needs of machines invariably took precedence over those of organics. Station, crew, and maintenance workers—not to mention travelers—all found themselves squeezed into smaller and smaller corridors and forced to take directions from programs or service droids that were themselves subject to minute-by-minute updating. It all made finding one's destination an exercise akin to negotiating the lowermost underlevels of the city itself.

Surrounded and delayed by agitated panglossia in dozens of tongues, the unavoidable reek of too-close-packed bodies, and the overriding cacophony of nonstop construction, one determined small group continued to force its way toward one of the farther launch pods. I-Five used a directed hypersonic pulse to ensure that his words would be heard over the din of the crowd. "Turn down the corridor to the left," the droid said. "It's a temporary elevated accessway that will let us bypass much of the major construction."

Jax noticed glowing letters floating above the entrance, along with a multilingual glyph for "danger." "It says CONSTRUCTION PERSONNEL ONLY," he said.

"That's us," responded the droid. "We're constructing a faster way to our destination."

Jax hesitated, but only until they entered the corridor. It was nearly deserted, and for the first time since arriving at the port they could actually advance unimpeded. Jax took a deep breath and relaxed.

Or rather, he tried to.

Now that they had temporarily bypassed the pandemonium, he realized that the Force was trying to tell him something. Actually, that was much too mild a phrase. It was more like being grabbed by the lapels and shaken violently. Before he realized it, the hilt of his newly acquired lightsaber was in his hand. He didn't ignite it yet, however; they were still in an all-too-public place.

A quick glance at Laranth confirmed that she had been warned as well; both hands were hovering near the twin DL-44s holstered on each hip. Jax looked warily about but saw nothing amiss. A few other species—mostly Niktos—walked or rode the slide-walks as well, but it made perfect sense that he and his cronies wouldn't be the only ones to risk a fine by making use of the construction accessway.

Den said, "Now what?" in a tone of voice usually only heard from H'nemthe grooms on their wedding nights.

"Hush!" It was menacing—that much was certain. But where was its source?

The relative quiet of the accessway was suddenly shattered by a loud throbbing, fluttering noise. Then an ornithopter rose nearby, its wings thrashing the air. At the same time Laranth shouted "Look out!" and shoved him to one side. Jax barely avoided being hit by a slashing emerald blade.

Laranth didn't.

twenty-nine

Jax landed on his side, rolled, and came to his feet in a single smooth motion, letting the Force do most of the work. At some point during the move he activated the lightsaber, though he couldn't have said when. The blade—crimson, a remote part of his mind noted—boiled out to its full length in a heartbeat.

Then he was on his feet and facing Aurra Sing.

Though he'd never met her before, her appearance left him with no doubt of her identity. He would have little time for doubt in any case, because her blade was already whistling toward him. It was a green lightsaber, and its glow painted everything the same shade of corroded brass. Everything, that is, except the Twi'lek's green skin—that it rendered the deep gray-green of ripe chee nuts.

Jax had just time enough to register that Laranth was either grievously wounded or already dead, and that she was directly in the path of the blade's second downward arc, before he lunged in a desperate attempt to block it.

He did, but just barely. The clashing blades crackled, the air was rent with ozone, and the two lightsabers rebounded. Sing's blade had been deflected just enough to miss Laranth. It sheared through the suspended floor of the elevated walkway, cutting supports. Jax backflipped and came down on the still-supported section, his lightsaber ready for another attack.

Behind him, his comrades fell into the abyss.

No time for even the briefest of reactions, as Sing was leaping at him again. Several meters below, an emergency-response tractor field automatically activated by the disintegration of the corridor caught his tumbling companions. They would slow-fall, but he didn't have time to watch; he barely had time to breathe. She rained down on him a fury of blows almost as vociferous as the oaths and curses that accompanied them.

"Fear me, Jedi! I am Aurra Sing, Nashtah, scourge of your kind! I haunt your darkest dreams! I drink Jedi blood; I nest in their guts! Your nightmares now have a name, hierophant, and that name is Aurra Sing!"

He felt the Force flowing around her. There was considerable might to it, but it was wild and undisciplined and, as such, difficult to anticipate. He'd never before felt anything quite like it, and he'd certainly never heard anything like it.

At last she paused for a moment in her tirade. Raising his lightsaber, he slid his right leg back and lifted the humming beam over his head.

"You'd be the bounty hunter, then," he said.

Hefting her own weapon, the woman grinned a feral grin at him. Externally, she was beautiful; even without an endocrine advantage, she could give Dejah a run for her credits. What Jax sensed within her, however, utterly obliterated any outward impression. She had an ugly soul.

"You handle a lightsaber well, prey." Suddenly she leaned forward, and her crimson eyes narrowed. Then rage filled them—*or at least,* he thought, *topped off the last little bit of sanity; it's not like there was a whole lot to begin with*—and she snarled, "Where did you get that?" She indicated his lightsaber.

He told her the truth: "An acquaintance sent it to me." He shrugged. "I guess he didn't want it anymore."

She came in, and she was incredibly fast; faster than anyone he had ever encountered. Only the Force allowed him to anticipate her reactions; otherwise he would have surely lost limbs in the first minute of action. It was all he could do to parry the hurricane of blows she threw at him: *cut-cut-cut-thrust-diagonalcut—!*

He leapt backward to escape, felt the heat of her lightsaber singe his right foot as it cut through his boot and sliced off part of the heel.

Maybe needling her into losing control wasn't such a good plan after all . . .

As he flew backward, Jax slashed behind himself with his weapon. A newly installed transparisteel pane shattered under the impact of his lightsaber, just in time for him to sail through unharmed. He landed on his feet on the roof.

In an instant, Sing followed. She flew through the opening, eyes narrowed, her arms held wide for balance. Her lightsaber was a viridian shaft in the semi-darkness.

She cut downward, hard, so fast! Without the

Force, he would have been bisected. Instead, before he could think, his body moved on its own, wrapped in lines of power. Unbidden, his hand snapped up to block her blade with his. Scarlet and emerald lightning once again blinded them both momentarily. Coupled with the force of her descent, her strike knocked him backward again, across the roof construction. He nearly fell off the far edge.

Behind him, several massive automata were hard at the business of demolition and construction. At a comfortable control station somewhere, a supervisory sentient was probably kicked back in a formchair, watching as the gigantic machines did all the work. Would he or she glance at a screen, take notice of the fight amid all the heavy work, set down the inevitable cup of caf and notify security? Would the fight even last long enough for help to arrive?

She came at him again. She was fast, strong, and good, but she was also reckless. She had said it herself: her passion lay in hunting Jedi, not fighting them. She was used to striking hard and fast, a streak of scarlet in the night. She wasn't used to fighting skilled opponents for any length of time.

Jax kept backing away, parrying, letting the Force completely control him. A wrong move and he would be chopped down. His best bet was to wait, to let her wear herself out before trying to take her down. Assuming he could outlast her. She was humanoid, but not human; there might be different rules for her kind. He was already certain that her fast-twitch muscle percentage was far higher than his. He was getting tired, and she seemed as fast and strong as when they'd started.

They were among the machines now. Heavy lifters and composite depositors, link checkers, emitters, and synthesizers whirred and hummed and rumbled all around them. Sing continued to push him back, back, always back. Jax went with it. He wanted her to be sure that she was winning.

Maybe she was . . .

At least she's stopped her diatribe. I was beginning to think she was trying to talk me to death.

"No need to die," she said, as if reading his mind. She threw a fast series of choppy attacks, none designed to do major damage, but rather to set him up for the killing stroke.

"Really? What do you think your boss plans to do with me? Buy me lunch?"

"Not my concern, Jedi. Surrender now and maybe you can negotiate something with him. Don't, and I kill you now. An iffy future is better than none, don't you agree?"

She charged in without waiting for an answer, and her attack sequence was too fast for him to follow consciously. The Force answered, its strings manipulating him like a marionette's, but his body wouldn't be able to keep up much longer. He blocked, counterattacked, was parried, and ducked just in time as she tried to take his head off.

This was not going well. He needed to do something, and soon, or—

Sing was growing impatient. The blasted Jedi refused to capitulate, even though the Force was all that was holding him up at this point.

She wasn't sure how he'd come upon her light-

saber; most likely he'd had an encounter of some sort
with Typho. The particulars didn't concern her—she
was intent on getting it back, and she wasn't too particular about how. If it meant prying it from the cold,
dead fingers of his severed hand, she was sure Lord
Vader would understand. But she wanted this to be
over, and soon. Her stamina would outlast most humanoid sentients, but when it faded, it faded fast.

Even acknowledging the possibility of failure was
not an option. She would defeat this upstart Jedi.
Anything else was unthinkable.

Movement out of the corner of his right eye caught
Jax's attention. The energy of their lightsabers clashed
and sizzled yet again, and he allowed the blow to
send him staggering back toward the activity he had
sensed. All he had time for was a quick look.

He couldn't fight any harder. He had to fight
smarter.

The machine was a large reposticator, or fabber. It
chewed up raw material that looked like sand from a
hopper, then laid a sheet of translucent plate onto the
roof for a hard, weatherproof coating. The hopper
had a safety field that glowed a pale blue, to keep
things from falling into the raw-materials bin. Wise,
because the fabber would ingest anything that fell
into it and restructure the material into its extrusion.

A desperate plan popped into his head.

He tried an attack, a basic, simple Form II series he
had learned early on. Not really much of a threat; the
moves were designed as defense against an opposing
lightsaber.

Sing did just that, easily blocking the attacks. She laughed.

"A defense unworthy of a Padawan? Come on, you can do better than that, can't you?"

"Not really," he said. But all he wanted was a little running room, which the moves had given him. He turned, sprinted three steps, and leapt with every bit of the Force he could muster, managing to land on the control bar above the fabber, arms windmilling in a charade of seeking balance—

Sing would be right behind him, he knew; he wouldn't even have time to turn and face her, and she would use the field guarding the raw-materials bin as a step before launching into a lunge that would easily unbalance him from his narrow perch.

He felt for her, using the Force—

The flashing red button on the control panel was just next to his damaged boot. Jax waited until he felt Sing land on the field—

Then he stepped on the button.

The field shut off.

Sing screamed as she fell into the churning sand. Her lightsaber cut a swath of molten energy through it, fusing the sand into lumpy green glass—then was snuffed out as she lost her grip on the hilt.

Sing looked up at him as she sank beneath the sand. It churned while it was sucked into the machine. The last he saw of her was a splotch of red hair.

He turned and started toward a nearby drop-tube, realizing that his friends should have reached the ground by now . . .

thirty

Jax had two bombshells dropped on him in quick succession soon after he got to the medcenter.

The first was from Dejah. She had checked out fine, her medscan showing no aftereffects from the fall. "We Zeltrons are a hardy breed," she said with a grin. She seemed quite a bit more cheerful—so much so, in fact, that Jax asked her what good news she must have received while in care.

"It's a decision I've made," she replied. "I'm staying here on Coruscant instead of returning to Zeltros. I want to be part of the resistance movement."

"What?" For a moment he wasn't sure he had heard her correctly. "You mean, after all the work and risk that members of the Whiplash took on to ensure your safe passage, that—?"

"I'm staying. Yes. I regret the trouble I've caused, but I think that, if you consider what I have to offer, you'll realize it's the best choice." She ticked off the reasons on her fingers as she spoke. "I'm basal humanoid, which means that with minimal cosmetic and prophylactic disguises, I can be a human, a Mirialan, or even a Twi'lek. I've got the whole pheromonic-telempathic thing going for me, which lets me manipulate a roomful of people without their suspecting a thing. And I'm rich and beautiful, which gives me access to some corridors of power. Face it, Jax—your group needs me."

He couldn't argue with that. She was headstrong, willful, accustomed to having her own way; in short, a real handful—and she was right. She could be an asset, no question about it.

He hoped Laranth wouldn't mind.

As it turned out, he didn't get a chance to ask.

She was in a private recovery room, he noted with surprise; unusual for someone with no grid references. He suspected that Dejah had worked her money and manipulation abilities already to get the Twi'lek the best possible care.

She was conscious when he entered, having just undergone extensive bacta tank regeneration. Her right arm had been almost completely severed, and the lightsaber had caused a grievous wound in her right side as well, damaging her liver and pancreas. Were it not for the cauterization that the energy blade's intense heat had caused as it did its damage, she would have bled to death before she'd hit the ground.

He looked at her face again, and was surprised to see her awake and watching him. Her gaze seemed even bleaker than usual. She didn't respond to his greeting; instead she said, simply, "I'm leaving."

"Leaving?"

"Your group. I've decided that I can accomplish more on my own, without the distractions of attempting to solve mysteries best left to the sector police." She raised her good hand to forestall any objections or questions. "I'll still be around, Jax. I'm sure our paths will cross. But I think it's best that we go our own ways."

Jax, still mentally reeling from the news that Dejah had just given him, found himself totally at a loss for words. He stood there, mouth agape like a Padawan who'd just seen his first Force demonstration. At last, unable to think of any other course of action, he sent his Force lines to her, questing for her feelings, expecting nothing more than the usual impenetrable armor in which she shielded herself.

To his shock, he found her wide open.

Hesitantly, he pushed farther. She still offered no resistance. *She's not exactly welcoming me with open arms, either,* he thought. Still, he knew it took an enormous amount of courage for the Paladin to go as far as she had.

Such trust demanded reciprocity. He opened himself, laid bare his inner feelings, his secrets, as best he could; he hadn't had much practice in self-examination and -realization, either. They were precepts he'd been learning as part of his adult training, before the Temple had been shattered. Nevertheless, he now stood as close to naked before the Force as he was capable of.

He felt her probe him, felt her mind within his; hesitant at first, but then with greater confidence, and finally with reckless abandon. She was looking for something . . .

He realized what it was just as he encountered the same emotion in her. She wasn't hiding it, though. Cautiously, tentatively, she was displaying it, like a war-torn pennant atop a battlement.

The revelation stunned him.

I—I never thought of you that way, he said mentally, letting the Force convey the essence of the message without unnecessary words.

Nor I you. But things change. She looked at him, and even though the tone of her thoughts was cool and controlled, the sense he received through the Force was anything but. It had all the truth and intensity of her passion for freedom and justice. And even as he felt its heat, he could feel it starting to wane, could feel its fires being brought under control.

Wait, he said, but it was too late. Her defenses had slammed back into place—that heavy mental armor, designed to contain the emotional equivalent of a thermal detonator, was aligned and seamless once more. She looked away from him. "As I said," she told him, "I'll be around. Now, if you'll excuse me, I'm tired." Her head lowered to the pillow as her eyes closed.

Jax left the room and wandered for a while, trying to cope with the change in personnel. He felt like a fool—but how was he to have known? His life inside the Temple had afforded him little opportunity to investigate the fairer sex and, while his life outside had offered opportunities aplenty, the class of beings he now ran with either weren't interested or used sex the same way they used everything else: as a bargaining chip, or a weapon.

He'd looked upon Laranth Tarak as a comrade in arms, but not in every possible sense of the phrase. Jax abruptly understood the Twi'lek's increasing moodiness and antipathy toward Dejah Duare. There was no way she could compete with the other woman; even without her extensive psychochemical arsenal, the Zeltron was a formidable opponent. She had money, beauty, and a fashion sense that made the top clothiers on the planet lick their chops like starving nexus. Compared with Dejah, Laranth was outclassed on every level.

All she could do was fight. All she had to offer was a heroic heart. All she gave was—everything.

"Something troubling you, Jax?" I-Five's voice broke into his thoughts.

"He means," Den's voice piped in, "that you look spacier than usual."

Jax blinked. He was down in the waiting area, which at the moment was giving half a dozen or so humans and humanoids places to wait—either for treatment or for news of others in worse shape than they. Den had gotten off with merely a long gash on his right ear, and the droid had sustained no damage at all.

Jax said, "I just saw Dejah and Laranth. They—"

"We heard the startling news from Dejah," I-Five said. "How is Laranth?"

"Alive and getting well," said Jax. "That's the good news."

As he continued to tell them of Laranth's decision, a realization struck him with such force that he stopped midsentence and laughed.

"Something funny that we're missing?" Den wanted to know.

"You might say that," Jax said. He composed himself, then said in sonorous tones, "Prioritize discreet vigilance anent fugitive recovery operation."

"That sounds familiar," Den mused. "Hey, wait a minute—that's the last thing the Cephalon told us."

"Exactly," Jax said. He shook his head. "It was trying to warn us about the bounty hunter. About Aurra Sing. We just figured it out a little after the fact." He laughed again.

"I thought this was supposed to be a grim and cheerless job," said a feminine voice from behind them. They turned as one to see Dejah Duare descending a nearby lift tube. She landed and walked toward them. She was wearing a dress that had something in common with the cloud dress of last night, only this one was in more of a liquid state. It was blue, and little wavelets began at her right shoulder and rippled across its length, to stop at her left hip and immediately begin again.

"Instead," Dejah continued, "I hear laughter. I see smiles. I must admit that, as a Zeltron, this gladdens me." She stoppd near the Jedi and smiled.

"Nice dress," he said.

"It's part of a set. Wait'll you see the final one—it's made of fire."

He grinned. He wasn't sure if her pheromones were working on him right now, and didn't really care. All he knew or cared to know was that he felt great. True, there were still problems to solve. There was the ongoing mystery of Vader's pursuit of him, and what actions he would take to avenge the murder of his father by the Sith. Also, he had not forgotten that realization, borne through the Force, that Anakin Skywalker was still alive. If so, it meant that he would have to find the young Jedi someday and return to him the pyronium nugget. And he had to decide what action to take regarding the bota distillate. All these decisions would have to be made—in time.

For now, however, it was enough to listen to Dejah's laughter, see her smile, and feel her touch.

Out of the corner of his eye, he saw Den shake his head and mutter something that sounded like *se'lahn*. I-Five nodded in agreement. He felt a momentary flare of annoyance before he realized that they didn't understand. Attitude was everything in this. It was what got you up in the morning, got you through the day alive. He'd much rather have someone like Dejah at his side than a grim and contained Laranth.

Someday they'd see that. Until then—

"Let's go," he said. "Rhinann's there by himself— we'd better make sure he hasn't auctioned off everything on the Net by now."

It was the droid, Rhinann realized. The droid was the key, somehow. It alone had been present at all the events. It linked them all together: the mysterious pursuit and slaughter on Coruscant, twenty years ago; the events on the planet Drongar, with the Jedi Barriss Offee; and the recovery of the data concerning the mysterious bota.

The droid was the connection. He knew it; could feel it.

Haninum Tyk Rhinann leaned back in his chair and smiled. It was a formidable puzzle, with some pieces more than two decades old and scattered halfway across the galaxy. And many of those pieces were hidden in places that were not only hard to find, but dangerous to access as well. It was worth it, however. If even a fraction of what he was begining to put together was true, it would be worth every effort and expenditure. With the power it promised, he could reclaim his former glory, and more—he could challenge the Emperor himself.

A challenging puzzle, without a doubt. But the Elomin were good at putting together puzzles.

Very good indeed.

Read on for a preview of

Star Wars: Coruscant Nights III: Patterns of Force

by Michael Reaves

Jax rose and padded out of his room into the larger main living area, noticing that the rest of his companions were either asleep or out. I-Five followed him.

As he moved to the front door of the con-apt, Jax sent out questing tendrils of the Force to the being on the opposite side of the barrier. In his mind's eye he "saw" the energy there, but perceived no telltale "threads" of the Force emanating from or connecting to them.

Every Jedi experienced and perceived the Force in intensely personal ways. Jax's particular sensibilities caused him to perceive it as threads of light or darkness that enrobed or enwrapped an individual and connected him or her to the Force itself and to other beings and things. In this case there seemed to be no threads . . . though there was a hint of a—well, a smudge was the only word Jax had that even vaguely fit.

Curious for the second time that morning, he opened the door, smiling a little as I-Five stepped to one side, taking up a defensive position where he would not immediately be seen by whoever was outside.

In the narrow, starkly lit corridor stood a short, stocky male Sakiyan in his sixties—or so Jax guessed—

dressed in clean but threadbare clothing. He blinked at Jax's appearance—he was wearing a loose pair of sleep pants and hadn't bothered to put on a tunic.

"I—I apologize for the hour," the Sakiyan stammered, blinking round eyes that seemed extraordinarily pale in his bronze face, "but the matter is urgent. I need to speak to Jax Pavan."

Jax scrutinized the Sakiyan man again, more thoroughly and with every sense he possessed. Sensing no ill intent, he introduced himself. "I'm Jax Pavan."

The visitor's face brightened and he heaved a huge sigh of relief. "By any chance, do you happen to own a protocol droid of the I-5YQ line?"

"I don't 'own' him," Jax replied cautiously. "But yes, he's here. What do you want with him, Citizen . . . ?"

The Sakiyan executed a slight bow. "I apologize for my extreme lack of manners. My name is—"

"Tuden Sal," I-Five said, stepping out of the shadows beside the door. The droid pointed an index finger at Tuden Sal. A red light gleamed at the tip—the muzzle of one of the twin lasers incorporated into his hands. His photoreceptors gleamed brightly.

"I've been waiting a long time for this . . ."